GW00683936

IF I
NEVER
WENT
HOME

IF I
NEVER
WENT
HOME

INGRID PERSAUD

BLUE CHINA
P R E S S

BLUE CHINA PRESS
30B Bellevue Road
London SW17 7EF
www.bluechinapress.com

IF I NEVER WENT HOME

Ingrid Persaud

Published in the United Kingdom by Blue China Press
ISBN: 978-0-9926977-0-9

For Avinash,
with love and gratitude

CHAPTER ONE

There was a sharp knock at the door, and a woman in light blue scrubs stuck her head into the room.

'Excuse me, doctor, but you wanted the file as soon as I got it.'

'Thanks,' said Bea Clark, taking the grey folder and placing it on her desk.

The woman backed out of the room and closed the door. Dr. Clark took off her brown suit jacket and hung it over the back of her chair.

'Sorry about that, Stephen,' she said.

Stephen shrugged and looked away.

'As I was saying,' Dr. Clark continued. 'Would you mind counting backwards in sevens? Start with one hundred.'

The burly nineteen-year-old stared across the room. At six feet and 250 pounds he could easily crush the young doctor, who had never made it to 100 pounds or past five feet.

'I'm not counting,' he growled. 'You think I'm some fucking retard that I can't even count?'

'I'm sure you can count. But humour me. Just try counting backwards in sevens. Start with one hundred.'

He sprang up from the chair. 'I said, I'm not counting. You deaf?'

'Stephen, I know how strange this must seem. Please sit

down. Believe me, I understand that you're scared. I understand more than you can imagine.'

He sat back down with a thud. 'What would you understand about me? You don't know nothing. I ain't scared of you. I ain't scared of nothing.'

Dr. Clark ignored him. 'The counting, the questions about dates, events, they all help me evaluate how well you're doing today.'

Stephen folded his arms and looked away. 'I ain't talking to no shrink.'

Bea propped up her chin with her interwoven fingers. She remembered her time in St. Anthony's Hospital. She was a different person then. She could not have offered Stephen any hope. She too had been reluctant to accept help, least of all from her parents Mira and Alan.

'Well, that's good, because I'm not a shrink,' she smiled. 'I'm what they call a clinical psychologist. A lot of my clients at this Crisis Centre have anxiety issues. Often they're confused or depressed. Might be self-harming. I work within a team. And yes, the team includes a psychiatrist to help people get better.'

'Call yourself what you like,' he said. 'I'm not saying nothing, so don't ask me about no bullshit numbers.'

'A few other people are going to need to speak with you. After our chat you're going to meet my colleague Dr. Payne. He's the head of this unit. Nice man. He has a lot of experience. In fact he's a world expert on depression, so you'll be in good hands.'

Stephen glared. 'What do I need with a world expert in depression? Don't be stupid. Men don't get depressed.'

'I don't know about that,' Bea said. 'It's not an illness that discriminates.'

He looked her up and down. 'You're not even American, are you?' he asked. 'Where're you from? India?'

She smiled. 'If I tell you something about me, you've got

to tell me something about you.'

He dug his fat fingers deep into his jeans pockets and parked his size-twelve, high-top sneakers on the edge of her desk.

'Take your feet off my desk,' she said, quiet but firm.

He hesitated for a few seconds, but put them down. He slumped further into the chair and pushed his long legs wide apart, his crotch in full view.

'I was born in Trinidad,' she said. 'But I've lived here in Boston on and off since college. Gosh, it's been twenty years.'

Stephen looked up at the ceiling.

'You want to tell me what happened this morning?' she asked.

'No,' he said, turning his attention to the tiled floor.

'I don't believe you,' said Dr. Clark, bending her head to catch his eyes. 'I think you're desperate to talk to me because, unlike friends or family, I am not here to judge you. My only job is to listen and help if I can. That's it.'

Stephen closed his legs and fidgeted in his chair.

'Is it your arms?' she asked. 'Please?'

He sighed, pushed his grey sweatshirt up a few inches and looked away. His big hands began shaking slightly.

'May I see?' she asked.

He continued to look away and said nothing.

Dr. Clark got up and walked around the desk. Even when she stood up, he seemed to tower over her. He held out his left arm and pushed the sleeve further up, his hand shaking. Crude cuts, in varying stages of healing, criss-crossed the flesh. Some would leave permanent scars. A few were very recent, still crusted with blood.

'Thank you, Stephen.'

He pulled the sleeve down and jerked his head violently against the wooden chair back.

'Don't hurt your head,' she said quietly.

He did it again, then bent forward, hugging his head between his knees.

'Stephen, do you understand why you're here?' she asked.

'They didn't need to call the cops,' he moaned. 'I wasn't going to hurt nobody. They didn't need to call the damn cops.'

She took a deep breath. 'Did you want to hurt yourself? Is that why you were on the roof of your apartment building?'

'Get out of my fucking face! If I want to end it, that's my business.' He curled his knees into his chest. For the first time Dr. Clark saw tears in his eyes. 'I don't need help.'

'It's my job,' she replied softly.

They were silent.

'Stephen, do you understand why people might have been concerned?' She paused. 'Stephen? Can you look at me?'

He put his hands over his face.

'What happened today?' she asked gently.

He was quiet.

'Stephen, we need to talk about today.'

He hugged himself. When he finally spoke, his voice was low. He was trying to hold back tears. 'It's my life. *My* life! They didn't need to bring me down here like some criminal. In a police car.' His voice cracked. 'Neighbours think I must've killed somebody.'

This time the tears did not stop. Dr. Clark sat back and looked at him, his muscular body hunched over, shaking as he sobbed. Soon, he would be able to talk about what took him to that rooftop. For now it was enough to sit, silently respecting his pain.

CHAPTER TWO

Bea Clark had not always worked with patients like Stephen. This new career had started only a few years ago. She couldn't remember exactly when she decided to go back to college in Boston and turn herself from a history professor into a psychologist, but the idea had been creeping up on her from the moment her father Alan was killed.

Bea could recall the details of his death a hundred times over, but they never made sense. Sudden deaths like his did not happen to ordinary people leading ordinary lives, unremarkable in every way until the moment of extinction. Was her father just in the wrong place at the wrong time? Was it chance, or fate? Bea had tried to concentrate on the phone call from her mother Mira in Trinidad.

'You mustn't grieve too much, darling,' Mira had said. 'He didn't suffer.'

'When?' Bea asked.

'I told you already,' Mira said. 'Today. A few hours ago.'

'And it was on the highway near Couva, you said?'

'No, not Couva,' said Mira, sounding irritated. 'Further south. By Claxton Bay. You remember the flyover?'

Bea hung up without saying goodbye. How could she react to something she did not understand?

The phone rang again. This time Mira's words were inescapable.

'Was anyone with him?' Bea asked. Her voice felt alien, as if someone else was speaking through her.

'He was alone.'

'And the other car?'

'It mash-up, mash-up.'

'And the driver?'

'That's the thing I can't understand. The man walked out of there with, what? Two, three little scratch. He didn't even need the hospital, but they keeping him in for observation.'

'But how?'

'Child, the man was stink drunk. He must have never even seen your father's car until he hit him.'

'But Dad was wearing a seatbelt?'

'I really don't know.' Mira paused. 'They say it was instant. He didn't suffer.'

'You sure?'

'The impact,' she said in a low voice. 'His neck. It broke his neck.'

Strange things happened around that spot. Bea had driven past the turnoff for Claxton Bay countless times; it was always a mesmerising place, but now in an acutely personal way. She could remember vividly the first time she heard of Claxton Bay.

'Where we going, Daddy?' she had asked.

'We going to see one of Daddy's friends,' Alan Clark replied.

'Who?'

'Is the Rahaman family. They know you, but you mightn't remember them.'

'They have little children?'

'They have a boy about six or seven. Your age. And I think they have a girl a little bit older.'

'Where they living?'

'Claxton Bay. Is not far. Now, your job, Miss Beezy, is to

read the road signs on the highway and tell me where the turnoff is.'

'Okay.'

They drove south from Port of Spain towards San Fernando, past Chaguanas, Couva and Preysal. Bea showed him the sign, partly obscured by tall sugarcane. Claxton Bay turnoff, one mile.

'You know, babes, they say is haunted around here.'

'For true?' Bea's eyes widened. 'Like jumbies will come and suck your blood?' She unwrapped a piece of chewing gum she had been saving and popped it into her mouth.

'Exactly. They say it have a ghost up here does haunt people all the time.'

She chewed noisily on the gum. 'You telling fibs, Daddy.'

'Somewhere up in Claxton Bay have a statue of a young girl that don't have a head.'

'Where the head gone?' she asked, frightened.

'Nobody know. They say as soon as the statue get put up, the head break off and fall down. Just so. Just so. Nobody touch the thing and it drop off. And every time they try to put it back on, in a few days it does fall off again.'

'And who is the girl in the statue?'

'They say is a young white girl. She was a pretty only child. Just like my pumpkin,' he said, leaning over to tickle little Bea's tummy. 'When she was about sixteen, the girl fall in love with a boy from the village. But her father say, no way no how she going marry a poor black boy working in the cement factory. But the girl and boy did really love each other, and they ran away.'

She spat the gum back into the wrapper and shoved it into a pocket of her shorts. 'Where'd they go?'

'Well, that is the thing. The story was that they didn't get far when a big snake drop on them from a tree. It was at least seven foot long. The snake tie itself round the girl neck. You ever see a snake long so?'

'No.' Bea trembled.

'The snake was ugly and fat. You must never go near one, okay, Beezy? They kill you before you have time to say boo.'

'So what happen to the girl and boy?'

'People say the big snake kill she right there on the spot.'

'Oh Lord,' said Bea, staring out at the dense lushness of the cane fields. 'We have any snakes by our house?'

'No, Beezy. Anyway, that is how come the parents put up the statue of the girl to remember she.'

'What happen to the boy?'

'Nobody know for sure. Some say the snake kill him too. But the girl ghost does haunt all about Claxton Bay area near the highway. Plenty people say they see she.'

'What she look like?'

'They say she pretty and does be wearing a long white dress like a nightie. But if you see her, is serious bad luck. You could bet your last dollar something real bad go happen to you soon after.'

'You ever see her?'

'No. Never.'

'Will we see her today, Daddy? I frighten.'

Alan gave a small steups, sucking his teeth. 'No, man. Jumbie can't take hot sun like this.'

'You sure?'

'Sure, sure. And even if there was a ghost lady in a white dress, Daddy will make sure nothing happens to his one and only Beezy-pumpkin.'

Bea meant to promise to protect her Daddy in return, but forgot.

The lady ghost was patient. One fresh spring day, when Bea was all grown up, a young history professor separated from her Daddy by thousands of miles, the ghost took her revenge. As Bea walked across Boston Common, she bent down to pick a lily as a token for Michael, a man she thought she might love. At that precise moment, her Daddy, driving past Claxton Bay, saw the young ghost in her white nightie standing in the middle of the road. Everything went blank. Daddy's head was broken off.

CHAPTER THREE

Miss Anna says we have to wait at the side of the stage and she will come for us when our name get called. I'm feeling queasy. The sorrel drink and ham sandwich like they fighting up in my tummy. Three of us reach the finals. I want to go to the toilet but if they call 'Tina Ramlogan' and I miss my turn I'll get disqualified. That's what happened to Cathy-Ann in the first round. I know my poem by heart. Every day I've been practising in front of Mummy's long bedroom mirror, saying the poem out loud. Miss Celia next door complain to Mummy that she know the whole poem too. I've been reciting it to our puppy Boo-Boo. But Boo-Boo doesn't always stay to the end where the little boy drop down and dead. I wonder if the poem frighten the dog. I never thought of that before.

They should hurry up with all them speech about the school and how the principal and teachers are an example to the nation and how crime would go down if more children took part in competitions like this. Oh, no. I feel a pee-pee coming.

'Miss Anna!'

'Sshhh.'

'Miss Anna, I have to go to the bathroom, please Miss.'

She want to know if I sure. Well, of course I sure. If I don't go right now I going to pee in my panty. The children's toilet is too far, so Miss Anna carry me to the teachers' toilet. If you see how nice that toilet is, and full of toilet paper. I could have stayed in there, but Miss Anna only saying hurry up Tina they starting. I push the wee out as fast as I could and we run back just as the big judge from the Ministry of Education was calling for Curtis.

'Curtis Thompson, come up to the stage please.'

Curtis thin as a piece of wire. He's ten like the rest of us, but if you didn't know you would say he's about eight years old.

'And what will you be reciting for us today, Curtis?'

'"Silver", by Walter de la Mare.'

'Very good.'

Curtis and his silver this and silver that poem. Everybody know gold more expensive. My Nanny said that when she dead she going to leave me a big fat gold bracelet that her Agee bring from India. She say I would never find a bracelet like that in Trinidad. Not even Marajsingh Jewellers have bracelet heavy like hers.

Next up is Joyce Mohammed. She win last year hands down and is the favourite to win again. Plus she's the brightest girl in the school. And on top of all that she only gone and choose a poem the whole school know. When she's on the stage reciting it the children them saying it too. All you see is children with their mouth opening and closing in time with her.

When I was sick and lay a-bed,
I had two pillows at my head,
And all my toys beside me lay,
To keep me happy all the day.

La, la, la, la, la. Oh and look how she curtseying. Bet she learn that in Miss Pauline ballet class. I used to do ballet. Miss Pauline ban me. She tell Mummy I am the first child she ever ban. 'Nalini, don't take this the wrong way but Tina don't have a single bone in she body that can dance.'

I don't remember what Mummy said to that. Miss Pauline said she should not waste she hard-earned cash on ballet lessons.

Sharp pains start in my tummy again.

'Miss Anna, I want to go to the toilet.'

She pretending not to hear me.

'Miss Anna, I have to go again.'

'Sshhh. You went already.'

'I know, but I have to go again.'

'Well you can't go now, so hold it in tight.'

'I can't!'

Just then Joyce finish.

'That was a splendid performance, Joyce. Excellent. If this is the kind of student St. Gabriel's is producing, then Trinidad's future is in good hands. Let us give Joyce another round of applause.'

Well, that's it. Madam win again. I want to please go to the toilet and stay there.

'Tina Ramlogan.'

I want to go home. Miss Anna come behind me and start pushing me out of the chair. Go on. Get up there quick and do your poem.

'Tina?'

'Yes, sir.'

'And what will you be reciting today?'

I gulp. My mouth tasting like Curtis silver poem.

'"The Story Of Augustus Who Would Not Have Any Soup", by Heinrich Hoffman.'

'I must say I'm not familiar with that one. Well, when you ready.'

My head feel it going to burst. When I look out at the audience I could see the whole school spread out on the assembly hall floor. The children not paying attention. They hear enough speech and poem for one day. I think I'm going to vomit up my ham sandwich. Then I see Mummy. She hiding in the corner. She smiling. So I take a deep breath and pretend I'm home saying it to her and Boo-Boo, but loud enough for Miss Celia to hear it too.

Augustus was a chubby lad;
Fat ruddy cheeks Augustus had –

I hear laughing. I not sure why they laughing. That part of the poem not even funny. But is when I reach the chorus that they really start to laugh.

Not any soup for me, I say!
Take the nasty soup away!
I won't have any soup today!

When I finish, people was clapping for so. I put my head down and walk back to my seat. I don't want to get jinx.

The judges say they taking a short break for their deliberations. I bolt straight for the toilet. This time I did a number two. Lucky thing I had kept paper from the teachers' toilet because I not seeing any paper here.

When I come out, people only poking me and saying, 'Not any soup for me I say! Take the nasty soup away!'

I want to go sit by Mummy, but teacher warn us to stay with our classmates until the bell ring.

The judges taking their cool time. Miss Anna bring them orange juice in tall glasses with ice and a napkin underneath. So now we have to wait for them to finish their juice. I wish they would drink fast, announce that Joyce win again, and let us all go home. I don't even remember why I went up for this contest. Look at Joyce sitting there with her hands folded in her lap. Little Miss Perfect. And skinny Curtis next to her grinning like a stupid fool. Mummy say I mustn't call anybody a stupid fool, but he does get on my nerves. I don't mind if Joyce win, but if Curtis come second that go make me feel real shame.

Oh look, they putting down the empty glasses and coming back to their table. The principal calling the main judge to the stage. He talk about all of us. He praise Curtis saying how he is a shining example, that boys don't always have to talk like they in a gangster video. Then he move on to Joyce. A credit to the school. Such a bright young lady with perfect diction. Then he reach me. My heart beating so fast I not sure I can understand what the man saying. I think he say something about how I entertain the crowd and how he nearly cry when Augustus died from starvation.

'And the winner of the second annual St. Gabriel's Primary School recitation competition is ...'

He stop. The children start shouting out names.

Joyce! Joyce!

Tina!

Curtis!

Joyce!

'And the winner is Miss Tina Ramlogan.'

Oh Lord, I can't believe it. Is me! I win? I look again to make sure is me. Yes, the judge calling me and hand over the trophy. Everybody clapping. I look at it. But they make a mistake. Mr Judge, I say. Please sir, is Joyce name on the trophy. He start to laugh. Joyce name was from last year. Don't worry, he say. They will engrave my name on it soon. But he say it loud and it get pick up by the microphone. Now people laughing at me for being so stupid.

Anyhow, I get rescue by the principal. He come up and say more thank you to this one and that one and ask that we close with the Lord's Prayer. I hold on to the trophy tight and close my eyes halfway so I could still see out while we praying. A girl from my class doing the same thing and we smile at each other. If the teacher catch you laughing or smiling during prayers it don't matter what you just win. She will make you stay behind and say the prayer over properly with your eyes shut tight.

When it over the principal wish us all a happy and holy Christmas. He say we should remember the true meaning of Christmas. It is not about getting the latest toys and gadgets.

Christmas is a time for celebrating the birth of baby Jesus, and with that school over till next year.

I holding on to the trophy tight and only now try to look at it properly. It big, but not too big. There's a person reaching forward and holding a bird with two hands, and on the base it says Joyce Mohammed. I still feel like I thief she first prize.

CHAPTER FOUR

It was nearly a decade already since Alan Clark died. Other family relationships had died with him. It was the end of any real connection between Bea and her mother Mira. Not that this bothered Bea much. At least, that is what she told herself. She had her work, and in the evenings there was the book club, the Boston Symphony, or the small group of friends she stayed loyal to. Her annual vacation was usually a cycling or walking holiday: she had been going with the same group for years. The pain of losing a love like Michael still simmered. She often felt the temptation of Internet sites that promised love was only a few clicks away. But she remembered the hurt, serious hurt. She resisted. She had had a lucky escape.

The morning session with Stephen had deteriorated. He saw no reason to live, and kept saying he wanted to be left alone to end it all. Dr. Payne and another psychiatrist had assessed him. She looked out of her office window at the garden outside, still stocked with bright summer flowers. She had tried hard with Stephen, but he had rejected her help and would have to be hospitalised involuntarily, to prevent a second, perhaps more successful suicide attempt. He would probably be transferred to Mount Russet Hospital or nearby St. Anthony's. She had asked if there was anyone to contact. Eventually he telephoned the copy shop where he worked, saying he would not be coming in for the rest of the week. She did not bother to correct him. There was no way he would be discharged that soon.

Two more assessments had filled the morning. A man who had exposed himself to some children in the park; a young woman who had been found wandering among the Back Bay alleyways, screaming that aliens from Pluto had invaded and were hiding in the garbage. Usually, more people would have been brought in by now. It was on warm summer days like this, under beautiful blue skies, that desperation, confusion and pain were hardest to keep at bay.

In the hours before her afternoon clinic at Mount Russet, Bea knew she ought to be working on her conference paper. She had promised it would be finished in a fortnight. Instead, she grabbed her handbag and headed out, telling the head nurse she was getting a coffee at the Coffee Bean café a block away. It would have been simpler to grab a latte from the vending machine, but she needed the walk. Her mind was racing.

The headache she felt coming on could be worry about the conference paper, or about the chores quietly piling up at home. But there was no use denying it. For days she had been carrying around Mira's unopened letter. The headache would stay until she dealt with that. Bea had no idea why her mother would write. Why not send a Facebook message or an email? They never invaded each other's lives beyond that. Whatever the reason for the intrusion, Bea knew it would be unwelcome news. She had neglected her mother for so long. Had Mira been diagnosed with some horrible illness? Then Bea would have to do the decent thing and help her through whatever it was. It was the least Mira should expect from her daughter, her only child.

She sipped the lukewarm coffee slowly, and bit into a banana muffin without tasting it. Mira never smoked, and kept herself fit by swimming. That was what Bea remembered. There was no family history of cancer or heart problems. No, it was something else. If Mira was not dying, then it was probably her maternal grandma, who had been ailing for years. Damn Mira for writing now, when life was good. But it was a life tightly wound, with little give to stretch and bend. It certainly didn't have space for Mira.

She fished the letter out from the jumbled contents of her handbag and stared at it again. Muffin crumbs fell on the envelope and smeared grease on the white surface. It didn't matter. It was beginning to look grubby anyway, after tossing around at the bottom of her bag. If Mira was writing to apologise properly after all these years, that was fine, as long as she understood it changed nothing. Too much time had passed to say sorry, and anyway sorry was not enough. Bea finished her coffee. Everyone had moved on, and she was not going to be dragged backwards into that whole Trinidad mess again. She shoved the unopened letter back into her bag. Whatever Mira had to say could wait.

Bea's life had changed drastically since she last saw Mira, and all for the better. She was no longer a history professor, for one thing. That was a lifetime ago. It had not been sustainable, not after that dark winter evening when she first came to the Crisis Centre.

She had sat fidgeting in the doctor's office that night. She had watched her reflection in the mirror: she looked like a brown-skin rag doll. She had turned her head to see if her thick black hair was as unruly at the sides as it was at the front. She wasn't sure where she was, but it had taken the ambulance about thirty minutes to drive from downtown Boston. Or maybe fifteen minutes. Time, wristwatch time, had stopped the moment she was bundled into the ambulance. A paramedic had given her an injection. Apart from a sprained ankle when she fell off her mountain bike, she had never been inside an American hospital before.

'Count backwards in sevens from one hundred,' Dr. Singh

had ordered.

Bea was still wearing her work clothes, a crisp grey suit and white shirt. She winced. 'Do I look like I can't count?'

He hunched his thin, lanky frame forward and stared at her from behind square, gold-framed glasses, their thick lenses protruding at the sides.

'Okay,' she said. 'One hundred. Ninety-three. Eighty-six. Seventy-nine. Seventy-two. Sixty-five.' She hesitated. 'Can I stop now?'

'Continue counting. I'll tell you when to stop.'

She sighed, a loud frustrated expulsion of air.

'Fifty-eight. Fifty-one. Forty-four. Thirty-seven. Thirty.'

He held his hand up. 'Okay, stop.'

Dr. Singh looked up from the notes he'd been scribbling and ran long, skeletal fingers through his crew-cut salt-and-pepper hair. 'When did the First World War start?'

She groaned. 'Why are you asking me these stupid questions? Are you a shrink?'

'I'm the admitting doctor. You'll see the psychiatrist later.'

'Okay, because I'm seeing a shrink every day. You might know her, Dr. Martin. She never asks weird questions like these.'

'When did the First World War start?'

Bea bit her lip.

'Miss Clark, this is part of the examination. Please answer.'

'1914, when they killed that insignificant Austrian.'

'Just the dates please. When did the Second World War start and finish?

'1939 to 1945.'

He rubbed his chin with his bony thumb and forefinger, then held up his other hand. 'How many fingers am I holding up?'

'Four.'

'How many voices do you hear?'

She rolled her eyes. 'Too many.'

'What?'

'Yours and mine.'

'Are there any others? Voices telling you to do bad things?'

Folding her arms, she scowled. 'Well, there is one tiny voice and it keeps telling me you have no sense of humour, Dr. Zing.'

'Miss Clark, I'd appreciate your full cooperation.'

She pushed on the arms of the chair to sit straighter, but that still left her size-three feet dangling above the floor. 'No voices. Yet.'

'Does your family have any history of mental illness, depression, bipolar disorder, schizophrenia? Anything of the sort?'

'My family? Nope. I'm the first fruitcake.'

'Have you had any surgery in the past ten years?'

'No.'

'Have you ever been pregnant?'

'You have to ask that? No.'

'Any allergies?'

She looked around his office and stared at the wooden bookshelves that lined the far wall. 'Actually, I'm allergic to dust.' She cleared her throat loudly a few times. 'I can't breathe when there's a lot of dust. Especially old magazines. Old office furniture. Stuff that should be thrown out.'

He lifted a bushy eyebrow. 'Any other allergies?'

'Grapefruit. Honest. I break out in a rash if I eat grapefruit.'

'Very well. I'll put in a request not to give you grapefruit. A nurse will come to take your temperature and blood pressure.' He put his notepad and pen down and rapped his long fingers on the desk. 'What part of India are you from? Gujarat?'

'Read my file. I'm not Indian.'

'Yes, you may be born elsewhere, but you are Indian, no?'

'I'm Trinidadian. Mother Indian, father mixed.'

'You look South Indian. Your mother's family are from India, no?'

'Long, long time ago. We're not Indians like you. Never even been to India.'

He mumbled something that sounded like Hindi or Urdu.

'I don't understand,' said Bea. 'Barely get by in English.'

'But you must be Hindu, no?'

'Catholic. Mass once a week like clockwork.'

'It's odd you don't know your Indian roots.'

She shrugged. 'Diaspora.'

'Well, as one Indian to another, I have to say something for your own good. This depression business is no good. No good at all. Who would want a daughter with mental illness? If you keep behaving like this you will be a grave disappointment to your parents. Grave disappointment. Try to stop it now. It's no good for anyone.' He shook a long finger at her. 'You are bringing shame on your family.'

She lowered her head and tried to squelch the tears behind her eyelids.

'And you must take into consideration that you do not have a husband. How will you get one if you are depressed, eh?'

The accusations sucked the air out of the room. He stood up and headed toward the door, smug satisfaction on his face.

'I hope you understand the wickedness of what you have done. Pray to Lord Vishnu and Mother Lakshmi. I will check on you again.' With that he opened the door and left.

She held her body rigid against his words, and stared at the tiled floor until she heard the door close behind him.

Check on me again? Did he think she was setting up home here?

She would have liked to dismiss him outright, but he was only saying what she knew already. Even if she was discharged tonight, her parents were entitled to be disappointed when they found out she had been brought here, and the circumstances surrounding her disgrace. Perhaps the truth could be hidden. There was no obligation to notify them.

She wept quietly. The tears flowed, trickled down her face, dripped onto the collar of her white shirt.

This is going to be a long, cold night.

*

'Hungry? I can get you a tuna sandwich, or maybe cheese,' the nurse offered.

'No thanks,' Bea said.

'Blood pressure's up a little.' The nurse removed the pressure cuff from Bea's arm. 'It's to be expected with all that's happened today. Go easy on the caffeine.'

'No one's telling me anything.' Bea pressed her thumbs in the space between her brows. 'In the ambulance they didn't even give the name of the hospital.'

'You're at the Crisis Centre of Mount Russet Hospital in Cambridge. We're a few miles north of Harvard Square.'

'What's going to happen to me?'

The nurse glanced at the clipboard in her hand. 'Let's see. Dr. Singh's checked you already, so the next person you'll be seeing is Dr. Payne. Everyone likes him. The young nurses are always going on about him.'

'What will he do?'

'He'll decide where we go from here. Don't worry. He's nice. Wait in the lounge and I'll come get you when he's ready.'

Bea made her way to the lounge. The straight-backed, moulded plastic chairs of institutional grey did not permit slouching. The dirty walls had a semblance of vanilla, but with the markings and smudges she couldn't be sure. Outside, it was snowing lightly.

The small room was crowded with eight people waiting. No one made eye contact as she settled into a chair in the far corner. From time to time blaring sirens broke the silence; tyres crunched on the ice as ambulances and police cars pulled up outside. Each new arrival intensified the atmosphere of the waiting lounge.

Sometimes a fellow patient would lean forward in a chair, perhaps straining for a snippet of conversation, some clue about the circumstances of the next person to join their cluster.

*

'Hi!' A handsome man with light brown hair and soft eyes of duck-egg blue pulled up two chairs in front of a black desk and offered Bea a seat. 'I'm Dr. Payne, the specialist on duty tonight.'

At least this one smiled.

Dr. Payne looked younger than Dr. Singh, maybe in his late forties. Average height, dressed in a deep blue suit and a light blue shirt set off by a flamboyant tie with paisley swirls of pink, green and blue. He stood out against the dirty grey environment. Bea understood what the nurse meant when she said the young women liked him: a handsome, exotic bird among a flock of common pigeons.

'Hi,' she mumbled with her head down, struggling not to stare up at him in spite of her curiosity.

'Sorry to have kept you waiting. As you can see, we've got

a full house tonight.'

He opened a brown file with her name scrawled in black marker across the front, and began flipping through the pages.

'Okay, let me have a look at your notes again for a moment. You were brought here this afternoon. Age twenty-nine. History professor. Unmarried. Seeing Dr. Martin for the past month. Okay. Yes.' He looked up. 'Right, tell me what happened.'

She instinctively covered her face with her hands.

'I know something of your circumstances,' he said. 'But I'd like to hear your version.'

Bea took a deep breath. 'I went in to see Dr. Martin today like I promised, and she had me brought here.'

'And you've been seeing her every day?'

'Yes.'

Despite the kindness in his voice she could not bring herself to look at him.

'In my opinion that means she thinks you're a high risk.'

'Not to anyone.' She peeped up at him. 'I'd never hurt anyone.'

'What about yourself? Would you hurt yourself?'

She pushed her chin into her chest and shut her eyes tight.

'Are you planning to hurt yourself?'

'I would never hurt anybody. If I hurt myself that's my affair.'

'May I call you Beatrice?'

She folded her arms tightly to her chest. 'Everyone calls me Bea.'

'Bea, are you planning to kill yourself?'

'Well, not much chance here. They took away my handbag, my belt. Like I'm some kind of criminal.'

'Dr. Martin was worried that you might kill yourself today. Was she right to be worried?'

Bea slid her hands under her thighs. 'I don't know, okay? I don't know.'

'Did you tell her that you were going to kill yourself?'

She massaged her temples. 'I've got a headache.'

'I can give you a painkiller if it persists.'

'I'm tired.'

Bea concentrated on the dark space beneath his desk. She desperately wanted to crawl into the cavity and curl up in a tight ball. It looked safe.

'Bea, do you understand why you're here?'

'I don't belong here,' she said. 'I'm not a criminal.'

'I'm sorry, but I have to keep you until we work out what's been happening.'

'It's all a misunderstanding,' she said with a loud sigh. 'I feel fine now.'

'I've worked with Dr. Martin for a long time and she's a solid person. She wouldn't have taken such drastic action without good reason.'

She shifted in her seat. 'Always a first time.'

'What were you doing to make her believe that if you weren't brought here you would be dead?'

She stared down at her hands, twisting them in her lap. 'I haven't done anything wrong. I haven't hurt anyone. Please let me go home.'

'I can't. From where I stand you are clearly distressed and must be looked after.'

'Well, that Dr. Singh has already made it clear I'm a disappointment.'

Dr. Payne's pen fell to the floor. 'Why would you say that?' He bent down to retrieve it. 'Dr. Singh was only doing the basics of checking you in.'

Bea wiped her face with both hands.

'He made time to let me know I was a disappointment to my family.'

Dr. Payne leant forward.

'I am sorry, Bea. That should never have happened. Never. I don't know what he was thinking. I promise you I will deal with it and you will not see him again. You understand that?'

Bea brushed away the tears. 'How long are you going to keep me locked up?'

The doctor smiled. 'That depends on you. You have to let me help you.'

'I want to go home. I'm exhausted.'

'How's your sleep?'

'I get about three or four hours a night.'

'No one can function properly on that little sleep. I'll prescribe something to help. And you're going to need a much higher dose of the anti-depressant than you're taking now, as well as something to augment it. We can't do much while there's a chemical imbalance.'

'Fine. Whatever. Look, I really need to get home. I have a class to teach in the morning.'

'You're not going to be doing any teaching for a while.'

For the first time she looked him in the eye. She felt faint. She touched her cheek. It was ice cold. 'It's my job. I need to work.'

'That's not possible right now,' he said, crossing his legs.

'You don't understand. My work is all I have left.'

'Bea, you have a major depressive disorder. When people are that ill they have to let others look after them until they're better.'

'But I'm fine. Please. You don't understand. I've grading to do.'

'It'll be taken care of.'

'No, it won't.'

'We've spoken to your dean. He's handling it. You'll go back when you're well. They only want you to get better.'

'Everyone knows?'

Dr. Payne did not answer.

Bea burst into tears. 'Oh God, everyone knows.'

'There is a high risk you will harm yourself. It's my job to ensure that doesn't happen.'

'I give you my word,' she sobbed. 'Please. I want to go home. I don't belong here. I'm so tired.'

'I can't allow you to go home alone. That will only increase your depression. It's too dangerous.'

Her tears tumbled down. 'Does anyone else know I'm here?'

He scanned the papers in the file. 'You haven't provided us with a next of kin. Do you have family we can call? Parents? Brother? Sister?'

'No. No one to call.'

'Are your parents around?'

'Yes.'

'I'm sure your family would want to know you're not well.'

'Not really.'

He handed her a tissue box. 'What about siblings?'

'None.' She took a tissue and dabbed her eyes. 'Well, none I know of anyway.'

'Okay. But I need a name and number in case of emergency. For the record. I won't contact anyone if you don't want me to.' He got up. 'Excuse me. I'll be back in a second.'

He returned before she had time to digest the implications of what had been said. 'I don't have a bed for you except on a closed ward,' Dr. Payne explained. 'It's not a pleasant environment. Will you be okay to stay here at the Clinic while I sort out a bed, or do you want to go to the ward?'

'I don't care.'

'Stay here then. We'll talk again in the morning.'

She tossed the hair off her shoulders and crossed her legs. 'Do I have a choice?'

'I'll be back in the morning once I finish my ward rounds,' he said and closed his files.

Stay here till tomorrow? The doctor talked as if she'd been booked into an inferior hotel room. *Madam, I'm sorry, but yours was a late booking and we don't have any free beds tonight. We can offer a temporary one for the night. We've checked and you have full coverage, so the expenses will all be taken care of.*

It was the other guests who were the real draw, like the man who claimed to be Captain Janeway from the starship *Voyager*. A teenager who had stabbed his mother with a butcher's knife. The voices in his head made him do it. A drug addict who had tried to jump out of a window on the thirty-ninth floor of a high-rise. An alcoholic who had trashed the family home and put his wife in intensive care. Then there was homeless Archie, a regular, with a passion for starting fires.

No, Ma'am, no other middle-class professionals due in tonight. But you never know. We are prepared for all eventualities. After all, we weren't expecting you tonight and here you are. She imagined herself as their lead character, a genuine university professor. Bea doubted they had ever had one of those before in this madhouse.

The duty nurse showed her where to find tea and coffee. The TV was permanently tuned to CNN, avoiding any argument over which channel clients could watch. Her cellphone was taken away. There was no Internet access. She was given a bag to put her clothes in and a medical gown to sleep in.

Who can rest in this fucking hellhole?

CHAPTER FIVE

Bea settled into a grey plastic chair in the far corner of the lounge and gazed at CNN. She flicked through dated magazines that chronicled the fashions and lives of celebrities. In spite of her exhaustion, she didn't close her eyes once during the night. A game of musical chairs took place around her as earlier occupants left and were replaced by others, equally troubled. The atmosphere was grim, tense with anticipation.

Sometimes a young overweight woman, wearing a dirty cut-off denim skirt and a pink sweater with a hole in the left sleeve, jumped up from her seat and addressed the room. 'I never killed myself before, okay?' she announced to no one in particular. 'I never did. Why are you all keeping me here? I never killed myself.' She would scan the room, muttering, and sit back down.

Most of the occupants were processed and transferred to the main hospital or other facilities nearby. A few were released into the care of a parent or partner. The nurse would appear with discharge papers and personal items – bags, coats, scarves, belts, shoelaces. Around one in the morning, a red-eyed boy in his late teens, head in his hands, was collected by a stony-faced man who promised to check him into a detox clinic downtown. 'Third time lucky,' the man said.

A loud buzzer meant that someone was being released: the locks clicked open on the thick glass door, the threshold to personal freedom. Bea knew she would not be stepping through that door for a while, but she looked up each time the nurses came in with news of an imminent departure, in case one was carrying her handbag, her coat, her belt.

I'm sorry but it's all been a terrible mistake, Miss Clark. Please sign here and you'll be free to leave. A taxi is waiting outside. You should be home in no time. Have a nice evening.

At some point, the dark night sky gave way to heavy grey morning light. A blanket of overnight snow was piled around the long low building. From the window she could see the ambulances and police cars come and go.

*

'The night duty nurse wrote that you were up all night watching TV,' said Dr. Payne as they walked from the lounge to his office.

'Couldn't sleep.'

'What about the sleeping tablets?'

'Didn't take them. You ever slept here? It's scary, really crazy people coming and going all night. And the sirens. The goddamn sirens.'

'Yes. It can be intimidating.' He opened the office door. 'You had breakfast?' He ushered her inside as he brushed snowflakes off his collar.

'Not hungry,' she replied.

He hung his flowing caramel coat on the back of the door and pulled up a chair next to hers. 'Let's not add another layer of problems.'

She pinched her stomach. 'I could do with losing a few pounds.'

'Bea, eat something! Actually, I haven't had breakfast

either. I'll get us a couple of bagels and coffee. How do you take your coffee?'

'I don't know. Okay, a cup of tea,' she said. 'Or coffee. You said coffee. A little milk. Whatever. I don't know.'

While he was out, she surveyed the room. There were two prints on the wall, framed without glass. All doctors' offices seemed to have the same art. There must be a School Of Art For Medical Facilities, with a code that banned bright colours or complex images and only allowed soothing scenes of pretty flowers and trees that bent to a breeze and blended with dingy cream walls. This office boasted a twinset of pink-and-lavender flowers that could not enliven any interior and had already received the last rites from a thick coat of dust.

'Bagels and tea.'

His voice startled her.

He sat down and handed her a cup. 'Hope that's enough milk.' He added cream to his coffee and took a sip. 'Now, what's been happening that's knocked you back so badly?'

Bea blew at the tea, watching the steam rise. 'Nothing.'

'From your notes, you've had outpatient treatment for severe depression. Do you know what triggers it?'

She sighed and closed her eyes. 'Do we have to talk about this now?'

'I'm afraid we do,' he said softly.

She kept her eyes shut tight. 'Losses,' she said quietly. 'The losses keep piling up.'

'What sort of losses?'

'Usual stuff.'

'And in the past, how have you coped?'

She opened her eyes and stared at the specks of dirt on her brown shoes. 'Meds. Therapy. You know the drill. Talk about your mother for a couple of years.'

'You haven't lost your sense of humour.'

She gave him a faint smile. 'Should've been a stand-up comic.'

'The medication hasn't helped?'

'Not really.'

'But do you take them as prescribed?'

'When I feel better I usually stop.'

He wagged a finger at her. 'Self-medication. Naughty, naughty.'

'I feel like a failure for taking them.'

'Why?'

She didn't answer.

'Bea, a chemical imbalance happens with depression. Willpower can't correct that. If you had diabetes I doubt you'd be telling me you feel a failure because you have to take drugs to deal with it.'

'Not the same.'

'It's exactly the same. You have to understand that, given your long history of depression, you may have to take meds for a while. It's not a reflection on your character.' He paused. 'Your notes mention a significant relationship ending.'

She crossed her arms tight across her chest, holding herself together.

'You've had a lot to deal with lately. When a relationship ends it's often like a death. That can make people without depression feel terrible.'

'Whatever.'

'What is it then?'

Her throat tightened. She tried to hold it back, but a sob escaped. 'I don't think things will ever be normal for me,' she whispered. 'You know, like having a family.'

'Why would you think that?'

'It's the way I'm made. I'm going to be alone for the rest of my life.'

'Well, that's something we'll explore.'

'Some things just are the way they are,' she said, turning away to wipe the tears with her sleeve.

'Talk me through how you came from Trinidad to Boston.'

'I went to college here. Did my graduate work here and was offered a job on the faculty. So I'm here by default really.'

'How long's that?'

'Ten years.' She thought about the cold outside that she had never become accustomed to. Ten Bostonian winters had attacked and retreated. She did not think she could survive this current onslaught.

'You like Boston? Have you got a good network?'

'It's okay, I guess.' She shrugged. 'I have a few friends.' She picked up a bagel, and put it back down without taking a bite. 'It's not home.'

'Home is Trinidad?'

'Sort of. Not sure.'

'Why not?'

'Been away too long. Never felt I belonged anyway.' She sat on her hands, staring at the floor. 'Never fitted in.'

'Why?'

'Always felt I was on the outside. It's easier in Boston. There's no pretence that I'll ever belong.'

Dr. Payne placed his empty coffee cup on the desk. 'All the time we've been talking, you've been staring at the floor. Is there a reason you won't look at me?'

'I can't.'

'Why not?'

Her hands blocked her face and she burst into tears.

'What are you afraid of?' he asked

'I don't belong here,' she whispered through the tears. 'I don't belong here.'

'No. You don't belong here.' He paused. 'But you do need help. Look at me.'

'I want to go home. Need some rest. This place is a prison.'

He nudged a box of tissues into her hand. 'You will get better.'

'You don't know that.' She slammed the box of tissues on the desk and hugged her knees. 'I've felt like this before. I can't keep living like this from one episode to another. I just can't.'

He tapped a pen on his desk. 'We're going to figure out the right medication. But it takes time. Unfortunately these drugs take a few weeks to kick in.'

Between sobs she blurted out, 'Don't believe you. No more. You don't know what it's like. No hope.'

'Sorry, what did you say?'

'I don't want any more hope.'

'You don't think you will get better?'

'No, I don't. And what drags me down is not the depression but the hope each time that this is the last time I'll ever go through this pain.'

'You're right. I can't promise you'll never have another acute episode. But there's a high probability that with the right medication and appropriate therapy you will get well. And I don't mean the therapy where you sit and talk about your mother for ages.'

Bea wished he would leave and hoped he would stay.

Dr. Payne explained that he wanted to admit her to a small hospital nearby where she would have the right medication and therapy. He mentioned something called mindfulness. But she was past caring. She begged to be allowed home. Dr. Payne was unyielding: she could go voluntarily or he would have to make her. It was time to let others help.

The room overwhelmed her as if an invisible toxic gas had been released. The poison of sadness. They sat facing each other in silence. The seconds ticked into minutes. Bea slipped further inside herself, longing to evaporate. Slowly she looked up. Dr. Payne's blue eyes stared intently at her.

'Bea, do you know how powerful your feelings are right now? I think you still want to kill yourself. But you have doubts, don't you?'

Through the tears she whispered, 'I don't know what to do.'

'Agree to the hospital care. I don't want to send you there involuntarily.'

'How long will I have to stay?'

'Depends. A few weeks. We'll see how it goes.'

'I can't even decide if to have tea or coffee.'

'Then let me help.'

He walked to the other side of the desk and started writing in her folder. He explained that an ambulance would take her to the hospital and he would come later to check on her. Bea telephoned her landlady, Mrs. Harris, who agreed to pack a bag of the things she would need and to drop it off. The hospital, St. Anthony's, was in a nearby suburb called Somerville.

'Don't be scared,' Dr. Payne said. 'It's a place where you can get better.'

She wiped damp palms over her tear-stained face and almost managed a smile.

'What's so funny?' he asked.

'I'm Catholic. St. Anthony is the patron saint of lost things. Lost things. Lost souls. Seems appropriate.'

She went back to the lounge, slumped into the grey plastic chair she had used the previous night, and waited for her name to be called.

CHAPTER SIX

Yesterday was payday for Mummy so she said after work today we going Christmas shopping. And – and – and she said she's buying me an extra present for winning the recitation competition. Thank you Augustus who would not drink his soup. I love shopping. We have to buy gifts for Aunty Indra, Uncle Ricky, and my three cousins Priya, Sammy and Hari. Priya is like my best friend although she is a year older. Sammy and Hari are too young to bother with. We bought a perfume set for Miss Celia next door that I helped choose. Nanny got a blue dress with a white collar. If I know Nanny she will wear it straightaway for church on Christmas Day. It's a secret but Nanny bought silver hoop earrings for me to give Mummy on Christmas Day. I wrapped them up and put the box in the bottom of my drawer with the card I made for her at school. No way she will find it under my pile of white socks.

We put up the tree since last week. Is only a small, plastic tree, same height as me. When I grow up and have my own house I'll have a real tree that goes right up to the ceiling with snow all over it. You can buy snow in a can in Clark's Hardware. I like Clark's Hardware. The man in there always wants to give me sweets or a dollar but Mummy tells him not to spoil the child. Anyway, me, my husband and two children – a girl and a boy – will sit by the tree and sing carols. Nanny and Mummy will sit in rocking chairs and lead the singing. If Priya's coming then I guess I'll have to invite Sammy and Hari as well. I hope by then they can talk about something except cars and trucks.

Apart from the tree, Christmas food is what I look forward to most. It's the best food you going to get whole year. You should see the enormous ham Mummy buy. When she ready to bake it Christmas Eve she will decorate it with cloves and pineapple. Aunty Indra drop off a parcel with a zillion pastels. If you never had a pastel you really missing out. It's a cornmeal pocket with chicken, pork or beef with currants and spices. Yummy in my tummy. We'll be eating pastels from this Christmas to the next. Miss Celia sent five bottles of sorrel that line up in the fridge. Somebody give us punch de crème but that is a big people drink. It got rum or something strong in it. Mummy made her famous fruit cake and shared it out already. Aunty Indra always telling people that her sister Nalini fruit cake is pure rum with a little bit of cake mixed in. You could get drunk eating it so don't eat and drive. I tried a tiny slice but it tasted yuk. Give me a chocolate cake with vanilla frosting any day.

Oh gosh, I just remember we didn't get Boo-Boo a present. I wonder what Trincity Mall has for dogs? If I were Boo-Boo I might want food, a slice of bacon or some cheese. And for Christmas Day itself I could make him a new collar from the ribbons we have to wrap gifts. I will plait three ribbons and then tie the plait around his neck. Boo-Boo will look so cute. He just came and curled up under my feet like he knows I am planning treats for him.

I wish Mummy would hurry up and come home so we can go to the mall. It's gone two o'clock and she doesn't finish till five. She's a dental nurse. I don't have a choice about brushing my teeth for at least two minutes, three times a day. It's embarrassing at school because I am always the only one brushing after lunch. Mummy says that I am leading by example. I would rather get a cavity. I am sure people laugh at me behind my back and I don't blame them.

Today's going by super slow. There's nothing good on TV, only shows for little kids or nature programmes with people walking up mountains or cutting through jungle. My favourite show is about these teams that compete to make the best cupcakes. The winner gets to make cupcakes for celebrities plus a cheque for thousands of dollars, and we talking real US not Trini money.

It would be amazing if I came home from school and Mummy was waiting for me with fresh chocolate cupcakes with vanilla frosting. But joke is joke – that never happening. For a start my Mummy would never give me that amount of sugar after school to rot my teeth. She always trying to scare me saying that when you look at plaque under a microscope it's like tiny white worms crawling over your teeth and gums. Yuk, yuk, yuk. Maybe I should brush my teeth again in case I missed any worms.

I always reach home before Mummy. We keep the key under the palm plant on the patio. I normally make a cheese sandwich, do my homework and wait for her to come home. I know not to let anybody in. If anything happen I only have to bawl hard and Miss Celia will hear me. The rule is that if it get real dark and Mummy not home yet I'm supposed to go and wait by Miss Celia. That doesn't happen often, but sometimes the bus don't run on time and taxi don't like to come in the back where we living.

Miss Celia's not a bad lady and I shouldn't really say anything about her because she's kind to Mummy and me and look at all the sorrel drink she done give us. But sometimes it not easy to bite my tongue. I'm by her waiting, listening for Mummy's footsteps, and for no good reason she would start asking me about my father.

'You don't find it strange that your mother never tell you your father name?'

'I don't mind.'

'Poor child. I can't imagine growing up not knowing who your father is.'

I pretend to be reading.

'Maybe she give you a hint and you forget?'

'No, Miss Celia. She never tell me nothing.'

'Well, he can't be full Indian because you come out mix-up. You have something else besides Indian.'

'I guess so. My hair not straight as Mummy's.'

'I'm not saying anything bad about your mother. Nalini is a hard-working woman, but your father, whoever he is, should be helping out.'

Miss Celia hesitated. 'I mean, on an evening like this when Nalini working late, it should be your father you go stay with. I not running you from the house, but suppose I was a woman who like to go out in the evening to church or take in a little karaoke? Where you would stay then, eh?'

I never knew what to say when Miss Celia started up like this. Mummy should let me wait in my own house till she come home. I can take care of myself. It's not like I had a Dad and then he left us. I never ever had a Dad, so I don't know different. Sometimes I think it would be nice to have one for parents' day at school or to take me to the beach. But it's not a big deal. Whenever I ask Mummy she either gets vex or looks sad. No matter how I beg, she said she made a vow on her father's grave never to say his name.

I thought Aunty Indra, as her only sister, might know something, so I asked her recently when Miss Celia's old-talk was starting to get on my nerves. She said is not her place to say anything, and if I find out it not going to be her doing. I ask if she could at least say if he alive or dead. Her eyes open big and she look like she was going to say something then she stop herself just in time. She said is up to my Mummy to decide if and when to tell me certain things. Then she said not to worry. Mummy will tell me when the time is right.

I am scared to bring up any talk of my Dad with Nanny, but if anybody know it go be she. Is her daughter we talking about. When I was spending the day with her I made up my mind to ask. She is a nice Nanny but she's strict and don't take nonsense from nobody. So when we were sitting together on the couch looking at TV I waited till the commercial about taking a luxury Caribbean cruise.

'Nanny, who is my father?'

'What?'

'Who is my father?'

'Why you asking me for?'

'Mummy says she made a vow on Nana's grave that she never going to tell a soul his name.'

'Well, if your mother make that kind of vow she must have her reasons.'

'But is my father. I have a right to know. I'm the only person in my school who doesn't know who their father is.'

Then the strangest thing happened. Nanny who don't like to hug up anybody, or give kiss unless it's your birthday, pull me towards her so my face in her chest and she drop a kiss on top of my head. That was weird. I don't think I should bother the old lady again.

CHAPTER SEVEN

The weight of Mira's letter increased every day until Bea could no longer lug it around. It had to be opened. Bea settled on doing the deed in a public place. Work seemed perfect. She laughed to herself: if she did lose control, what better place than a Crisis Centre? Mira's words could be explosive.

On the drive to Mount Russet she decided to wait until there was a lull in the morning, settle in with a double espresso, and consume the letter slowly. Once that decision was made, her heart rate soared and her foot pressed down on the accelerator. What did the damn woman have to say that could only be done by a letter? Was this going to disrupt her contained, ordered life? Her brakes screeched as she swung into her regular parking spot. She turned off the engine and grabbed her bag. She couldn't wait any longer. Her hands quivered as she tore the envelope open and pulled out a handwritten letter wrapped around a pretty pink-and-white card.

The trembling spread from her hands to her whole body. She could barely hold the card steady enough to read it. It was a party invitation. Her paternal grandmother, Granny Gwen, would be celebrating her ninetieth birthday at the Royal Savannah Hotel, Port of Spain, at the beginning of October. She made a quick calculation: forty days and counting. Mira's letter was plain and brief. She was sorry for the pain that had been caused between them. No one was getting younger and it was high time they buried the past. Granny Gwen's deepest wish was to have all the family together for this milestone birthday. For her grandmother's sake she should come home. It was signed 'Love, Mom'.

Only five lines, but she read them until she knew them by heart. She felt pure anger. It pulsed through her body and took shape as trembling, sweaty palms and a throbbing head. Ten long years and this was it? This was the hand of reconciliation? Five lines? Was time itself enough reason to forgive?

The letter did not even raise the problem of Bea's former boyfriend, Michael. Why write after all this time and not mention him? Did Mira hope that she had forgotten? Was he to be rolled into a bundle along with a pile of other spiky hurts and hidden in a box in the basement? She could almost stomach seeing Mira, but not Michael, especially if he was now embedded in her family. Mira should have said something. How sorry was she really if Michael remained taboo? *Bury the past?* That was precisely the problem. They were a family of gravediggers continually burying the inconvenient and unpalatable. Bea had spent long, lonely years doing her own exhausting private excavations and reburials. It had been mandatory for her second career. Burying the past because time had rotted it to near invisibility was not an option.

Bea sank back into the car seat and looked up. People hurried past towards the Mount Russet Hospital compound. Anonymous faces, their hurts tucked away in pockets, bags and bodies. She gripped the steering wheel to steady herself.

A sharp rap on her window jolted her upright. It was Nick Payne. She wound the glass down and forced a smile.

'You planning on actually making it inside?' he asked,

smiling.

'Yes. Yes. Hi, Nick!' She spoke fast. 'Collecting my thoughts before I face the zoo.'

'Come on. Sitting there isn't going to make it easier.'

He had the kindest blue eyes. She stuffed the card back into her overflowing bag and climbed out of the car.

'You okay?' he asked.

'Yeah, it's nothing,' said Bea. Her convincing tone took even her by surprise.

'I've been meaning to ask you when you're going to organise a hike for the staff,' he said. 'Summer's gone.'

'Gosh, haven't thought about it.'

'But you're the one who always plans these great outings. Please let's do something before the cold sets in.'

They parted inside the Crisis Centre. Bea headed for the nurses' station. Where would she find the cheeriness to bring the staff together? That was Nick Payne's job as director. In his easy, charming way he had shifted the burden to her. Well, she owed him big time. Putting together a staff hike and picnic was a tiny repayment of the debt. The clock over the coffee machine said it was three minutes to nine and already she was exhausted. She collected her files. Through the thick glass door at the end of the corridor she spotted a police officer staring at the TV and another hovering by the window. A heavy-set man, extensively tattooed, maybe early fifties, was joined to the officer at the wrist by steel cuffs.

Bea was glad for the protection. Being attacked by aggressive patients was a real risk: she knew at first hand several horror stories about psychologists being attacked. In one particularly awful case a colleague at the Crisis Centre had lost her partner in 9/11 and then, a decade later, with a new partner and a new baby, was stabbed by a patient and left permanently wheelchair-bound.

She thought of what Stephen had said about his neighbours seeing him being taken away. She had wanted to tell him that she too remembered the police taking her forcibly to this very Crisis Centre, years ago. Being hauled from your workplace was even worse than being carted away from your home. She was not a criminal – not so much as an outstanding parking ticket to her name. But the police had been involved. No point in denying that shame. She liked to think that her experiences made her a better, more empathetic psychologist. Or perhaps it was a sign that she was inherently too weak to mine the horrors her clients stashed inside themselves.

*

That first day, when she was transferred to St. Anthony's, only an ambulance was needed. No police. No sirens. The day had passed in a flurry of form-filling and examinations. She was bounced from one strange room to another to be prodded, poked and questioned. When she was finally sent back to her single room she crawled into the narrow bed, fully clothed, and stared at the dull cream ceiling and walls. That unidentifiable dingy paint seemed standard issue in hospitals everywhere. At least the room had an en-suite – compact, but with a clever mirrored wall of safety glass that made it seem more spacious. Apart from bars on the window, there were no architectural reminders of the ward's purpose. But her peace was short-lived. The chatter and movement outside her room got louder and closer. She lay silent, her eyes shut. Whatever was happening would stop soon. She did not need to be involved.

'Beatrice?' asked a sharp voice. Bea shot up. A nurse stood in the doorway.

'It's Bea,' she answered.

'All right, Bea,' said the nurse. 'Time for dinner and meds. You go to the nurses' station for your meds and then down to the ground floor. You must have been shown where the canteen is. Eat there or bring up your tray to the lounge.'

Bea got up reluctantly and followed the nurse. There were a few people ahead of her, waiting for their medication. No one turned round as she joined the queue. She waited, arms folded, staring at the ground. When her turn came she was asked to confirm her name and silently accepted a small cup with two red capsules and two white.

'What are these?' she asked.

One of the nurses looked up at her, then checked her clipboard. 'Dr. Payne prescribed an increase in Venlafaxine and added Quetiapine.'

It was an unfamiliar combination, but she swallowed them quickly and stepped aside without meeting anyone's eyes.

The patients ahead of her were walking towards the exit, so Bea followed the trail down two flights of stairs to the dining room. She kept her head down but could not help noticing as they passed the floor below that its only access was through a closed, reinforced door with a tiny glass window. Whatever she had done wrong, it had not landed her behind that door. She was one floor up and determined she would stay that way while she was at St. Anthony's.

At the entrance to the dining room a handwritten notice on the chalkboard proclaimed that the mains of the day were beef and potato stew, couscous with tangy chicken, or vegetarian chilli with garlic bread. Bea had not eaten since the bagel and tea Dr. Payne had brought her that morning. The kitchen aromas were warm and tempting. She glanced around the dining room, taking in the choices. Time ticked by. A man joined the queue behind her. It was time to choose. What to eat? Chicken was nice. But was the vegetarian chilli better? And what about beef? She was hungry. Or maybe she did not need a meal now. She felt impatient eyes on her back so she grabbed what was closest – a cold plate of fruit, vegetable sticks and cheese – and hurried off to sit in the farthest corner. If she could summon a magical power right now it would be a cloak of invisibility, to get through whatever time she had to serve at St. Anthony's quietly, quickly, and overlooked.

Once Bea had settled into her meal and was sure no one would intrude, she dared to look around. Everyone looked so ordinary. Hospitals usually displayed their wounded but at St. Anthony's no one walked around in pyjamas, bandaged, or attached to tubes. There were no wheelchairs or crutches, no oppressive stench of illness masked by lemon-scented disinfectant. Just a group of about fifty ordinary people, dressed in unremarkable clothes, concentrating on their humdrum dinner.

Bea finished her vegetable sticks and started slowly on the thin slices of apple. She looked up again and instantly regretted it as she caught the eye of a pale young man from her ward. They had been introduced earlier. His name might be Dave – she was not sure. He quickly looked away. Maybe he recognised her distress, or maybe he too wanted nothing more than to be left alone. Whichever – it was a sign that she had been in the dining room long enough. She took her half-empty plate to the corner where other dirty dishes were stacked on trays. As she walked back to the exit she noticed for the first time a small room off the main dining area. The shapes of several diners were silhouetted against the cheap white screen that protected their identities. No one was talking. Another place to avoid being sent to. She had better behave.

About seven o'clock she came back to the ward and was told by a passing nurse that Dr. Payne was there and would be checking on her soon. Bea went to her room and sat in the small stiff armchair next to the barred window. Hooting and cheering from a television game show mixed with the general mêlée of movement and talk from down the hallway. Bea chewed her already short nails and waited for Dr. Payne.

When he finally put his head around the door she had trouble containing her relief at seeing a familiar face. She gave him her chair and sat on the bed opposite. Dr. Payne smiled as he asked if everything was fine and had she been shown around places like the dining room and gym. He urged her to get in touch with friends who were welcome during visiting hours. Bea managed a weak smile but knew that was impossible. She asked if she could leave on her own to go shopping or have a coffee. Not yet. He felt it was too early. And then he was done, promising to check on her the following day.

With Dr. Payne gone, Bea sat on the bed, unsure what was expected of her. It was too early to sleep. Television held no interest for her. There was a shelf of books in the lounge, but there was no way she was going to risk having to make small talk while retrieving one. Indecision gave way to anxiety, and anxiety morphed into numbing fear. Forty-eight hours earlier she had been free and knew what she had to do. Now she was in a room she could not leave, in a place she did not understand. Sitting on the bed much longer might attract the attention of the patrolling nurses, but what else was she to do? Outside her room the passing foot traffic seemed to be lessening, the noises more muted. It was at least thirty minutes before she forced herself to move and change into her nightdress. She turned off the light and was surprised at how heavy with sleep she suddenly felt.

*

In her office, Bea put the teacup on her desk and turned on the lights. Few had made her journey from one side of the desk to the other. She should be proud. There was no reason to think it would all unravel because of a short visit to Trinidad. She was stronger than that. If this was a test of her worth and everything she had achieved in the intervening years, then she would not be found wanting. Thriving in voluntary exile, far away from the site of memories and dreams, might have been enough in the early years. But surely those she had left behind could get a look in now. After all, the visit could be kept to a long weekend.

She sipped her tea and thumbed through the files she had collected. It all seemed routine apart from the client outside, handcuffed to the police. He had tried to stab his girlfriend when she announced she was leaving him and taking their baby son. It was Bea's job to do the first interview, brief Dr. Payne, and then sit in on any further client assessment. She needed to be alert, focused to pick up signs of psychosis, drug abuse, anything that might explain today's behaviour or indicate future risks.

But even as she gathered her iPad and headed off to the assessment room her mind was wandering. Mira and Granny Gwen aside, there were people and places she missed. It was strange what popped into her head. On the drive from Piarco airport to Mira's house in Port of Spain, they always passed that bleak monastery built into the side of the northern range of mountains. The sprawling, castle-like Mount St. Benedict stood so high up that low cumulus clouds often sliced off the tops of the buildings. Her kindergarten school was somewhere up that mountainside. She remembered unsmiling nuns. Was it her imagination, or did they really smack tiny hands with a wooden ruler for the slightest perceived wrong?

Then they would swish past the chaotically sprawled-out shopping mall at Valsayn. And the Nestlé factory. Her child's mind had imagined huge metal vats inside with unlimited supplies of Milo milk chocolate drink or smooth chocolate to be pressed into bars, a Caribbean version of *Charlie and the Chocolate Factory* that she might get to enter one day. And as they neared home they always had to go around the Savannah in the heart of Port of Spain, ringed by once splendid mansions from a bygone age. She loved it when they stopped at one of the coconut vendors. Before their eyes he would slice the top off a nut with his machete and they would drink the ice-cold water inside. Port of Spain may boast five-star hotels and an imitation Sydney Opera House, but she hoped there was still space in town for a simple coconut vendor.

No decision was necessary today. She would get on with her work and let the invitation wait. Anger, fear and nostalgia would have to wrestle a final decision out of her.

CHAPTER EIGHT

Bea slept fitfully that first night at St. Anthony's, fearful of the unfamiliar surroundings and the nighttime din. Nurses stopped regularly by her room to shine a torch on her face. Routine hospital policy, they explained. The drugs helped her doze off at first, but her anxieties broke through and by three in the morning she gave up trying to sleep. Why was she being forcibly kept alive in this jailhouse? The goodbyes had already been said. Her papers were either shredded or in a neat pile on her kitchen table. Yes, she had more doubts now, but nothing had fundamentally changed. And she resented not being allowed to end the semester neatly, with grades properly delivered. All she had left to live for were her beloved students, and that one last goodbye had not happened – at least not in the way she had planned. Well, they couldn't lock her up for ever. Besides, the medical insurance was bound to cut off funds at some point. Best to do as she was told and not draw unnecessary attention to herself. Soon she would be in control again.

Breakfast was tea from the machine on the ward – she could not face the canteen again so soon. She gulped it down, went back to bed and curled up under the blankets, weary and weighed down. In recent weeks, routine matters of personal hygiene – brushing teeth, showering, choosing her clothes, getting dressed – had become exhausting challenges. Only a lazy failure would take almost three hours over basic ablutions. The woman who held a university post and could be washed, changed, breakfasted and out the door in less than thirty minutes had disappeared, leaving behind this inept doppelgänger.

'Morning. Weather getting good!' said a woman in pink-and-green scrubs as she pushed her head around the unlocked door to Bea's room. 'I'm Sharon, one of the nursing assistants here on the ward. I hear you is a Trini?'

Bea sat up and took in the broad flat face of this dark, buxom, middle-aged woman. The cloying smell of cheap perfume filled the room.

'Yes. I'm from Trinidad,' Bea said softly. 'You too?'

'No man,' said Sharon, settling herself in the armchair. 'Grenadian. Been here a good thirty years now. Imagine that.' She looked around the bare room. 'You sleep sound?'

'Not really,' said Bea, and immediately regretted it. 'Actually it was okay. I'm fine.'

'Why you don't put on a little TV to keep you company? That's why they have it put up in the room.'

'Don't know why, but I find I can't watch TV.'

'Well, get a book then. I hear you working in the university. A bright girl like you must like book.'

Bea sat up. 'I'll get one today.'

Sharon stole a quick glance outside Bea's door. 'This not the kind of thing I supposed to say to people, but you is different. This place ain't good for we people,' she whispered. 'We so don't get these kind of sickness in the head. That is a white people thing. How much people you know back home does get put in hospital when things ain't too right? I working here long and is them white people that does be here idling. They idling instead of getting up and going to work. If you ask me them have it too easy. We not like them, girl. If you know what good for you, you would start getting better fast-fast.'

Bea managed a slight nod. Getting out of St. Anthony's fast-fast was her goal. But Sharon had it wrong. The reason 'we people' weren't in places like St. Anthony's was because 'we people' didn't have facilities like this in Trinidad or Grenada. But arguing with Sharon was the last thing she felt able to do.

When Sharon left, Bea looked for the first time at the papers she had been given, outlining her programme. Group therapy was later that morning. She mentally rehearsed the sequence of actions that would take her from the bedroom to the group therapy room one floor up.

Swing legs over side of bed.

Stand up.

Put on slippers.

Possibly.

Not sure.

Okay, no slippers.

Walk three paces to bathroom door.

She had been warned there were no locks on the doors. Hospital policy.

Shower.

Shampoo hair today?

No energy. Hair's greasy. Oh shit.

She pulled the hair off her face and into a ponytail.

Wash it tomorrow. No one will notice.

Her armpit hair was longer than she normally allowed. It would need shaving soon.

Why bother? Nobody's going to look.

She opened the closet door and stared at her blue and black jeans. She decided on the black pair and matched them with a crumpled black T-shirt, then pulled a black sweater on and slipped into a pair of black flats. The clock showed a few minutes before eight. She had been up for almost five hours and still she struggled to face the day.

Dirty, lazy, woman.

No wonder he left me.

She stayed in her room, unable to take the final step into the public area of the ward. It was only when she heard voices outside talking about the group therapy that she forced herself into the corridor. The pale young man she had seen yesterday in the canteen introduced himself again as Dave, and she followed his lead into a windowless room with armchairs arranged in a circle. As the newest person, she had to say her name first, then the dozen or so patients introduced themselves.

The facilitator, a gentle soft-spoken woman called Melanie, encouraged the gathering to talk about how things were with them that morning. Dave was expecting his first visitor in the three weeks he had been there. A former girlfriend, actually his only girlfriend ever, had promised to come by after work. His whole body jittered with excitement. Bea found it hard to tell how old he was with his skinny pale body and open child-like face. He must be younger than her – early twenties at most. Why would such a sweet man-boy be here?

Sarah, who sat cross-legged, was due to go home for the weekend and unsure of coping. Her husband had given her an ultimatum. After years of unsuccessful attempts he wanted her to forget about ever having a baby. It had destroyed them emotionally and financially. If she could not let go, then he could not stay. Sarah wanted her marriage, but did she want a baby at any price? During the six weeks she had been at St. Anthony's she had felt calmer. The visit home might help her decide. Bea could hardly believe that anyone would be here for that long. Six weeks? She expected to be gone in a week, two tops.

She felt complete relief when the hour-and-a-half session ended and she had not been made to chip in with the discussion. But Dave was waiting for her as they walked out. Did she know about the art and craft classes every afternoon?

He had made an enamel brooch last week. Today they were going to try making paper. Bea smiled politely, knowing she would not be there unless Dr. Payne specifically prescribed it.

In the time before lunch Dave invited her to have a coffee with him in the canteen. There was something gentle and vulnerable in his bearing that made it rude to refuse him.

'Why are you here?' he asked quietly almost as soon as they had sat down.

'Not sure,' she said, looking around.

'It's no big deal.' He sipped his tea. 'I was knocking back the booze. Took too many pills one night and now I'm here.'

Bea concentrated on her coffee.

'I thought maybe I was an alcoholic,' he went on. 'But since I've been here I know that's not me.'

Bea nodded in agreement and took another gulp of too-hot coffee.

'It's the abuse that got me drinking,' Dave said, biting his nails. 'Stepdad. Every chance he got it was bathroom door locked. Down on the floor. He only stopped last year. I suspect he's abusing my little nephew too.'

He looked up and beyond her. 'I'm not gay. I'm not. I've had a girlfriend and everything. Melanie says just because he did that to me doesn't make me gay.'

Bea's coffee suddenly tasted bitter. She had no business being here.

Towards lunchtime people began to flow into the canteen. Some joined their table. Bea felt boxed in, but afraid to offend by leaving. She only relaxed a little when it became clear there was no need to talk. A listener was valued. Smells of cooking wafted through to the table while the group sat chatting. Sarah was the first to investigate. She was sure she smelt spicy chilli. Then a group of about ten people burst noisily into the canteen, a swagger of silk, leather, and sunglasses. At least two of them sported cowboy boots. Could these be in-patients? They must have wandered in accidentally. Their flamboyance silenced Bea's group. Compared to these wild things, they looked like unsophisticated country cousins on a supervised day trip to the big city.

Bea leaned over to Dave. 'Who are they?' she whispered.

'Fourth floor. Addicts. They don't talk to the rest of us.'

'Do we ever do stuff with them?'

'No. They have their own groups and everything. I only ever see them in here.'

She thought for a moment about this new tribe. They seemed happier than her bunch.

She leaned back over to Dave. 'Yesterday there were people eating behind that partition off to the side. It wasn't them, was it?'

'No.' He took a breath in and bit his lip. 'That's the eating disorders group.'

'Oh. Sorry.'

'They don't do much with us either. They're on the fifth floor.'

'Can we go there?'

'Don't know. Don't think so. Well, I've never been up there.'

Bea could feel anxiety welling up inside. She wanted to leave, but she could smell the warm, spicy food. She should not eat. Eating would only prolong a life she was ambivalent about. An apple would be enough. But there was only one fruit on display: grapefruit. Menacing grapefruit, cut in half with a cherry in the middle, like an evil eye searching for victims to devour. She was afraid to ask if they might have a bigger selection squirrelled away behind the counter. Maybe she could have a Diet Coke as well? That had no nutritional value. But they had Sprite Zero too. So many decisions. Her hands began to shake. She abandoned the idea of fruit or a drink. Suddenly, from one second to the next, she knew she had to leave the canteen.

Don't run.

Don't draw attention to yourself.

Walk quickly.

Her leg muscles felt weak and it took all her will to concentrate on walking. Sweat began pouring down into her eyes, blurring her vision. She was almost there. She had to keep focusing as she climbed up the stairs.

You're on the ward now.

Down the corridor.

Third door on the left.

You can do it.

A few more steps.

She collapsed on the bed and burst into tears. She heard low whimpering sounds, and it was some time before she realised they were coming from deep inside herself.

Nurse Sharon found her curled in a ball. 'What wrong now?'

Bea didn't answer.

'You hurt yourself?'

Silence.

'Somebody make you cry?'

Bea wished the nurse would go away or shut up.

'Well, I going sit down here little bit,' she said. 'I right here, girl. Rest yourself. This go pass.'

Pain swelled up inside her like a balloon being slowly inflated. It moved from the pit of her stomach, up through her chest, down through her arms, out through her fingertips, into her thighs, through her knees, and settled on the tips of her toes. She was a single, bloated mass of unnameable pain. The room teetered, then slipped and slid, taking her far away to a hilly suburb in the north of Trinidad. She was about five years old.

*

'Is every day so I have to tell you to take your nasty elbows off the table!' screamed Mira.

'Why do I have to eat a whole grapefruit and a bowl of cereal?' whined Bea. 'I only want the grapefruit.'

'Hurry up and eat what I give you. Lord Jesus, give me patience.'

Mira scraped her long jet black hair into a ponytail and pulled an elastic band around it. Bea was a miniature version of her, with the same golden-brown complexion and thick straight hair that swished down her back.

Her mother picked up a wooden spoon and shook it in front of little Bea's eyes. 'Every morning is a big headache dealing with you, madam. The day ain't even start good yet and I already dead tired.'

Bea picked up her fork and dug into the fruit until she had pulled a mouthful of the tart flesh free from its membrane. She brought each small forkful to eye level and inspected its tight, cellular structure before savouring it.

'Stop eating so slow, child. You want to kill me?'

'Mummy, you forget it's Saturday. No school.'

Her mother rolled her eyes to the ceiling. 'I have a whole heap of things to do! When I was your age I was helping my mother in the house. But you? Whole day you in the yard or next door playing. Stay inside and read a book today.'

'I promised Michael we'd finish making the play house behind the Julie mango tree.'

'You think I reach where I is in life playing dolly house every day so? Go play. See if you don't end up like your father.'

Bea continued excavating the grapefruit. 'So what if I come out like Daddy?'

'Don't be rude, child. And stay out of big people business.'

Bea bent her head. 'Sorry.'

'I hope you sorry for true. My life would be a lot better if it wasn't for you and your damn father. I don't get a minute to myself because of all you.'

Her father Alan Clark, tall, slim, almond-brown with curly black hair, walked into the kitchen, wiping the corners of his eyes clean. Even with his rumpled morning face there was no mistaking that he was a handsome man. He smiled at Bea. 'Morning, Beezy.'

She smiled back. 'Morning, Daddy. Can we go for a long long long long long drive today?'

'No problem, pumpkin. Where you want to go?'

As Alan turned to pick up the kettle he bumped into Mira. Her coffee mug crashed to the floor and shattered, spilling hot coffee over the counter and cupboards, staining her dress and puddling the floor.

'Look at the mess you make! You nearly burn me real bad!' Mira shouted. 'But don't worry.' She jabbed her finger at her chest. 'The maid here will clean up and finish cooking the food!'

Alan looked around, probably searching for a rag. 'Woman, have a heart. I just wake up. It was an accident. You need help today?'

'Need help? Well look at my crosses. Only a real stupid fool would ask a question like that. The house don't clean itself, you know!'

'Let me help you clean up the kitchen and then we go do the rest of the house tomorrow. We planning a little cook by Zyda and Derek them. And Mama say she want me to take she to see Tanti June quite up in Arima. And you know Tanti living in real bush.'

'Why you always have to be the one to take she here, there and everywhere?' snapped Mira. 'She don't have other children? Last I check she have more than one son.'

'Look, she asked me to help she out.' Alan wiped the counter with a paper towel. 'And I go take Bea for the drive so you will get some peace and quiet.'

Mira opened drawers, searching for another rag. 'She always want something doing. Go here. Do this. Do that. Want. Want. Want. Man, I fed up with your blasted mother!'

That's when he grabbed a meat knife off the countertop, gripped Mira's arm and pushed it at her throat. 'You don't tell me nothing about my mother!' he hissed.

The tip of the long blade pressed against Mira's skin. The kitchen was deadly quiet. With Mira's hard breathing the knife could easily draw blood.

Bea did not remember how long the standoff lasted. Eventually Alan threw the knife on the kitchen counter and marched out. The attack was over as abruptly as it had started. All the while Bea had sat frozen to her chair with a spoonful of grapefruit poised in mid-air. Mira stood still on the spot where Alan had pinned her. Outside the car door slammed shut. The engine started. He was gone.

Bea had eaten her last grapefruit.

CHAPTER NINE

I t's funny how when it's holidays the time goes fast like a racing car. When it's school time it slows right down like one of those African snails that we have in our yard. If you don't have African snails then you lucky. They are the ugliest-est creatures in the whole wide universe, with a big fat brown body and a huge shell that can grow big as my fist. When I see them in the yard I used to stamp my foot on the shell and kill them. Nasty slimy giants. Apparently you not supposed to do that. Miss Celia see me killing one the other day and shout out that I doing it wrong because that don't kill the eggs and each one of them disgusting snails have hundreds of eggs inside. The only way to make sure you kill off the snail and the eggs is to pour salt on it. Since then I have my own bag of salt I keep on the veranda. As soon as I wake up I go outside to check for snails. As the salt touches them they curl up, go fizzle-fizzle-fizzle and boops they dead. It's probably a sin but I like to hear the sound of them snails dying. Fizzzz. I try to kill as many as I can before eating my cereal.

Even if the holidays rushing by I think I will always remember this as the best Christmas ever. Mummy (who still writes the card 'from Santa') gave me a games console and Aunty Indra's family added three games to go with it. Nanny bought a four-poster bedroom set and a three-piece living room set for my dolly house. They are amazing. I wish we had real furniture like that in our house. I even get a gift from Miss Celia. It was a book of children's Bible stories and to be honest I know all the stories already but she is a poor old lady and I'm not even her family or anything.

Every Sunday when Mummy cook lunch she makes me take some for Miss Celia. If you see how much food she does cook: rice, pigeon peas, stew chicken, macaroni pie, plantain and ground provision. Only things we don't eat are pork and beef. Mummy say proper Indian people don't eat pork because it dirty and they don't eat cow because it holy. We always have enough left over for Monday and Tuesday even after giving Miss Celia food. It makes up for the other days when Mummy too tired to cook and we make do with bread and cheese or corned beef and rice. I want to learn to cook but Mummy said I'm too small to light the stove. Next year I should be old enough.

We missed church this morning. Mummy got up late and went straight in the kitchen. Apparently the Lord will have to wait till she done cooking. We aiming for the seven o'clock service tonight and as school not opening till Wednesday it won't interfere with bedtime. I don't see why we can't skip church this one Sunday. Is not like God didn't see us plenty times over Christmas and New Year, but I best keep that thought to myself. The one thing you don't want to see is my mother when she vex.

So is church we heading to, never mind it started raining. We catch a maxi-taxi that take us right outside the church. Still it had enough puddles to jump over from the road to inside the church. Hardly anybody in the congregation – only some old people who look like they might drop down and dead before the service finish. The man in front of us must be at least forty he so old. During the sermon – which was the story of the good Samaritan – I count thirty people in church. But is the singing that does bring down the service.

Not a single one of them old-timers could sing 'Great is thy Faithfulness' in tune. On top of that the rain like it want to mash up the church roof. You can't include Mummy in the singing because she don't sing. She does pretend she singing but you don't hear a sound coming out her mouth. Today every hymn we sing ending up sounding like we at a funeral – as if the Bible ban happiness in church or else the Lord will strike us down.

At least the service didn't go over time and, since this wasn't the usual group we worship with, Mummy had no excuse to stay behind and talk to this body and that body. As soon as I step out into the churchyard I accidentally land in a puddle with water up to my ankles. I could feel the rain pelting at my chest, my arms and my legs. It seemed to be coming at you sideways so the umbrella not much help. We stood up by the side of the road waiting for a maxi-taxi or a bus. Every time a car pass you have to pray you don't get spray with dirty water because of course it don't have a pavement and I in a dress.

We wait, we wait, we wait, and no taxi passing and the few that whoosh by full up. Maybe is because it's Sunday or maybe is because it raining hard but the road them empty. No cars and no people. Plus the street lights not all working. Even the moon look like it afraid of the rain because I can't see it in the sky. My dress clinging to me and my teeth chattering. All I want to do is reach home, get dry off and watch TV in Mummy's bed. If we don't catch a ride soon we going to miss 'Law and Order' on TV tonight.

Well, it look like we not reaching home any time soon. No taxi. No bus. Is Mummy's fault. If she had let us skip church this one little Sunday then we wouldn't be out here in the dark getting wet. Now she want us to walk up the road. There's a place to shelter across the road from that big field where they sometimes put up a tent and have church with loud singing and clapping. She keep saying hurry up, you walking too slow. I'm walking as fast as I can with two shoes full of water. We should be home like everybody else and is all because my holy mother can't miss a single Sunday service. Jesus better bless us specially. If you want us to win the lottery, Lord, we wouldn't say no and we would share it with Nanny and Aunty Indra and even Miss Celia will get some change. Just a thought, Jesus, if you looking down on us getting soaked.

It seemed like we walk half an hour to reach the shelter. You could hear the water swishing about in my good shoes. Mummy said to stop complaining, we only walked five minutes. And yes the shelter better than waiting in the rain, but I'm sure I'm going to catch a nasty cold. Where the good Samaritan they talk about now, eh? Maybe he still riding donkey rather than motor car or bus. Please, Jesus, please – I want to go home. I promise if you send a taxi right now I won't give Boo-Boo my carrots when Mummy not looking. And I will never answer back when Mummy talking to me. Please send a taxi now. Now please.

And who say prayers don't get answered? I hardly finish when we see a van coming towards us. Mummy said to stay under the shelter. At last a maxi-taxi going our way. Mummy step out into the road, rain pelting down, and start waving for the van to stop. But he not stopping. Mummy waving and he still coming towards us. She waving and he coming. She waving and waving. He getting closer and closer. Then bam.

He didn't stop.

I ran to her. Her face mash up and she not moving or saying anything and I screaming Mummy, Mummy, but she not answering. Rain pelting down on her. Blood like a river running off to the side of the road. Her arm looks funny. Her legs look funny. The driver stop up the road and start to reverse back. He come running out the van holding an umbrella.

'I hit she?'

'Mummy! Mummy! Answer me! You all right Mummy?'

'Oh God! I thought it was a cow. I swear is a cow I hit.'

'Is not a cow you stupid fool!'

He's on his cellphone but I can't hear what he shouting. I'm crying so hard. She not opening her eyes and she not talking.

'Mummy!'

I'm trying to hold her but I can't.

'Mummy! Mummy!'

The man say an ambulance coming.

Get the ambulance fast!

The driver tried to pull me off Mummy but I bite his hand so hard he bawl out. The rain not easing up at all. It must be hurting her to be on the hard road.

'Mummy! You hearing me? The ambulance coming. Hold on. It coming now.'

The man only saying it look just like a dark cow. Now he telling me that we can't move her out of the road and the rain because we might hurt her more. Why she not waking up? Her head bleeding. It must be hurting her so much. Mummy! I'm on my knees in the road. Lord, make sure she not hurt too bad even if she don't look good now. Save my Mummy, please Jesus. She always in church, Jesus. You must know what a good person she is, Lord. Stop the bleeding, please Jesus. Please Lord Jesus. Please Lord.

It take me a minute to realise the man kneeling down next to me and praying too.

Thy kingdom come, Thy will be done on earth as it is in heaven, Give us this day our daily bread, And forgive us our trespasses –

Mummy you going to be all right. The man say the ambulance here soon.

As we forgive those who trespass against us, And lead us not into temptation –

Please Jesus.

But deliver us from evil, For thine is the kingdom, the power and the glory,

For ever and ever, Amen. Our father, who art in heaven, hallowed be –

The sirens – the sirens getting louder. The ambulance here, Mummy. But I only seeing the police. Where the ambulance? Okay, it pulling up behind. Please Jesus help my Mummy.

They pushing me aside and I hear someone screaming and it take me a second to realise is me but I can't stop. They pull out a stretcher and they lifting her on it. Oh Lord there's so much blood on her dress you can hardly make out it was yellow before. You have to tiptoe around to not step in her blood. She's in the back of the ambulance now.

'Mummy! I want to stay with my Mummy!'

A policeman pick me up and I shove him away as hard as I could and a next one come and the two of them hold me down and put me in the police car. I was kicking to go in the ambulance but one of them holding on tight and he saying how we going to the hospital in the police car and it don't have room in the ambulance. I don't want to leave my Mummy.

'Stop bawling. What is your name?'

'The woman that get knocked down is your mother?'

'What is her name?'

The police want to know all kind of thing. Where my father? I tell him I don't know but to call my Aunty Indra and my Nanny. How I manage to remember Aunty Indra number I will never know because my mind jumbled up. One of the police saying not to worry, that my aunty will come for me. Where they taking my Mummy? How far to the hospital? She not going to dead is she? When I was talking to her she wasn't talking back. She lost so much blood. What happen if you loose all that blood? She will need stitches? I don't know what happen to her arm, and one leg was fold up under her. You think she break her leg? The police keep saying not to worry, my aunty coming just now. He already call her and she coming straight to the hospital. Not long now. Don't worry. The doctors will look after your Mummy. We nearly there. Hold on, child. We nearly reach.

CHAPTER TEN

Bea understood that showing up for Granny Gwen's ninetieth was not the same as living in the daily chaos of Trinidadian family life. But no matter how hard she tried, she trembled whenever she thought of a visit. In the quiet cool of early Sunday morning she put on her running shoes and joined the others pounding a path along the Charles River, hoping that the act of slow running would release her from this anxiety. Of course, ostrich-like, she could ignore the celebrations. Let the event pass without her. Who would really miss her? Granny Gwen might be a little put out, but she must be accustomed to Bea's absence. Once Alan and Mira had divorced, little Bea had felt irrelevant to Granny Gwen – that had only changed with Alan's death, when she became the remaining, much-valued link.

Later that day, weary and unquiet, Bea sat surrounded by half-scanned weekend papers, and absently began flicking through the Web for flights to Trinidad. The birthday party was only a month away. More than one airline offered specials, including packages with cut-rate hotel rooms. Each click melted the practical obstacles to taking the trip. It was affordable, and she had overdue holiday leave. What she still needed was an emotional battle plan that would get her back to Boston with at most superficial emotional scars. No more cutting – she had long since given up that release. Sometimes that early exposure to St. Anthony's still gnawed as if it was yesterday. She remembered all too well the early days of being there, queuing up with Dave for their happy pills.

'We've got music therapy this afternoon,' Dave had said. 'You coming?'

'Not if I can help it.'

'It's kind of nice.'

'Sorry. Not my thing.'

'See you after, then?'

'I'm not leaving.'

They shuffled forward in an orderly queue. Bea was the last to receive the morning's medical rations.

'Hi, there,' the nurse said. '400mg Venlafaxine, and Dr. Payne has increased your Quetiapine to 400mg.'

'Thanks.' Bea accepted the communion in two tiny paper cups, one with red and yellow pills and the other with water. The nurse watched while Bea gulped down the capsules, then ticked her off the list. 'Good girl.'

Body and blood. Amen.

Tonight we'll be lining up again.

Body and blood. Amen.

As the nurse turned back toward the work station, Bea summoned up the courage to tap her on the shoulder.

The nurse spun around. 'Yes?' she answered brusquely.

'I wonder,' Bea hesitated, 'is it possible, I mean, maybe, if I could ... I need a razor to shave? I need to shave my legs and underarms.'

'You're not down for sharps.'

'I only want one for a few minutes.'

'You can have a razor any time you like. Ask any of the nurses and we'll stay with you while you shave.'

'You have to stay with me the whole time?'

'Those are the rules.'

'But I'm not cutting,' said Bea. 'Look.' She yanked up the sleeves of her sweater to expose unbroken skin.

'I believe you,' the nurse sneered. 'There're no cutters on my ward.'

Bea walked off. That stupid cunt didn't even know she preferred cutting into her scalp. They could keep the fucking razor.

But that moment belonged to a different age. Now she worked with nurses like the ones she had met as an in-patient at St. Anthony's. At first she had been afraid someone might recognise her. She even dreamed about being unmasked for the imposter she still felt she was, deep inside. And it took an imposter to be afraid of time alone with your own innocent family. She made up her mind to talk to Nick about it at their next debriefing.

*

Dr. Payne looked through his notes on Beatrice Clark. He had made a list of her strengths:

Ability to comprehend English.
Ability to read and write.
Neat appearance.
Appropriate social behaviours.
Good hygiene.
Artistic.
No criminal record.
Superior educational skills present.
Vocational skills present.
Occupational skills present.
Willingness to take necessary medications.
Willingness to participate in ongoing treatment.
A knock at the door interrupted his thoughts.
'Your nine o'clock is here, Dr. Payne.'
'Thanks.'
He strolled out to the waiting room. 'Bea! Good to see

you. Come in.'

She followed him into his office.

'So how are things with you this week?'

'Fine,' she whispered, looking at the floor.

'How are you feeling?'

'All right I guess.' Her voice was barely audible.

'Why are you whispering?'

She looked up at him. 'I'm not,' she said in a low, raspy tone. 'I've lost my voice.'

'A cold?'

She put her hand to her throat and took a deep breath to push the words out. 'No. Just lost my voice.'

'Completely?'

'Yes.'

He smiled. 'If you didn't want to talk to me all you had to do was say.'

Bea attempted a brief smile.

'Has this ever happened before?' he asked. 'I mean, without an underlying physical cause?'

'Yes,' she said, avoiding his eyes. 'It comes and goes of its own free will. It doesn't usually leave me for more than a week.'

'I'll try my best to hear what you say. Now, what else has been happening?'

'Not much,' she squeaked.

'You've been at St. Anthony's nearly a month now. Have you settled in okay?'

She shrugged her shoulders, turning her head to the side. 'Yeah.'

'I understand you haven't been taking part in many of the activities.'

'Origami for beginners? Play with clay? Give me a break,' she said, rolling her eyes.

'Often doing something physical and creative can soothe the mind.'

'Well, it stresses me out.'

'And the group therapy?'

She wrung her hands. 'Super stressful,' she said, glancing around the room. 'There's this new guy who runs it and he doesn't like me.'

Dr. Payne crossed his legs. 'Why do you say that?'

'He keeps making sarcastic remarks about me being an academic. Makes out that I think I'm better than everyone, which I don't think I do at all. It's starting to bug me.'

'Is that why you lost your voice?'

She touched her throat. 'No.'

'It stands to reason that if you have no voice he can't say much about you.'

'Yeah, well, he's made fun of me losing my voice as well.'

'But you're still going to the sessions, I hope?'

'Of course. The other patients are nice and their stories are eye-openers. Human beings survive such horrors.'

He nodded. 'They do. And what about visitors?'

Bea sighed. 'Don't want to see anyone here.'

'There's no shame in being hospitalised.'

'Really?' she snapped in her little mouse voice. 'Ever happened to you?'

'If you broke your leg and were in hospital you would want friends to visit.'

'Don't pretend this is the same.'

'Many people suffer from depression. Perhaps not all as acutely as you are experiencing now, but far more people than you think. It's the equivalent of the common cold in psychiatry.'

'It's a mental hospital.' Her voice sounded as if it was deep inside the pit of her belly. 'In the real world that makes me a freaking basket case. Completely humiliating.' She paused. 'And I didn't want to come here. You made me.'

Tears came again. She pulled her body in tightly and covered her face with her hands. The room went quiet.

'Have you had any side effects from the medication?' he asked. 'Headaches? Nausea?'

'No.'

'And you're sleeping OK?'

'Yes. The Quetiapine makes me drowsy.'

'Okay, so we'll stick with the regime for now.'

He looked at the young woman in front of him, hugging herself and staring at the floor. She looked more like nineteen than twenty-nine.

'How did things get like this?' he asked. 'Help me understand what's going on in that head of yours.'

Bea looked up and for the first time made eye contact with him. 'Thought I could cope with it all,' she whispered.

'What were you coping with?'

'Work. Relationships. Everything. The usual.'

'Tell me about the relationships.'

'What do you want to know?'

'What about the last significant relationship?'

'Not much to tell. Last one was married. Had kids. Went on for two years. The end was brutal.'

'How long ago was that?'

'About three months before I came into hospital. In Pizza Hut.'

'Sorry, can't hear you.'

'Three months before I came here.' Her tiny voice tried to rise. 'He dumped me at Pizza Hut.'

'You're making that up.'

Bea hugged herself tighter, her knuckles pale against her caramel skin. 'No. The bastard took me for pizza and dumped me.' She was half smiling as she wiped the tears from her face. 'Two years we'd been together.'

'Were things deteriorating, or was it a shock?'

'Big shock. A few weeks earlier we had been working out details of when he would move in. Then wham! Guess I deserved it. Married man and all.' The tears stained her face and neck. 'I thought I was going for a Pepperoni Supreme. Next thing I know it's being served with a side of deep-fried heartbreak.'

Dr. Payne looked like he was having a hard time not smiling. 'You make it sound comical,' he said. 'But I imagine it was devastating.'

'I miss him so much,' she said, roughly wiping her tears away. 'I thought we'd be together. Maybe have kids. We were so compatible. But then he tells me, right there in Pizza Hut, that he's met someone else and he's in love with this new person and doesn't know what to do. He didn't want to hurt his family. He never mentioned anything about us. He didn't once consider how I might feel.'

Dr. Payne could barely hear her tiny voice through the sobs.

'I understand why this happened,' she said. 'Really, I do.'

'Understanding intellectually doesn't make it any easier. You still need to grieve.'

She cried even louder. 'He's not coming back,' she croaked. 'He didn't love me. Just a bit of pussy on the side.'

'I don't know the guy, but what's clear is he couldn't or wouldn't give you what you needed.'

'No one stays. Ever. Just something about me.'

He waited for her to continue but she stared at the floor.

'Why do you say that no one ever stays?' he asked quietly.

He regarded her for a few moments as the tears streamed down her arms and dripped on the floor. It was as if little by little her sadness displaced the oxygen in the room.

'Is this about the Pizza Man or something else?' he asked.

Bea bit her lip. 'His name is Paul, not Pizza Man.'

'Is this about Paul or your father?'

Bea closed her eyes. She couldn't wait for the session to be over. 'This has nothing to do with my father.'

'Are you sure?'

She kept her eyes shut tight. Dr. Payne pressed on. 'Did your depression start after the break-up?'

She opened her eyes. 'You want to know when it started?' She sighed and looked up. 'I'm so tired.'

'I understand that.'

'I felt it bad from August when I was preparing for the new semester. Bit like a surfer waiting for a wave. I knew something would happen. Wasn't sure exactly what or how or when.'

She paused and blew her nose.

'Before the breakup things were bad,' she sniffed. 'But the pizza thing made life hell.'

CHAPTER ELEVEN

Bea's main objection to being an in-patient at St. Anthony's was simple: she was not sick. There were days when she might be a bit gloomy, but so would anyone confined here. And if the low winter sun intensified the fog of dread she stumbled around in every day, it must do the same for thousands. Who would not be more focused under a summer sun than under grey skies and prematurely dark nights? The aloneness was the same whether she was among colleagues and students or nurses, doctors and patients. Her insides had been cold and numb for so long that she did not remember a time of warmth and light. St. Anthony's had done nothing to reverse that dark ache.

And while she hung around endlessly waiting for the next therapy session or the next visit from Dr. Payne, she felt pure shame at the laziness of her days. Here was time free of teaching that should be invested in unwritten articles and chapters of books she had failed to deliver these past months. Instead she remained paralysed by worthlessness, unable to concentrate and hating herself more each day.

She had some unexpected relief when one night Boston was assaulted by a blizzard that shut down the city and closed the airport. While the TV warned of possible loss of life and damage to property, she took comfort in the pounding snow that obscured the window panes. For one night at least, the gods showed empathy with the random chaos and anxiety that swirled and twisted its way through her.

When she woke from the dreamless sleep that the medication provided, the storm outside had passed. From her window she saw city workers shovelling snow off the sidewalks, while ploughs were beginning to make the main roads passable. Superficially, she too was calm and clear. But her only certainty was that her daily tempest would erupt and rage again.

The blizzard meant that the therapist for group work did not come in, and Dr. Payne could not guarantee he would be at St. Anthony's either. Bea retreated to her room pretending to be absorbed in a *Good Housekeeping* magazine. But the others too were bored and restless. Dave wandered in, established himself in her armchair, and showed no sign of moving soon. She listened to his intimacies. His ex-girlfriend had visited but was unlikely to appear again. The hospital, the admission of being abused – it was too much for her to take on.

He was sobbing quietly. 'At least she was honest and upfront.'

Bea gently reached for his hand. He tightened his grip around her fingers, while the other hand mopped the tears pouring down his face. For the first time in ages Bea felt true calm inside. She was useful to someone, if only for a moment.

Dr. Payne pushed his head around the door. Calm changed to embarrassment. Would he think there was something beyond friendship developing between them?

'Sorry I'm late,' he said. 'You must have heard how bad it is out there.'

'No problem, Doctor,' said Bea, straightening up.

Dave made his exit, eyes firmly downcast. Dr. Payne closed the door behind him.

'He's a nice man.'

'Yes,' replied Bea.

'Good to hear your voice is back.'

Bea scowled.

'And how are things with you today?'

She hesitated. 'Okay.'

Dr. Payne sat down and crossed his legs. 'Bea, you know that recovery is never straightforward. You're doing well, but it's okay to still feel low or anxious.'

She stared at the window. 'I should be better by now. I should be going home.'

'And you will, but not yet. You need to give yourself more time.'

She did not answer.

'You haven't lost anything. When you're better, you have your job waiting for you. Your friends.'

'I'm not so sure,' she said, her voice breaking. 'No one misses me.'

'That's the depression talking. Once these increased meds take effect things will begin to look a lot different.' He paused. 'You're not the person you were just a few weeks ago, Bea. You're doing so well. I wouldn't say that if I didn't believe it.'

Through eyes blurred with tears, she tried to focus on the awful abstract painting in reds and blues that hung behind the armchair.

'Back in Trinidad, in the countryside, there are men who can be rounded up to attend any funeral for rum or a few dollars. Knowing the dead person is optional. They'll turn up wearing black and might even cry.'

'Really?'

'I swear,' she said crossing herself. 'For my funeral they're going to have to pass by a rum shop and bribe a few guys to come and mourn for me just to have a decent show.'

'Stop talking like that. I know that quite a few people have called for you. And these flowers in your room. They came from people who care about what happens to Bea Clark.'

She could not return his gaze.

He shifted in his seat. 'By the way, who are the lovely roses from?'

'A colleague. Actually that was a surprise, because it's an older professor that I haven't had much dealings with.'

'There are good people around you,' he said smiling. 'You have to give them a chance, Bea.'

Something about the talk of roses made Bea burst into tears again. He waited until she was calmer and accepted the tissues he offered.

'I know it's not easy,' he said softly.

She wiped the tears across her sticky face and took a deep breath.

'My Dad gave me a dozen red roses for my sixteenth birthday. He showed up with them on the actual day. You have to understand that this is a man who if he turned up with a present in the same month you were born you'd say he remembered. I was so touched I cried.'

Dr. Payne sat silently.

'That was only once, and it happened a long time ago.'

'What does it feel like when you remember these gestures?'

She bent her head and remained silent.

'Bea?'

'I'm so tired. So tired.'

'But you're sleeping better?'

'I get about five hours most nights.'

'That's certainly better, but you need more.'

She kept her head down and whispered to the carpeted floor. 'I've been thinking about Paul.'

'The infamous Pizza Man?'

'Yes.' She nodded. 'That one.' She let out a long sigh.

'What about him?'

'I don't know. Miss him, I guess.'

'What do you miss?'

'A lot of stuff.' She shrugged. 'I miss his smell. And he wasn't much of a cook but he made the best pancakes in the entire universe. Never cared for pancakes till I met him. Now I cry if they serve them in the canteen. Silly things like that.'

'It's not silly,' he replied. 'Often it's the little things that trigger a whole new wave of grief when we least expect it.'

Bea wiped away fresh tears.

Dr. Payne leaned forward. 'We've all been there before, Bea. Everything I say will sound like a platitude, but time does heal. You have every reason to hope for a fulfilling life. He wasn't good enough for you.'

'His favourite movie was *Casablanca*. That's how we met. It was a special showing at Brattle Theater in Harvard Square. He was sitting two seats away. I told him to shush because he was whispering the lines along with the actors. He knows the entire movie word for word. He'd stop for a bit then start again. Then he moved to the seat next to me and started telling me when the good lines were coming up.'

She sat on her hands and began rocking gently. 'Fancies himself as Rick,' she smiled. 'You know the bit where the Captain says, *What in heaven's name brought you to Casablanca?* And Rick says, *My health. I came to Casablanca for the waters.* The Captain looks puzzled. *The waters? What waters? We're in the desert.* And Rick says, *I was misinformed.* My guy used to crack up as if he was hearing that line for the first time.'

She blew a loud breath, frowning. 'Where am I going to find another romantic idiot like that?'

'Pizza Man was married with two kids and left you because he got himself another mistress,' said Dr. Payne. 'You don't want someone like that in your life. Doesn't look like it now, but when you're ready you will find someone who loves you properly.'

'Yeah, right. I'm not the kind of girl men want to keep. Just a plaything. Toss aside when you're finished.'

'Why do you say that?'

'No one ever stays,' she said, biting her lips. 'Good enough to fuck but never good enough to love.' She stared into the middle distance and continued to chew on her lips.

'Is this about your father?' asked Dr. Payne.

She clenched her jaw.

'You told me he left when you were very young.'

The silence became heavier.

Dr. Payne was saying something about wounds that never heal, but she couldn't be sure. It was taking all her concentration to keep from shaking.

'I don't always know where I am,' she whispered, and instinctively put a hand over her mouth. But the words had already escaped.

'What do you mean?' he asked.

She pulled air deep into her lungs and exhaled with a weary sigh. 'I'll start thinking about Paul and end up seeing my Dad's face. It's like I'm little again, and I get confused between the people and the events. I feel everything like it's happening all over again. Am I crying about now or then? I must be crazier than I thought.'

'What events?'

'People leaving.'

'What was it like when your Dad left?'

'I don't want to talk about it,' she said with conviction. 'I get confused about where I am, and what's happening, and who I'm talking about.'

'You're not crazy, as you put it. I haven't seen any sign of psychosis,' he said. 'If we don't deal with issues, they simply wait for us. We fool ourselves that they're buried for good, but that's really not possible. And for you, recent events have unleashed some powerful stuff you're going to have to face up to.'

'Oh, please. My parents are good, decent people. I'm not blaming them for my fuck-up.'

'I'm sure they are good people,' he said, smiling. 'But why won't you tell them you're having a rough time and need their support?'

'They wouldn't understand. We don't have nutcases in our family. Lots of gamblers and drunks and a few religious fanatics, but I'm the very first certified mad person. I am the proud owner of a legal document that committed me against my will to a place of safety for fear I would harm myself. Signed by two doctors. Proper girls from respectable homes like mine are supposed to become lawyers, doctors. Maybe at a push they'll settle for an accountant. They marry other lawyers, doctors and accountants. They do not get put into the looney bin.'

'I don't deny the stigma,' he said. 'But you're their only child. They would feel terrible if they knew you were facing this on your own.'

'Anyway, I'm fine now,' said Bea, wiping her face and straightening her back. 'Our time must be up.'

'We have a few more minutes.'

'Well, you're a busy man,' she said, throwing her legs off the side of the bed.

'Bea, do you think that I will reject you?'

'That's a weird thing to say. I don't care what you think.'

'Do you think if I get to know you better I wouldn't like you?'

She stared out at the snow.

'Think about it,' he said.

'Fine,' she said, looking past him at the door.

'Good. I'll see you tomorrow then,' he said. 'Of course, if there's a problem before, they can always page me. With this weather I don't know how long it would take me to get back here again. But we can always talk on the phone.'

'Thank you, but I'm fine,' she said.

Dr. Payne folded his arms. 'One day you will have to acknowledge the anger you feel.'

She looked at him and for the first time felt violent rage. 'You know Dave who was in here? Well, he hasn't had a visit from any family members. Not one. He said they're embarrassed. His brother's in jail for burglary or something, but their mother never misses a single visit to that son. That is how much people look down on us. So please don't tell me to contact my parents who are proudly telling everyone about their goddamn successful daughter in Boston.'

Bea shook with anger as she stood for him to leave.

Dr. Payne stayed where he stood for several seconds.

'One day at a time, Bea,' he said. 'One day at a time.'

CHAPTER TWELVE

They say two wrongs don't make a right and that was definitely the case with Mummy. She thought he was a maxi-taxi van. He thought she was a cow. Two wrongs and she gone. I don't remember how we got from the hospital to Aunty Indra's house. They gave me Priya's room and Priya's clothes. Nanny promised to take me to my own house but I heard her crying in the kitchen saying how she can't face seeing all Nalini's things. The next day a doctor came to the house and gave me two pink tablets that made me sleep whole day till six o'clock in the evening. He tried to get Nanny to take the pink tablets too but she shout at the man that nothing going to stop her from doing right by the dead. She go have plenty time to sleep after the dead bury.

I certainly did a lot of sleeping. I would get up and it would hit me like a cricket bat cracking a six that Mummy not coming back to take me home. As soon as I start crying someone would make me take more pink tablets. This morning at breakfast my cousins all had on their school uniforms. My school must be opening today too but Aunty Indra want me to stay home this week while things get sort out. I don't want to ever go back to school. People will look at me strange – the girl with no parents. No other child in my school missing both parents. I could hear them already, happy that the winner of the recitation competition ain't all that. Poor Tina – she used to only have a mother, now she don't even have that. Maybe I won't be able to attend normal school now. Maybe the principal doesn't like to mix normal children with orphans in case that jinx the proper families.

People keep coming by Aunty Indra house to sit around, cry and drink juice. Some bring food to share. A lady I never see before came and put a bag of sugar cakes and tamarind balls in my hand. People I don't know coming up to hug me. They tell me my mother was an angel and I should pray for her soul in heaven. Of course she was an angel. I don't know how they know since I never see them before.

One old lady made me sit on her lap. She asking if I know her. I told her straight – I have no idea who she is.

'Yes man. You must know me. I see you with your mammy and your cousins in our hardware. You don't remember the time all you come in for paint because you wanted your room paint pink? You remember that?'

That was last year during the August holidays. Mummy don't like pink. I mean didn't like pink. But she let me have a pink room. She said as long as is only my room she don't care. Or she didn't care. I don't even know how I suppose to talk about her now.

The old lady damp with old lady sweat. She put her hand down the front of her dress and took out a handkerchief to wipe her face. I tried to get up but she hold me down. She not even talking to me any more but she still pin me down on she lap. She and Nanny start to talk about me as if I not even there.

'She went to school yet?'

'No. I say leave it till after the funeral.'

'Yes, that is the best thing to do.'

The sweaty old lady took another swipe of her face with the hanky and then stuffed it back into her bra. She keep trying to jig me up and down on her lap even though I'm not a baby. I will be eleven this year.

'All you decide what to do with Tina?'

Nanny didn't answer. Aunty Indra passed by same time carrying a tray of empty glasses.

'Indra, what all you going to do with Tina? She staying by you from now on?'

Aunty Indra and Nanny both screw up their faces like they smelling something bad.

'Nothing fixed for certain yet, Granny Gwen. And the way you holding on to Tina it look like you want to take my niece home with you.'

'She have a sweet little face. And you know something? She remind me of my granddaughter Bea when she was little so. I wish I could take her home. Still, I too old to look after more children.'

The lady Aunty Indra had called Granny Gwen was sweating even more. This time she wiped her face on the back of my T-shirt. Then she held my cheeks and pulled my face close to her. I could see big beads of sweat in her hair.

'Tina child, you must think of me as another granny. When the funeral and thing done, and you settle, get your Nanny or your Aunty to come bring you by me. We have a big chenette tree and pomerac in season now. I will get one of the yard boys to pick for you.'

She loosened her grip a little and I tried to make a dash for it.

'Come back here, child.'

She catch my hand. Oh Lord, I stuck with her again. She opened her purse and put a crumpled-up twenty dollars in my hand.

'Take that to buy sweeties.'

Nanny give me one hard look.

'What you say to Granny Gwen?'

'Thanks, Miss Granny Gwen.'

I ran to Priya's room so fast. I couldn't take another hug-up from that lady. I rather give back the twenty dollars than get pin down on her damp lap again. But twenty dollars is a lot of money. Me and Priya will share it. When Priya came home from school I showed her the money. She didn't look too happy.

'So she give you all that money just because your mother dead?'

'I guess so.'

'Well, that don't seem fair to me. A whole twenty for nothing.'

Priya doesn't get it, that I would give all the money in the world to have my Mummy back. I hate Priya.

But hate her or not, I am staying by her house and sleeping in her bedroom. I heard her complaining to Aunty Indra that she need her room back to do her homework. Aunty Indra tell her something in a whisper and she start whining how that's not fair and how I should go stay by Nanny. Whatever Aunty say make her march off and slam the door to her brothers' room. I wanted to go and tell her I don't want to live in her stupid house either. I want my Mummy so bad.

There doesn't seem to be a moment when the house empty of people coming to say they sorry about Mummy. I can't even cry in peace or think about her without someone wanting to hug me up and kiss me or look at me like they never see anything sadder than me. But I guess she was loved. All her church group came. The people from the dentist office came, even the big dentist Dr. Cameron. I heard him say that the cheque in the envelope is what was owed to Mummy and some extra to help with the funeral. Nanny said we will manage by the grace of God. She said Nalini had life insurance plus an insurance to pay for funeral expenses. And, not that they counting on it, but that driver's insurance go have to pay up. The problem is what to do with Tina.

I was sitting on the other side of the living room so

Nanny must think I can't hear her, but I hearing real good. She telling Dr. Cameron that how they not sure where I should live. Indra already have three children and she could manage a next one but it go be a stretch. Her husband okay with it. Still, is a big deal to take on another girl child. Nanny not sure she able. The question is whether she have any choice. At least she said she love me bad. It's only that she getting old and don't know where she will find the energy for a youngster.

'In two-twos Tina will be in high school and then it go be boyfriend problems and all that. I tired just thinking about it. Bringing up Indra and Nalini was enough, you hear.'

'What about Tina's father?' Dr. Cameron wanted to know.

'As God is my witness I don't know who the Daddy is,' said Nanny.

'She never tell anybody?'

'No. She always say she wanted the baby and so that is that.'

Nanny leaned closer to Dr. Cameron. 'But that don't mean I ain't have my suspicions.' She rocked back in the armchair and shook her head. 'We don't know for sure and now she gone, Lord rest her soul, we will never know unless he come forward. That poor child. It not easy never knowing who to call Daddy.'

I went in Priya's bedroom and lay down with the blanket over my face and pretended to be sleeping. I want my Mummy. The sun hot outside but it feels cold even under the blanket. I want to stay here and never come out. Why God would take away my Mummy? They have plenty bad people on the news that he should take first. But no. He had to take my Mummy who everybody loved. I want my Mummy back now. My head hurting. I want to scream and scream but I must be quiet. If I make plenty noise they could put me out. This is not my house, as Priya keeps telling me. Strange how she used to be my best friend and now she's such a pig.

And Nanny has no right to be talking we family business with strangers. Not because people come to say they sorry about Mummy don't mean they have to know about my not having a father. She not thinking how embarrassed I am with everybody telling me they sorry for me. When they find out I don't have a father they look even more sorry. One church lady even ask Aunty Indra if we don't have relatives in Canada or America that could take me in. She sure somebody must like to have a girl to help around the house and I will still get to go to school. Aunty Indra said she can't think of anybody off the top of her head but she knows we have some pumpkin-vine family living in Alberta.

The thing is that not once has Nanny or Aunty Indra asked me where I would want to live. Nobody even take me back to the house to get my clothes. Uncle Ricky went and got clothes for me like he know what I like to wear. He pick up some things and shove them in a bag. So what going to happen to the place now? I know we were renting it from Mr. George so I suppose he will take it back and rent it to someone else. In fact I heard the receptionist from the dentist office already asking if the place go be free soon because she looking for something in the area that not too expensive. Mummy not even bury yet and people want our home. And what going to happen to Boo-Boo? Nanny and Aunty Indra both hate dogs. Apparently Miss Celia looking after him for now. Lord you know how much I miss my puppy.

I am so mad at Mummy. She should have stayed under the shelter. It was raining too hard to know if it was a taxi from so far. She should have stayed under the shelter and see what it is when it reach us. And that stupid, stupid man. I know they sometimes have cows in the field near the shelter but how he could think Mummy was a cow? She wasn't even fat. In the hospital the doctor said she died instantly. At least she didn't feel the blood flowing from her head. But she had no right to die and leave me here alone. And to die without telling me who my father is make me so vex. How he going to find me now and take me home with him?

CHAPTER THIRTEEN

The endless nothing days at St. Anthony's stretched out to ten weeks, shaped by therapy sessions and mealtimes. Bea saw others come and go, and was no longer surprised by who might join their ranks. A few from her original group were still there. Sarah was back home and seemed to have accepted she would not become a mother. She still attended sessions twice a week. Dave remained, slowly gaining weight and getting colour into his sallow cheeks. He looked less like a lost child. A Japanese diplomat joined them for two weeks. She never said much and rarely left her room, but it was understood that she had stopped taking her medication for manic depression and had suffered a difficult and public relapse. A college student entered their world for a few days plagued by obsessive, compulsive anxiety that was making it impossible to do his courses. His mother swooped in from Texas and took him home before anyone had made friends with him.

Bea still had days when the escape route of suicide would overwhelm her and she would be unable to leave her room. She gradually learnt to be grateful for the longer gaps between such days. New patients, unsure of the routines, found her quietly helpful. It gave her some fleeting self-worth, to be useful like this. She had more privileges now. She could go for walks in the grounds outside by herself, though the freezing conditions made that a redundant concession. The staff occasionally took patients at Bea's stage of recovery for accompanied walks to the coffee shop nearby or the Wal-Mart for essentials that were not stocked by the on-site kiosk. She was allowed a laptop and cellphone.

But Bea was working up the courage to ask for another concession. She was ticking all the boxes – taking her medication, practising daily mindfulness, and taking her therapy seriously. It was time to put this progress into practice. When Dr. Payne came for one of his now twice-weekly visits she was ready. In spite of all the lines she had rehearsed the words tumbled out just minutes after he sat down.

'So what do you think?' she asked, anxiously searching his face for approval.

He looked at her for a long moment then smiled.

'You have no idea what a big step this is. I'm really delighted for you.'

'So I can go?'

'Of course.'

It felt like Christmas in February. She was being allowed to go out on her own to have her hair done and walk around the shops. Her whole demeanour changed. She could not have been happier if she had been given a trip to the moon.

'You'll make sure the nurses know I have permission to go on my own?' she asked.

'I'll do it right away.'

The next morning she showered and changed carefully, layering up against the cold. When she stepped outside she wished she had her sunglasses to face the dazzling, cloudless blue sky. Sinking her hands deep into her coat pockets she set off trembling with excitement and barely feeling the cold. People on their regular morning rush hustled past. They had no idea what it meant to be able to do what you like, go where you like, without your competence being constantly scrutinised and analysed. She breathed in the freezing air and didn't mind that it burnt her throat. When you are floating, little can spoil the moment. She thought of taking a bus into the shopping centre of Boston but pulled back. That was too much to navigate. She would go where her feet took her: and her feet took her to a row of trendy Somerville shops she vaguely knew.

After a while she found herself in front of Universal Cuts, a glass-fronted salon. Inside, an older woman was having a haircut and chatting intensely to the young woman with the scissors. Two other people, probably stylists, were sitting unoccupied. Bea stared inside. One of the idle stylists, an Asian woman, looked up and returned her stare, absent-mindedly twirling the ends of her long jet-black hair. Bea suddenly felt intensely nauseous and dizzy.

The memories were as sudden as a violent earthquake. She clutched her stomach tight and kept walking. When she was young, friends would taunt her about her long rod-straight hair. Her mother had explained that eating tomatoes encouraged curls like those of adorable Carlene who lived on the same street. But munching a daily tomato instead of an apple had failed to cajole a single strand into a beautiful bounce or charming curl.

As she got older, Bea's hair had acquired another significance. Men in particular found it dazzling. The more praise it attracted, the greater her discomfort. Slowly she became aware that her hair merely crowned a blossoming body with breasts that filled a decent-sized bra.

'Stop pushing yourself up so by every man you see,' Mira complained.

Thirteen year-old Bea hung her head.

Mira continued to badger her. 'You should see yourself laughing and carrying on like you is a big woman. Have some decency about you. You is still a little child.'

If only she had inherited Alan's coarse wavy hair, life would have been easier. She said this to her maternal grandmother.

'Listen, little madam,' her grandmother had replied. 'Stop right there. You don't know how lucky you is to get good hair from we side of the family. That so-called father of yours have hair picky-picky and curl-up. Them does have to straighten it regular to make it good. You don't have to do nothing and your hair come down straight. Young people today! They never appreciate what the good Lord give them. Always wanting what they don't have.'

'But, Ma, I want it bouncy like Carlene's hair. Why can't mine be like that? And it's too long. I don't want it past my shoulders.'

'You mad or what?' shrieked her grandmother. 'Don't let me hear a scissors touch that head. Cut it and it will never grow back long so again. Mark my words.'

'Well, I don't like it,' said Bea, pulling it into a bun.

'When you get to be a big woman you could do what you want. But right now I can't see your mother letting you cut the hair. Take it from an old lady. Leave the hair alone.'

'Daddy said I could cut it if I want.'

'If your mother hear you talking like that she go wash out your mouth with blue soap. He does do anything for you? When was the last time he come and see you, eh? Mira tell me how he forget your birthday. I lie? Didn't do nothing. Not even a card. That is any kind of father to have?'

Bea did not answer.

'School holidays come and gone and not once he say, well, he go take you to the beach, or take you to spend a two days by he. You think he give one shit about you? You hear me? You only have father in name.'

Bea had fought back tears, retreating to the relative safety of her room and her books.

The next opportunity came when she was at the hair-dresser's, waiting while her mother had her hair done. Bea dared to ask directly if she could have shorter hair. Judy, the hairdresser, ran her fingers through the dark thick mane.

'Let we cut it in layers,' Judy said. 'Man, that go look real good. Mira, the child have good hair.'

'Nah. Nah. Nah. We not doing nothing so,' her mother had retorted. 'Leave the hair. You can't see how she hot with sheself already? If you give she some fancy style I go can't control this force-ripe madam.'

Her mother had swung her chair so she faced the rest of the salon. 'I look like I ready to be anybody grandmother?'

The half-dozen ladies in the cramped salon all burst out laughing.

'Put the pill in she Milo-tea,' urged Judy, grinning. 'It never too early these days. You ain't see in the papers how that high school girl, must be same age as Bea, making baby for a schoolboy still in short pants?'

The women nodded in collective agreement.

'Mira, girl, you have your hands full,' Judy continued. 'I thank the Lord I don't have no girl children to worry about so. My two sons don't give me no trouble.'

'Judy, you don't know how hard it does be. Sometimes I wish I had a son, yes.' Her mother had sighed. 'Bea looking innocent because she so small. But let me tell you something. She ain't easy, you hear? Just the other day we was on the beach and she laughing and running up and down playing cricket. Next thing you know a fellow come and want to take out she picture. Well, I make she sit down by me straightaway. The child need to learn some decency.'

Bea had sat next to her in silent humiliation. The salon ladies picked her over with their gazes like vultures pecking on a rotting carcass.

'I don't know what to do,' said Mira. 'Is me alone. I have to be mother, father, everything.'

'She father don't help out?' asked a woman from under her hair dryer.

'Help out?' echoed Mira. 'He feel if he give me a little

change for the child that he done he work as a father. But ask him to keep she to ease me up little bit and he can't do that. He always have somewhere to go running behind all them Jezebel.'

'Man, forget about he,' said Judy. 'You still young. Take a next man.'

'You see any nice man between Port of Spain and San Fernando? If you see any that ain't going to thief your money or horn you with your best friend then let me know.'

The salon ladies laughed in agreement.

'Oh Lord, you talking truth, yes,' Judy laughed. 'Them man them real worthless. And mind you, all of them the same. Coolie, black, white, mix-up. Them all make the same damn way.'

'I don't know if they all the same. My mother cry when I tell she I was marrying Bea father. Man, that woman cry for days. She say how if my father was alive it would have been licks for so. He wasn't having no black man for a son-in-law. And she say Bea father look like he go run down plenty woman. Well, so said, so done. If you go against your parents it does come back to bite you in your, excuse my French, bite you in your backside.'

Judy nodded. She was spraying Mira's hair. 'Right, I done,' she said. 'Take a look.'

'Judy, you real know how to do my hair,' replied Mira, inspecting the back of her head in a mirror. 'Thanks. Let me settle up with you.'

Judy waved away Mira's purse. 'Man, put that away. You think I forget is your birthday?'

'Oh, Lord, girl, is how you know I turn twenty-one again today? You is a real good friend. Thanks, Judy.' Mira turned to the rest of the salon and waved. 'Ladies, I gone. Bea, hurry up and come.'

Bea had gone home encrusted in a loneliness and isolation she could not understand. If only her father would take her away. He used to love her. She was sure of it. As a little girl she went everywhere with him – every cricket match he played, every visit to friends and relatives. She was his little Beezy, his princess, and he would boast to his friends about how bright and pretty she was. But after he left them, the time between visits gradually stretched from days to weeks, and then months would go by without even a phone call. She thought about the distance between their homes. Less than five miles separated them, but he might as well have been living in a different country.

Bea hid in her room reading until Mira shouted it was time to change for the small birthday celebrations they were hosting at home. She had slipped into a long blue dress when she heard a soft knock on the bedroom door.

'Who is it?' she asked.

'Uncle Fred,' said a low voice.

'I'm changing. Be down in a minute.'

To her shock he pushed the bedroom door open.

Bea quickly pulled the dress down and smoothed it out. 'I'm changing.'

'Yes, well, I come to see you. You looking real nice.'

'Uncle Fred, let me finish changing. I'll come down just now.'

Instead he moved further into the room and sat on the edge of her bed. 'We could talk right here. You look like you nearly ready.'

Bea anxiously took a brush and attacked her hair. Uncle Fred, a long-standing family friend, was not someone she had private conversations with.

'I never tell you before but I always love your long hair. Don't cut it. When you bathe I bet it does look nice wet, hanging down your back.'

In one swift move he reached out and pulled her backwards so that she was pinned between his legs, his hard crotch pushed into her backside.

She froze. She wanted to say something but couldn't. His hands groped her hips, stomach, thighs and breasts. He whispered in a deep low voice she had never heard him use before.

'Oh God, you growing up sweet, girl. Them boobies like two ripe mango.' He moved his grip from her hips and massaged her breasts. 'You like me, Bea?' he whispered. 'Ain't I is always nice to you? I bring a big Fruit and Nut chocolate for you. It downstairs in the kitchen.'

His fingers clamped her nipples hard. She felt tears spring up in her eyes. 'Please stop, Uncle Fred.'

'No, man. You feeling hot. I know you want me.'

The tears dripped down her face. 'Please, stop.'

'I know you don't want me to stop nothing. You do it yet, Bea?'

She shook her head. 'Please, stop.'

'You worried about your mother? Don't worry. She busy downstairs.'

His huge rough hands reached between her legs and rubbed back and forth. 'You ever let anybody fuck this pussy, Bea?'

'Please. Please stop.'

'It must be a real tight pussy. I go break you in good. You go love it. I know you going to be a real good fuck.'

'Please stop.'

'I fuck your mother already. You know that? Remember when I come to fix the microwave last week? I fuck she in the spare room right there when you was watching TV. Your mother know how to suck a cock dry. She beg me. You should hear she. Fred, I don't want nothing from you. Fred, come and fuck me. Please, baby, I ain't get it long time. Fred, nobody have to know we business. But is really you I did want. I just give she a little something to keep she sweet.'

He slid one of his hands down the front of his pants and shoved the other hand between her legs.

Bea closed her eyes tight. 'You're hurting me,' she whispered. 'Please stop.'

But Uncle Fred was not listening. 'When she not home you must call me up and I go come and do you. You get it from behind and I sure you go be bawling for more. Just now you go be bawling for me to come fuck you day and night.'

He got up and pulled her round to face him. 'Baby, kiss me.' He clamped his moustached face down hard on her small mouth. His big wet tongue pushed to the back of her throat. Although the urge to gag was overwhelming, Bea tried to stay perfectly still.

'Bea!' Her mother's voice rang from downstairs.

He let her go instantly.

'Hurry up! I need help in the kitchen!'

Bea ran out the room and down the stairs.

Mira sneered as she passed by, oblivious of Bea's tear-stained face. 'You wearing that good dress? Anybody would think is your birthday.'

Bea looked at her feet. 'I don't want to change. Please.'

'It don't have time for that. Come put out the plates and cutlery.'

In a haze she took down the good china plates, reserved for guests, and set the table for dinner with trembling hands. As she laid the knives and forks neatly, it occurred to her that of all the many ways she had imagined, this was never how she dreamed her first grown-up kiss would be.

*

She had walked almost the whole way to Harvard Square. Her feet were damp and cold. A bus was approaching on the other side of the road. She dodged the traffic and ran to catch it, getting off at the end of the street where she had seen the salon, Universal Cuts. She didn't notice anything until she was inside the door.

'Can I help?' asked the young Asian woman she had seen earlier.

'I'd like a haircut now, please.'

'Let me see. One second,' she said as she pored over a huge notebook. 'Oscar can do it. Just have a seat and I'll go get him.'

Oscar turned out to be an amiable young Australian. 'So what are we doing today? Don't tell me you want to cut this beautiful hair off.'

'I want it short. Very short. Maybe a number three razor all over.'

His fingers weaved through her hair, pulling it in all directions. 'Honey, I don't do razor cuts. You have fabulous hair. Let me shape it a bit. Take some of the weight out of it for you.'

Bea closed her eyes and saw Uncle Fred's moustached mouth. She could almost hear him telling her never to cut her long hair. She cringed and opened her eyes. 'I don't care what style you choose as long as it's short. If you don't want to, then I'll find someone who will.'

He shook his head, his lips in a tight thin line, and led her to the shampoo basin.

CHAPTER FOURTEEN

St. Anthony's had been Bea's home for over three months now, and she had to admit she had begun to appreciate being there. She lived without the daily responsibility of details like grocery shopping or work. And it was clear to all that she was more robust – no longer constantly exhausted or obsessed with secret thoughts of how best to end her life. Having fought admission, she now dreaded being discharged back to her apartment in Mrs. Harris's brownstone conversion.

And then it happened.

She was in her room debating with Nurse Sharon the calibre of Trinidad Carnival versus Toronto's Caribana. Sharon had a sister living in Scarborough, and for the past ten years the sisters had bought costumes and jumped up on the streets of Toronto. Yes, Trinidad Carnival might be bigger, but she was sure she would not have a better time there. Bea defended Trinidad based on her observation and research. She had never actually taken part in the two-day beads-and-bikini parade. Then another nursing assistant interrupted the banter: Bea had a visitor.

'There must be a mistake. I don't have visitors.'

'No,' said the woman. 'There's someone here to see you. He's waiting in the lounge.'

Bea felt as if her insides had been placed in a freezer and

began shivering at the cold only she could feel in this well-heated building. So far, she had managed to bar everyone who showed an interest in her well-being at St. Anthony's. Who would be so bold as to turn up unannounced, against her explicit requests? Nurse Sharon squeezed her hand.

'Don't mind, darling. I sure it go be somebody you did want to see.'

Bea continued shaking as she sat on her bed.

'Come,' said Nurse Sharon gently. 'Get up and I will walk with you. Don't be frighten.'

Bea took a deep breath and trailed slowly behind Sharon as they walked the few steps to the lounge. She tried to catch a glimpse of who it might be before going in, but all she could make out were some dark brown boots and blue jeans belonging to a man's crossed legs. Nurse Sharon stepped aside and nodded at Bea to go through the doorway. The legs quickly uncrossed and a vaguely familiar, olive-skinned man stood up.

'Beezy?' he asked smiling.

'Yes?'

'You don't recognise me? Michael? Michael Singh? From Trinidad? You remember?'

'No way,' said Bea looking him up and down. 'What are you doing here? How did you find me?'

The stranger reached forward and bent to give her a hug.

'How did you find me? Who told you I was here?'

'It wasn't easy.'

He beamed at her and held her hand. 'You look exactly as I thought you would. Except for the short hair. I remember you with long hair.'

'I only cut it a few days ago. It was always long.'

Bea became aware that others were captivated by this abrupt reunion. 'Come with me to the canteen for a coffee or something.'

He followed happily, grinning at her as they walked.

'It's so good to see you again,' he said.

They planted themselves in a far corner and began to talk in earnest. He had moved to Boston from London in the last year and kept meaning to get in touch, but finding an apartment and getting to grips with a new job had gobbled up his time. Their mothers periodically exchanged emails and he had been given Bea's contact details. Both work and home numbers went automatically to voicemail. But earlier that day he had been near the university and decided to find her. There was a note on her office door explaining that Professor Clark was on leave, giving details of her administrative assistant. Michael had tracked down the assistant and, claiming to be a family member, was directed to St. Anthony's. He had taken a taxi and come straight here from the university.

'My assistant gave you the name of the hospital just like that?' asked Bea.

'I may have made it seem like I forgot the address and was directly off the plane from Trinidad,' he said. 'Please don't blame her. Once I heard you weren't well I really had to see you.'

'I'm actually okay. Probably going home soon.'

'You don't have to tell me anything,' he said, looking her straight in the eye. 'I live here and I would want to help any friend, but especially one who was my best buddy from childhood.'

When Beatrice Clark had been brought home from the Port of Spain General Hospital, a healthy six pounds four ounces, Michael was already next door, having arrived a couple of months earlier. Neither child had siblings, so they clung to each other right up to the moment when his family moved to the UK soon after his eighth birthday. Since then she recalled several Christmas and birthday cards, usually with long rhyming verses stressing the importance of both the occasion and the recipient. Sometimes these cards included photos where he took on a new persona – distant and exotic in thick overcoats and boots set against the even more mysterious landscape of the Scottish Highlands. But the gaps between letters had lengthened over time. It had taken nearly two decades for them to find each other again.

Bea was slightly ashamed and surprised that she noticed how handsome he was with his dark hair and smooth olive skin even in deep winter, the result of having an Indian father and an Irish mother. She could discern the outline of his slim, gym-honed body. But it was his eyes she reconnected with most – vivid green and unafraid.

'I don't mean to be rude, but I have not allowed visitors.' She hesitated. 'My family, well, they don't know anything about me being ill. And I would appreciate it if you could keep this confidential.' In spite of herself a tear escaped and rolled down her cheek. 'Please don't tell anyone,' she mumbled. 'I couldn't bear it if anyone in Trinidad found out.'

'I won't,' he said handing her a paper napkin. 'I understand about wanting privacy.'

She looked up at him. 'Your Mom might tell mine,' she whispered.

Michael laughed. 'No she won't, because she will never find out. Okay?'

He squeezed her hand tight. Bea recalled that his parents had started married life in Trinidad, but work in the oil industry had soon taken them to the United Kingdom. Michael filled in the gaps. He had stayed there for university and then his first job out of college. Now an experienced computer engineer, he had secured work with an international firm out of Boston with projects that would take him to Latin America and the Caribbean. They reminisced about two small children in their play house made of old bits of cloth strung from the branches of a spreading Julie mango tree. Days were spent digging holes, mango juice-stained faces grinning wildly as they ran amok.

'Beezy, do you need anything?' he asked. 'I could go get whatever you need.'

'No. Thanks. I'm fine,' she said. 'Seeing you after all this time is enough.'

'I'm really glad.'

'You probably want to know why I'm here.'

'If you want to tell me. I don't need to know.'

Bea paused. 'How're your parents?'

'Doing well. They keep saying they want to retire in Trinidad, but I doubt they'll move back after all these years.'

They chatted some more, recounting the births, marriages and deaths of people they knew in common. Less than an hour after he had swept into her life he stood up to go.

'I don't want to intrude, Beezy, but if you can stand to see me again I'd like to visit.'

Bea looked down so he would not see the flush she felt burning her cheeks.

'I'd like you to visit,' she said in a faint voice.

'Can I come tomorrow?'

'Sure.'

'Are there special visiting hours?'

'They prefer visitors from three to seven in the evening.'

'I'll come after work. It might be close to six if that's okay?'

Bea merely nodded, afraid to let her face show that her heart was bursting with happiness at the prospect of seeing him again. They walked together to the main entrance and before he left he pressed each of her cheeks with a goodbye kiss. She floated back up to her room.

'Somebody looking happy,' said Nurse Sharon. 'That the boyfriend?'

'No. He's an old friend from childhood. I haven't seen him for years.'

'And look how he find you,' Sharon laughed. She bent close to Bea's ear. 'He coming back again?'

'Yes.'

'Oh Lord. Well look how things changing for Miss Clark. I better keep an eye on you.'

True to his word, Michael did visit the next day, and the day after that. On the third visit she asked him if he would like to go somewhere outside the clinic.

'I didn't know you could leave.'

'I'm due to be discharged next week, and my doctor has been encouraging me to go out more often, to get back into normal life.'

'Cool. I'm going to take you to one of my favourite places.'

'Yes?'

'It's in Harvard Square. Bet you know all the restaurants, but the surprise will be which one it is.'

Bea took a deep breath. He had no idea how much of a step it was for her go out with someone, to take a taxi and to have a meal in a public space. Such seemingly simple undertakings all had to be remastered. But she wanted this to succeed – to be better, to do normal things again.

The taxi stopped on Brattle Street outside a Mediterranean restaurant that used to make her smile whenever she passed it, if only for the name.

'This is your favourite place?' she asked.

'Yup. I love the food. You've been?'

'I have.'

'You're okay with us going here, Beezy?'

'Sure. Casablanca's food is divine and I adore the mural of the movie they have on the wall.'

'Oh, me too.'

She sighed. Of all the gin joints, in all the towns, in all the world, Michael had to pick this one for her first outing.

'Fuck you, Paul,' she murmured under her breath as she walked into the restaurant.

'You said something, Beezy?'

'No. Just talking to myself. Bad habit.'

Once they were settled in a booth by the window and the difficult part of ordering had been taken care of, Bea, without any prompting, began talking about St. Anthony's. As casually as she could, without making eye contact, she told him of her depression and how much better she was. There was no need for the shameful details of the route by which she had arrived at St. Anthony's. Michael admitted knowing little about mental illness. She joked about the different types of treatment she had been offered in the past.

'You won't believe what this one doctor suggested,' she said.

He smiled. 'What?'

'He said I should join a choir.'

Michael nearly spluttered his grilled chicken breast all over the table. 'He said what?'

'A choir. Do you remember my singing? I got expelled from our Sunday school choir. I was that bad.'

He giggled, wiping his mouth with a napkin. 'You might have improved with age.'

'Nope. Still can't sing.' She moved her mashed potato around the plate. 'Sometimes I think it would be best to run away from it all. But not sure where I would go.'

'I ran away once,' said Michael, between mouthfuls.

Her eyes lit with curiosity.

'Nothing alarming,' he said. 'I must have been about six, so still living next door to you.'

'I don't recall you running away,' said Bea, as she tasted a tiny piece of her lamb.

'I was angry with my mom, so I took a suitcase and loaded it up with my most cherished possessions, the brand new volumes of the *Encyclopaedia Britannica*.'

'See, that's the difference between us,' laughed Bea. 'At six you thought the key to survival was the *Encyclopaedia Britannica*. I would have taken chocolate and my Barbie doll.'

'The bloody thing was too heavy to take far. I remember the agony of trying to drag that dead weight through the house. Think I got as far as the front porch.' He took another mouthful. 'Gave up after that and snuck back into the house through the back door. I had a sore back for ages.'

She reached over and ruffled his floppy dark hair. 'Poor baby.'

Michael scraped the last bit of chicken off the plate. 'Well? What about you?'

She was silent. He smiled and touched her cheek with the back of his hand. 'You ever ran away?'

'What? Apart from my whole life of running away?' she asked. 'Yes. Actually I was a repeat offender. Must have been a phase.'

He drained his water glass. 'How many times?'

'Quite a few,' she said. 'Problem was, no one seemed to realise I was running away.'

'You weren't missed?'

'Not really.'

The waitress came to their table and cleared away the empty plates. 'Can I show you the dessert menu?'

'Actually, can I have a glass of house red, please?' asked Michael.

'And for you?' asked the waitress turning to Bea.

'I'm fine for now, thanks,' said Bea.

'Okay, where were we?' Michael asked.

'I was telling you how I ran away. See, I wanted to live with my Dad. So I put some clothes in a plastic bag and set off down the street. Never got far. Maybe as far as Carlene's house. You remember Carlene? She lived down that steep street off the main road. They had this big red house with a cherry tree in the front and a swing at the back. Well, you know Trini people. Each day they welcomed me in as if they were expecting me.'

'How long would you stay?' he asked.

'Don't know. Few hours. I was a latchkey kid, so if Mom came home and I wasn't there she just checked at your house or Carlene's and brought me home. Don't think she ever realised I didn't want to be home.'

The waitress brought Michael's wine.

Bea continued. 'After a couple times she began stopping on her way home and beeping the horn. I would come out and we'd go home.'

'What about the bag?'

'She asked once,' said Bea. 'I mumbled something and she laughed it off. We never talked about it.'

He sipped the wine. 'This is good. You want to taste it?'

He handed her the glass by its delicate stem, letting his fingers touch hers for a few seconds longer than necessary.

'You're right,' she said. 'It is good. But I should stay off the booze for now.'

'Are you still running away, Beezy?' he asked quietly.

She glanced away. 'Probably.'

He touched her hand. 'When will you stop?'

'When I make it home,' she whispered.

CHAPTER FIFTEEN

Well, it's been a whole year since they bury Mummy, and I'm living by Nanny now. I didn't get a choice. Boo-Boo remained with Miss Celia. Nanny put she foot down and say she not minding child and dog same time. And I'm in secondary school now – Queen's College, same as Priya. She's one year ahead of me and has her own friends. I like this school. The teachers and students only know me as living by my grandmother. Some kids ask about my parents but most aren't bothered. And there are other kids who live with relatives. I don't stick out like I did at St. Gabriel's. My dream would be to live in a big city like New York or even London where everybody busy and no one knows your business.

My favourite subjects are English and History. We had this assignment in English the other day where you had to pretend to be a character from a story and write a new short story from that character's point of view. I wrote about 'The Three Little Pigs'. In it there was a Mummy pig and twin baby pigs. I was one of the baby pigs. We all lived happily together in a house made of bricks. The big bad wolf would often creep up at night and huff and puff and blow with all his might but he never managed to cause the slightest damage to our brick house.

Then one dark night when Mummy pig was outside

looking for the moon she was snatched. We never saw her again. The evil wizard who took her also used his magic powers to make our brick house vanish. We baby pigs had no bricks and no clue how to build a new house. We were super frightened. My twin curled her tail with mine and together we set off through the countryside looking for a new home. After walking all day we came across a house made of straw belonging to a kind rabbit called Finn. Rabbit Finn said that it was not safe for baby pigs to be walking in the wild by themselves. The wizard was sure to come back and this time he would eat us alive. So Rabbit Finn took us in and made us macaroni pie, baked chicken, red velvet cake and vanilla ice cream. During the day we played and helped around the house but at night we would quiver under our blankets wondering if the big bad wolf might return. If he huffed and puffed he would mash up Rabbit Finn's house. It was only a matter of time. The End.

Don't think I wrote about the pigs because Nanny has a little old house. It might be old but nothing – no hurricane or wolf – going to blow it down. Nana was a joiner by trade and he built this little house from scratch. It must have been something when it was first built. The problem Nanny has is finding people, like when the wooden fretwork was breaking off. She's always complaining people nowadays don't do good work like Nana, God rest his soul, used to do. I wonder how much longer Nanny will live. She's real old. She even smells old. Old people have that sickly-sweet talcum-powder-rolled-up-with-sweat smell. She left school when she was twelve and became a seamstress so she's no use with my homework. She's even too old to sew much now. It has to be something extra special before she will take out the sewing machine and run up a dress.

We had parents' day last Friday. Nanny came, and Aunty Indra and Uncle Ricky were there too, but they only came to see Priya's teachers. Nanny kept holding on to my wrist real tight and dragging me around. The normal parents were walking from teacher to teacher with their child. They did not hold on like they were afraid their secondary school kid would get lost in her own school grounds or that she might run away. And before that there was sports day. I wanted to dig a hole in the stadium and hide. Nanny up in the front cheering loud-loud for every race I was in. She wouldn't stay in the bleachers like the other parents. Mummy never carried on so. Sports day she would be too busy chatting to the other moms to bother with me and my friends.

I know I am complaining when I should be grateful, but one last thing really bugging me. Nanny doesn't like me going to the mall to hang out with my friends or go to the movies. She thinks I will get in trouble, though exactly what kind of trouble she trying to avoid she don't say. If I wanted to get in trouble I don't have to go to any mall or cinema. There was a girl and boy who found trouble right behind the church but the priest catch them. I better not say anything or Nanny might really lock me up in my bedroom till I turn eighteen like she keep saying she going to do. I bet if Mummy were alive she would let me go out with my friends. And who knows, if my Daddy found out about me and came to get me to live with him, he would take me to the mall and the cinema and we would have lots of friends and his house would always have people liming and laughing.

The only time I can go out is when Nanny's church group plan an excursion to the beach or one time we went to the Pitch Lake in La Brea. Usually I am the only person under a hundred. Is always a set of half dead church elders. Actually, that is not completely true. We also get invited to every single wedding, christening and funeral happening in St. Theresa's church. Nanny has worshipped there since her wedding about a million years ago. Aunty Indra and Uncle Ricky got married in St. Theresa's. Nana's funeral was there, but that was before I was born. Mummy's service was there too. All Nanny's grandchildren get christened there. In fact in our family you can't pick your nose without first notifying St. Theresa's.

Most of the time we stay home. We don't have many visitors. Miss Celia has come a few times. That Granny Gwen old lady is a regular. She likes visiting on a Saturday after the hardware closes up. Once she reach, the two old ladies like to sink into the Morris rocking chairs and is old talk and Bible reading until it get dark. I usually settle myself in front the TV or finish my homework. I don't mind Granny Gwen. Since that time she made me sit on her sweaty lap we cool. We have a routine. It's one kiss when she reach and one kiss when she going – no matter how damp and sticky her cheek feels I always do my duty.

Today we had some sad news. Granny Gwen has a son called Mr. Alan. His name is not Mr. Alan exactly but that is how everyone use to call him so I followed suit. His proper name would be Mr. Alan Clark. People should have called the man Mr. Clark instead of Mr. Alan but that is Trinidad for you. Anyway, when Aunty Indra came to pick up Priya from school today she told me to get in the car. Nanny was going to be home late tonight so I was to spend the night by her. She had packed my overnight bag and it was already in Aunty Indra's car trunk. Priya made it clear she was not sharing her room. Aunty said Uncle Ricky will fix up the sofa bed in the living room. When did Priya stop liking me?

It is not Nanny's style to go out and on a school night to boot. Aunty said that Granny Gwen's son Mr. Alan had passed away that same day. She only heard part of the story but it seemed that he was driving after drinking too much rum and crashed his car. Or maybe someone else was drinking rum and crashed into his car. We'll have to wait for the full story. One way or another Mr. Alan end up dead. His brother, who I know as Mr. Robin, had to go all the way to San Fernando General Hospital to identify the body. The doctor had given Granny Gwen sleeping tablets. The St. Theresa's ladies didn't miss a beat. They had already organised a rota so she always had a sister from the church by her side, morning, noon and night. Nanny was doing the evening shift and wanted to stay as late as she was needed.

One night at Aunty Indra's turned into a full week on that lumpy sofa bed. Nanny seemed to have moved into Granny Gwen's house. Whenever she came to check up on me she was full of excitement. First they had to wait for the body to be released and then they had to wait for Mr. Alan's daughter to come from America. And we finally get the story straight. Mr. Alan was the one who get hit by a drunk driver. He dead but the drunk driver not only living but he hardly get a scratch. At least the police charged him. You see how life not fair. I feel for his daughter. I suppose she still has a mother although nobody mention a Mrs. Alan.

The way Nanny excited you would think is a wedding they organising. The family put up a tent behind the hardware and every night is big wake. She say night after night people turning up with one set of food. People nearby have used that hardware to buy everything from mop bucket to hacksaw so they would have known Mr. Alan by face if not by name. He must have been a good man to bring in a crowd every night. My Mummy had a little crowd too.

I got to sample the buzz firsthand when Nanny took me to the wake one night. But it was the funeral in St. Theresa's church that I'm not going to forget for a long time. The church was packed as if roti and curry chicken was sharing. Everybody squish up on the pews so your arms pushed tight against your sides. Small children had to sit on their parents' lap. People who didn't get there at least half an hour before the service started could only stand at the side or in the back. The place was hot like hell and me in my thick black dress. I could feel the sweat rolling in the crease down the middle of my back. Some ladies were using the thin programmes to fan themselves. There was absolutely no breeze to cool down the amount of bodies stacked up in the church. If we weren't sitting down I would have fainted before the service even started.

The casket was open at the front of the church. Nanny told us that Granny Gwen had insisted on an open casket and Chatoo Funeral Services had had a hard time fixing to make him look respectable. His face had gone right through the windscreen. Aunty Indra march straight up, take a good look and cross herself. Nanny was right behind. I don't normally want to look at dead people but after getting all the details for days I had to take a peek. Mr. Alan looked like I remembered, but I only saw him a few times. He had on thick foundation and lipstick and look peaceful like when you pulling a good sleep. Mummy had looked peaceful too. Sometimes I can't believe she really gone.

Well, the service started the way every funeral does start with hymns and scripture readings and things like that. Mr. Robin, the brother, did the first reading. Granny Gwen was in the front pew so I could only see her back. She was holding herself up stiff like the guards outside the prime minister's office. Her white hanky kept coming out and getting shoved back up her long sleeves. Thank God she was not stuffing it down her bra this time. Poor old lady. I'm not sure if it's sweat or tears she wiping. Next to her is this tiny person who Aunty Indra mumbled is Mr. Alan's daughter. When the girl get up she so little I think she look like a midget. She walk up to do the eulogy but if you weren't near the front I don't know how you would see her. She definitely didn't take after her tall father. It wasn't only that she was short but she was small like a dolly. They should have put a box for her to stand up on.

This was one special funeral for St. Theresa's congregation to remember. The service hadn't even reach halfway when a woman started to shout out all kind of craziness. People trying to get her to keep quiet but she keeping up one big noise. The cute midget, who had a surprisingly strong voice, was trying to give her little speech only to be interrupted by the woman bawling down the church. I didn't get what the crazy lady was saying but it was something about how much she did love Mr. Alan and how much she hate Granny Gwen. I tried to turn around to see who it was but Aunty Indra push me down in my seat. I don't see why – everybody else was straining to see who it was. The lady bawl so hard that the little midget-girl stop talking and we sang a hymn instead. I whispering to Priya but she didn't know who it was either. Someone must have tried to take the bawling lady out of the church because she yell that if anybody touch her again she going to call police for them. Priya and I were trying not to giggle because Nanny was looking at us hard with her eyes open big.

Then the sweet Mr. Alan daughter made another try to say what she had to say – something about building a wall. She must have been talking about the walls of Jericho. It wasn't easy to understand because all through the speech Miss Bawling Lady was carrying on for so. I'm not sure if she finally shut up because someone tape up her mouth and took her outside or she got fed up and left, but eventually the service went back to normal. No. You can't call this bacchanal normal. Well, it normal for Trinidad. I doubt church in Canada and America does see this kind of confusion. Mr. Alan, I wonder if you know what trouble you make at your own funeral?

CHAPTER SIXTEEN

It was April before Bea was finally discharged from St. Anthony's. She looked out of the taxi window as it moved through the city, driving her away from the hospital and back to her previous life. Although she had spent years uncovering and absorbing its secrets, Boston today seemed uncharted, out of step with all she had known. It wasn't only that when she last walked these streets there were huge piles of dirty snow, the wind whipping through her coat. Nor was it because the city sidewalks were now lined with explosions of vibrant yellow crocuses and tulips in a myriad of colours from milk white to deep regal purple. Something more fundamental had occurred. Bea's eyes had a new optic nerve, replacing the one severed last year when she said a final goodbye to these streets. Now she registered each skyscraper, each road sign, each passing face, as if for the first time.

Spring was everywhere as the taxi crawled through morning rush-hour traffic on the main street, past the antique furniture shop and overpriced deli, turning right at the corner with Macpherson's Pharmacy – landmarks Bea found familiar but today were simultaneously alien.

'It's the third house on the left,' she told the taxi driver. 'That brownstone with the blue front door.'

'Fancy part of town,' said the driver.

She got out and stood on the pavement with her battered duffle bag. Last December she should have returned to this apartment for the last time. After teaching the final class of the semester there was to have been one last subway ride. Everything was prepared, waiting in the locked bedside drawer. Untouched.

That moment had passed. Now, in a different time, she needed to climb the five small steps that led to the blue front door. But even that simple act demanded extensive mental preparation.

Insert key in lock. Turn.

Push door open.

The apartment would be visible at the end of the short inner passageway. A few more rehearsals and she'd be ready. Well, as ready as anyone can be returning to a house that looked like your home but really wasn't.

Bea kept reminding herself it was the same one-bedroom apartment. Had the taxi transported her to a twin planet where everything looks the same but feels different?

Insert key in lock. Turn.

Push door.

Walk straight ahead.

Apartment with letter C on white door.

Insert key in lock.

Turn.

Push door.

Home again.

Time paused while Bea hovered on the spot where she had alighted from the taxi. Over and over she rehearsed in her mind the progression from pavement to apartment, but each time her feet refused to budge. Rigid bones collided with a thumping, panic-stricken chest, finally settling in small, tight fists.

She wondered what would happen if she turned around and walked away. What if she never went through the blue front door? To the untrained eye it was an old building converted into three apartments like many others on that street. Concealed layers of memory silently seeped from the chinks of its honeystone façade, spilling onto the dark wood floors and soaking through cracks in the white ceilings. Home had morphed into a three-storey monument mocking her shame.

'What are you doing here, Bea?'

Startled, she span around to find the voice belonged to her landlady, Mrs. Harris. 'I didn't know you were coming out of hospital today,' she said. 'I could've picked you up.' She put an arm around Bea. 'Why are you out here, dear? Come inside.' She took a frayed tissue out of her pocket and thrust it at Bea. 'Don't cry. It's okay.'

Mrs. Harris took hold of the old duffle bag and marched up to the blue front door.

Bea shuffled slowly behind. 'I'm really sorry for this trouble, Mrs. Harris,' she said, sniffling. She opened her apartment door. 'I'm fine now.'

'You're sure? Can I get you anything? Help you settle back in?'

'You're so kind. It's a little difficult coming home.'

'Well, I'm only upstairs. If you need anything, dear, anything at all, just bang your broomstick on the ceiling.'

'Thanks.'

'Now, I mean it, young lady. I'm only upstairs.'

Mrs. Harris was barely out the door when Bea hurried to the bedroom and the bedside cupboard. It was still there, untouched. The package of white powder had been in hiding all these months: two ounces of hateful accusations. She perched on the edge of the bed staring at the little plastic bag, unable to decide what to do next. Why so many decisions when today she couldn't even choose between tea or coffee?

Bea glanced up at the clock on her wall. Unbelievably,

nearly two hours had passed since she had been delivered home from St. Anthony's, and she had not moved from where she sat on the bed. She was aware of the pressure on her bladder. It was time to pee, unpack, shower and have lunch, but her mind would not slow down long enough to focus on completing any one of these elementary tasks.

With some effort, she placed the plastic bag of white powder back in the bedside cabinet. A surgical removal was too strenuous. Maybe tomorrow. Besides, if she didn't get to the toilet soon her jeans would be soaked.

Too late. As she stood up, warm liquid squirted straight through her panties and jeans, and trickled down her inner thighs. Soon a sticky little golden pool surrounded her feet.

I can't even pee properly.

She rubbed her forehead, groaning.

In the bathroom the cracked bar of soap from more than four months earlier was still caked to its white plastic dish next to the half-empty bottle of shampoo. There was no reason why it should not be there. Only she had not expected to be in this shower again, rubbing that bar of soap across her body, massaging that shampoo into her scalp. Four months to erase the pain from her body, and now this sour smell of piss.

She attacked her skin with a loofah, reducing it to a patchwork of brown and red. Grime and urine vanished down the plughole. But the smell of St. Anthony's had bonded with cells far below the epidermis and remained untroubled by lathers of Camay Softly Scented Bath Bar. Exhausted, Bea went back to her bedroom and lay down. The bed was soft with clean white welcoming sheets, and even though it was the middle of the day she crawled in, naked and damp.

Slowly she traced the contours of her breasts, then down across her stomach. Here lay a woman surplus to requirements, but written on her body were fragments – moments of connection – that would always exist, even if Bogart never came back. Why did he still fill her thoughts? What about Michael? Could he be the one? They were easy in each other's company. He did not judge her. But she reminded herself that he did not know the kind of woman she had become, not really. Once he found out, he too would disappear and not look back.

Could she still feel?

Closing her eyes, she imagined feeling her heart beat against his lips.

His tongue seeking her out.

Her hips reaching for his.

Her mind swirled with images of his naked body.

She held his head in her hands.

She sensed his urgent kisses. All over.

Sucking. All over.

Licking. All over.

His fingers reaching. All over.

Searching. All over.

Over, all over.

Flicking. Dipping.

The spasms of tight, warm muscles thumped and pulsed rhythmically, clenching wet against her fingers.

All over.

*

The university gave Bea generous paid leave, effectively providing time out until the new academic year. Late spring and a long summer stretched ahead. The dean wrote, reminding her of the contribution she had already made, the research that had received critical approval and the teaching awards she had secured. He knew she would come back refreshed and ready to continue a promising career.

Colleagues surprised her with their kindness. She had an

inbox of emails with offers of places to stay and invitations to break bread. She was at a loss to explain that sharing a family meal or staying at a house beside a lake would be wonderful but for her inability to assume even the minimum of social graces. She could manage with Michael or maybe Dave, but no one else. Not yet. In a perfect world she would exist in a deaf-mute state, without demands, and only the barest of acknowledgements from others.

So Bea locked her apartment door and retreated inside.

But hiding wasn't straightforward either. Life continued to happen around her. Bills had to be paid, trash had to be taken out and laundry had to be done. During her daily trip to the local grocery, Bea filled her basket with one banana, one Diet Coke, one microwavable meal and one small container of two percent milk. Sometimes she included a tube of Colgate toothpaste or a couple rolls of Charmin Ultra toilet paper.

'Hi, how are you?' asked the cashier. 'Getting the usual?'

Bea had seen her often enough. Her air of authority suggested she must be the owner or manager of the store.

'Back for the same stuff,' Bea replied.

'You know you could save yourself this trip every day. We'll deliver for free if the bags are too heavy for you to walk home with.'

'Thanks, but I like the walk. Gets me out,' said Bea. 'See what's happening in the world.'

'No problem, but anytime you need a hand I'll have Ed bring the groceries round. You live nearby, don't you?'

'Just at the bottom of Mount Vernon Street.'

'That's no distance. We could do that any time.'

What Bea could not say was that, while she was better, she had not actively embraced life either. She had thrived in the safety of St. Anthony's, but in this twilight world of not quite living – with its dry cleaners, trash days, bills and newspapers – it would take time to adjust. So she lurched from one daily purchase to another with no action plan and no future that required a stockpile of daily provisions. Life proceeded with pills, one banana, one ready meal, one Diet Coke at a time. Her only other outings were the required medical checkups.

But slowly, unrelentingly, the future unfurled into brighter, longer days. The trees regained luscious green canopies. Pink cherry blossom punctured the landscape; people shed heavy clothing and inhibitions as soon as the merest glint of sunshine lit the sky. It was impossible to avoid a sense of rejuvenation. Bea still found it gruelling to do much beyond the daily walk to and from the grocery store. But at least it was a routine anchoring her day. Michael called often and their almost weekly outings for coffee or meals became the high-water mark of her existence.

After being back at her own apartment for over a month, she awoke one morning to find the darkness had descended again, unexpectedly and completely. It was impossible to get out of bed. Her body knew the sequence of movements but, for reasons unknown, her mind could not be willed into submission. Her heart thumped louder and louder as the minutes turned to hours and she had not left her bed, in spite of wanting to. She shivered in the warm room. Her cotton nightshirt was soaked in sweat. The white powder, still unopened, sprung to mind.

She held her head in her hands, shaking.

I'm supposed to be well. I'm supposed to be well.

For almost a week she stayed in her apartment, existing on bits of food, refusing to answer the telephone or turn on her computer. She could hear Mrs. Harris's footsteps on the landing outside as she went about life. Bea made no attempt to pick her mail off the floor and before long a mound of flyers, magazines and letters barricaded her in.

A rancid smell came from under the duvet, and Bea was shocked to discover it was her own filthy flesh. Biting back tears, she reached out and dialled.

'Day clinic, good morning.'

'I'd like an appointment with Dr. Payne please,' she said in a weak voice.

'When for?'

'Today if possible.'

'He's got a fairly full diary at the moment. Who's calling?'

'Bea. Beatrice Clark.'

'Hang on a minute, let's see what I can do.'

Music displaced the silence while she held on. It was a familiar Bach piece that for some reason made her even sadder. It stopped as abruptly as it had started when the woman came back on the phone. 'Sorry for the wait. I spoke to Dr. Payne and he'll see you at five o'clock. Can you make that?'

'Yes. Thanks.'

'Have a good day now.'

'Bye.'

Bea knew the six hours before her appointment would be filled with getting herself ready and taking the short cab ride to Dr. Payne's downtown office. Six hours to have breakfast, wash, and take a two-mile cab ride.

*

'Hi! Come on in,' said Dr. Payne, rising from his desk and gesturing at the two faded armchairs. There was always a deliberate ease in his gait, shoulders back, looking taller than his actual height. A shaft of sunlight fell on his face as he sat down, shifting slightly to his left to avoid the glare. For a moment Bea could see the boy he might have been – thick, light brown hair, almost blond, and smooth skin tautly stretched over chiselled bones. But the eyes would have been the same as now. Time would always preserve the kindness in those pale-blue eyes.

'Thanks for seeing me today,' said Bea, fidgeting to fit her fragile frame comfortably in the overstuffed armchair.

'This worked out well,' he replied. 'Tell me what's been happening.'

Bea didn't answer.

'Has it been difficult adjusting to the big bad world?' he asked.

She could not stop the tears from leaking down her cheeks. She finally managed to find her voice. 'I was doing okay. Really I was.'

He nodded.

'Then out of nowhere it got worse again. I can't sleep. I can't leave the apartment. This is the first place I've gone to in over a week.'

'But you did it. You got yourself here.'

'I suppose.'

Dr. Payne slumped lower into the chair, interlocked his fingers and waited.

'My heart felt like it was going a million miles an hour and I was soaked in sweat and my jaws hurt. Think I've been grinding my teeth.'

'When you were first at St. Anthony's you had a couple of panic attacks like that, didn't you?'

'Yes, but this is the first time I've felt like this since I came out of hospital,' Bea said, drying her eyes.

'It's tough when you first get back out there and you don't have much support. At least, none you will accept.'

'Maybe I should be back at St. Anthony's.'

He sighed. 'No. We can always keep it as an option, but right now you need to try getting into life gently. You can do this. I truly believe this is a temporary setback that we can overcome.'

Bea said nothing.

'Have you been eating? You look like you've lost weight.'

'Not much,' she mumbled.

'You have to eat with the meds you're taking, or you're not going to get better, and you can even get worse.'

Bea stared at the wall to the left of his head.

'Why don't we try having you come in twice a week for now, so this kind of low feeling isn't allowed to fester?'

'Okay,' she said meekly and took her coat off the arm of the chair.

'What are you doing this evening?'

'Nothing.'

'Try to get out of the apartment at least once a day, even if it's to walk to the end of the street and back.'

'I'll try.'

'Okay, so I'll see you in two days' time. I'll get my assistant to phone you with an exact time. She's left for the day already.'

'Thanks.'

'Bea, you will get better. You have to believe that.'

She wanted to believe, but today it didn't feel possible.

CHAPTER SEVENTEEN

Summer was Bea's favourite season. This July was perfect, with none of the unpredictability of June and still some way from the fiery August heat. Her mind drifted to her father. She wondered if he'd enjoy this clear Boston sky reflected in the Charles River.

Alan Clark had travelled some – Barbados, St. Vincent, New York, Toronto, and even London. But he had never expressed an interest in visiting Boston, nor had Bea pressed him. After any trip abroad he would say there wasn't anything as lovely as the clear blue sky at home. Trinidad was crowned by a canopy of purest blue, uncluttered except for a few apologetic wisps of stray clouds.

What was he doing now, she wondered? At four in the afternoon there was a good chance he would be sitting in a battered plastic garden chair under the shade of the ancient chenette tree. Taking the breeze. Perhaps he would be checking the latest political intrigue in the Express and chain-smoking his Marlboros. Always chain-smoking.

Home and work had merged after the divorce, when he returned to live in his childhood house, keeping his lonely mother company. They had always lived above the small family hardware store that Alan managed. For him, the arrangement had the dual advantage of minimal responsibility and minimal costs. As a bonus there was his doting mother, Granny Gwen, tending to his every whim, cooking his favourite stew chicken with peas and rice, even making his bed and picking his dirty clothes off the bathroom floor. His older brother Robin, who also worked in the business, was so efficient that Alan's role was almost ceremonial, certainly marginal. Granny Gwen was determined never to let this favourite son leave home again. No woman had ever – could ever – look after him, love him, honour him like she did. That Indian bitch Mira, whom he had erroneously married, was confirmation enough if any was needed. But that was all thankfully in the past. Mother and son were reunited and would remain so for ever, at peace under one roof.

Did he still have a relationship with the woman Bea met last year on her annual summer visit? Alan's women came and went with slippery ease, their phone calls unanswered if they dared state needs of their own. He lived on his own terms, asking little of others, or indeed of himself. Disappointment, regret, anxiety were all rare occurrences. For as long as he still had his good looks and the stamina to play mas in a Carnival band, and could afford a few weeks holiday abroad, life was sweet.

And Bea's mother, where was she this balmy July afternoon? Intelligence and complete dedication had driven her rise through the ranks of the finance ministry to become one of the most senior career civil servants. Wednesdays, unless stopped by thunderstorms, she and a group of ladies walked the perimeter of the Savannah, Port of Spain's main park. Then Mira would head home and potter around in her little garden, tending her exotic but temperamental orchids or coaxing pigeon peas, tomatoes, okra and melongene into ripeness. She had not remarried either. A couple of serious relationships after Alan, with the attendant emotional battering as each failed, had left her determined to be self-sufficient. Anyone who would listen knew that she was a woman with her own house and her own car and didn't need a man confusing her head. Though in quieter moments, Mira had confessed to missing the companionship and intimacy that transformed a house into a home, a less lonely place to be.

When Bea left Trinidad on a scholarship that took her to a colder place, her relationship with both parents – never close to begin with – had deteriorated rapidly. Communication was hampered by her father's dislike of computers, though Bea doubted that this would have changed anything between them. They settled on a rhythm of twice-yearly contact, acknowledging Christmas and birthdays. Alan's preference was for oversized cards with long flowery verses executed in cursive script. The instant Bea received a card headlined 'To A Darling Daughter At Christmas' or 'For A Special Daughter Overseas' she knew Alan, rather than practical Mira, had sent it. Beyond signing the card 'Your loving father' he did not inquire into her world or offer details of his own. By last summer's visit it was sadly evident that father and daughter related to each other as strangers.

Mira had made an effort to stay in touch with Bea, but it was not reciprocated. Occasionally her frustration at Bea's silence spilled over into an angry phone call or email.

'If you was living by your father growing up, you think you would end up teaching in a university? You think so?' she screeched down the telephone. 'Let me tell you something, you ungrateful wretch. You would've end up like all the rest of them no-good Clarks. You wanted to spend your life selling sandpaper and paint? Is because of me you get where you is, and now you can't even pick up the phone to give your mother a call once in a blue moon. I don't know what to say. I don't know what I do wrong in this life to deserve a child like you.'

Each of Mira's outbursts worsened the strained relationship and led to further estrangement between mother and daughter. Bea knew her unexplained absence this summer was hurtful to both parents, a sign that the little contact they had was no longer sacred. Perhaps she should visit at Christmas. With goodwill and rum flowing, fruit cake almost a food group of its own, and a soundtrack of sweet parang music in the air, rapprochement was a possibility. It was worth considering.

In a session with Dr Payne, Bea asked if she should go to Trinidad for Christmas.

He seemed excited about the idea. 'Excellent. Great chance to see your family. And when it's freezing cold here you'll be enjoying the Caribbean sunshine. I'm envious already.'

'Growing up I just assumed I'd live there for ever. The beauty of driving through the mountains to Maracas Bay. It takes your breath away. When I was little, every summer we would stuff our tiny Vauxhall full of clothes and food and set off to Mayaro beach for a holiday. They say you don't appreciate what you have until it's gone.'

'They are called clichés for a reason.'

Bea laughed. 'But there's no point in longing for those days. They're not coming back. They don't belong to me any more, or I don't belong any more. Don't know which. Maybe it'll feel homey at Christmas. Trinidadians go all out then. Even if you haven't seen someone all year, and you pop by for a visit, they'll welcome you and insist you have fresh sorrel juice and a pastel to eat. That's how Trini people operate. Food and drink everywhere you go.'

'Sounds delightful.'

'But it doesn't last. And if you make the mistake of believing that you belong, you're screwed.'

Bea looked suddenly agitated, wringing her hands.

'You seem anxious.'

She looked away, still wringing her hands.

'Bea, because your parents weren't able to give you the sense of belonging you needed, doesn't mean you can't create it for yourself now.'

She smiled shyly. 'You're trying to tell me to grow up?'

His eyes smiled. 'I'm saying that the isolation you feel is in part a choice. There are other choices you can make.'

'Fine.' She looked down and mumbled, 'Can we talk about something else? Please.'

Dr. Payne rocked back in his chair and took a deep, audible breath. 'Just an observation, but whenever I mention your parents, you become a different person.'

She did not answer and after a few moments he continued, 'So what's been happening otherwise? Going into the office?'

She looked up in relief. 'Yup. Getting ready for next semester. Luckily I'm not teaching any new courses. Only updating ones I've taught before.'

'Take it slowly,' he urged. 'When does the new semester start?'

'End of August. I've got a bit more time.'

'I'm sorry, I know you've told me before,' he said scratching his head. 'What sort of history do you teach?'

'I teach courses with a transnational approach to history. So I do a course on comparative approaches to anti-colonial politics and ideologies, comparing colonial India with, say, nationalism in Vietnam. And I also teach more theoretical courses that consider major themes in world history like colonialism, imperialism and post-colonialism.'

He leaned forward. 'I can see you're passionate about this.'

'Yup.' She nodded, pulling her shoulders back in pride. It felt good, talking about something other than tweaking the antidepressants to mitigate side effects such as her perpetually dry mouth or the feeling of constant, low-level sedation. 'Wouldn't want to be doing anything else.'

'Few people can say that.'

'Guess I'm lucky.' She paused for a second then blurted out, 'Do you like what you do?'

'Sure. Especially when you see someone go from being really quite ill to functioning in society.' He leaned back in his chair and crossed his legs. 'I definitely have a rescue fantasy.'

A shaft of sunlight burst through the window, warming her, giving her a sense of comfort with the conversation. 'I don't want you to break any confidences,' she said, biting her bottom lip. 'But do you have a case that makes you specially happy?'

He rubbed his chin. 'Well, maybe the ones where the patient is desperate to be free of emotional pain and can't see a way out except through suicide. When you prevent that and help the patient back to health. Yes, those are the ones I feel good about.'

It was only a snippet of his life, but she clamped down on that information and stored it in her memory. Rescue fantasy.

He can rescue me any time.

He pulled her out of her thoughts. 'That's enough about me. What about the guy you've been seeing? Michael?'

Bea blushed. 'Don't know why, but he comes by every week. Not sure what he's getting out of it.'

'He would not still be seeing you if he did not find you a bright, interesting woman.'

'Maybe I'm his charity case.'

'Don't put yourself down. Now, what about your colleagues? How've they reacted to you being back?'

'Everyone's kind. At least to my face.' She shrugged. 'Maybe behind my back they're calling me a nutcase.'

'No one's calling you a nutcase.'

'I guess. It feels genuine enough. But I still hide in my office. It's easier to deal with people by email rather than face to face.'

'You understand that you still have to work toward increasing proper human contact. We can't let this social phobia get out of control.'

She sighed. 'That's tough.'

'It's a goal, not something you have to do today,' he said. 'And physically, how're you feeling?'

'Sleeping better. Most nights I get around seven hours. The meds make me drowsy. And I'm eating better.'

'Good.'

He looked at her in a curious way. 'I know this is unprofessional, but I still can't get accustomed to this very short hair of yours. You look completely different from when we first met.'

She touched the sides of her hair. 'Good different or bad different?'

'The contrast is stark. Much tougher than your old style.'

'Well, I like it, and for a girl I don't have to blow dry it. Wash and wear. Just like a man.'

He nodded. 'You do seem to be doing a lot better.'

'I am. Even bought enough food for a week. Really shocked the grocery lady. She made her sidekick, Ed, wheel it to my place in a trolley.'

'That's fantastic.' He uncrossed his legs and leaned forward, staring her straight in the eyes. 'This doesn't mean you stop taking the medication. I want you to stay at this dose for a while. We'll review it of course, but let's get a good period of stability going before even thinking of reducing it.'

Bea folded her arms around her body. 'Okay.'

'It's important you understand that feeling better for a couple of weeks is not enough. When you start teaching again, you'll be facing another set of challenges.'

'I've been teaching for a while, you know.'

'Yes, but these are early days of your recovery. In an ideal world I'd give you another month off before full-time work.'

'I can cope.'

'And you will cope. Just don't fall into the trap of underestimating what you've been through and how fragile you still are.' He wagged his finger in mock accusation. 'Don't start self-medicating. I'm the doctor.'

'Promise. I won't,' she said in an exaggeratedly meek voice.

'I don't mean to sound like you're on the naughty step. You're doing great and we want to keep it that way.'

'Yes, Doctor Payne.'

He pulled a face at her, rolling his eyes. 'The things we doctors have to put up with.'

He was dressed in a casual blazer and was not wearing a tie. Bea liked the informality. It made him more accessible – like a real man she could have rather than a distant doctor.

'Bea?'

'Sorry, yes. You were asking?'

'Are you going to the group therapy sessions?'

'Sometimes.'

'Isn't there one today?'

'Yeah. I guess I should go. By bedtime I'll be up to my eyeballs in analysis.'

'Before you go I need to tell you about the next few weeks. I'll be away for three weeks. There is another doctor if you need to see someone.'

'Who is it? Anyone from St. Anthony's?'

'No. His name's Dr. Wise. Josh Wise. Hopefully you won't need to see him, and I'll be back right after your semester starts. We can take it from there.'

Bea smiled. 'Full of wisdom, is he?'

'Tut-tut.'

'Well, you're called Dr. Payne. The only thing worse would be Dr. Hurt.'

'I wondered how long it would take you to make fun of me. My whole family dines out on it. My sister especially is always telling people I became a doctor just to call myself Dr. Payne.'

'I'm sorry. That was a bit wicked,' she conceded. 'So, is this vacation?'

'A combination. I'm giving a paper at a conference, then taking a holiday.'

Bea considered the odds of having another opportunity like this. 'You're taking your family with you?' she asked, her voice as disinterested as she could manage.

He hesitated. 'I'm on my own. Might meet up with friends along the trip.'

She felt emboldened by his willingness to reveal these scraps of personal information. 'Where are you going?'

'Starting off in London for the conference. After that I catch a bit of the Edinburgh fringe theatre festival and then head back home.'

'Hope you have a good time.'

'I need a break,' he replied sighing. 'And I'm not going to come back and find you're flipping pancakes with Pizza Man or self-harming, am I? Of course your hair is so short now you can't hide cuts in your scalp.'

'You're like a mother hen. And you know I've not been cutting myself. Honest, I feel, well, how should I put it? It's not jubilant but not down either. Kind of level. Neutral.'

'Good. So I'll see you in about three weeks?'

'Yeah. See you. Don't forget to come back – your patients need you.'

'I'll be back before you notice I was gone.'

CHAPTER EIGHTEEN

Queen's College is putting on the Bump and Wine Fete the weekend before Carnival to raise money for computer equipment. It's an all-day fete and the PTA is organising food stalls and running the bars. They are having a corn soup station, a doubles[1] station, a shark-and-bake stall, a roti section, and a tent with the usual peas and rice and stew chicken and that kind of food. If you still have room they're making old-fashioned ice cream right there – coconut, soursop, and rum and raisin. DJ Mad Menz playing the latest soca tunes and Indian chutney music and Krazy Kool steelband from Laventille will keep the vibes going. One tune I can't get out of my head is all about how a wasp (we call it a jep) sting this girl name Naina on she behind. I know it sound real foolish but I been singing it nonstop.

Everybody in Queen's get two tickets that we must sell, but you can sell more if you want. When I brought home the tickets you should hear how Nanny start to carry on. Carnival is the devil's doing. People does use it as an excuse to prance about half-naked and get on bad. The kind of grinding-up you see these days, they might as well be having full sexual intercourse in public. And is the women them who really doing the dirty, not the men. No sir, she not spending she little pension on no Carnival fete ticket. I explained how all of us have to sell at least the two tickets they sent home, but Nanny not budging.

'Charmaine going with her family to the fete,' I said.

'Who is this Charmaine?'

'Remember I went by her house during Christmas holidays? Is not like I went by anybody else.'

'The white girl with curly dark hair?'

'Yes.'

'How much years she have?'

'Same as me. Fourteen. Nearly fifteen.'

'And what a girl with fourteen years doing going Carnival fete?'

'She's not the only one. Other girls in my class going. Is no big deal.'

'No big deal? Well, all I have to say is that them can't be proper Christian people. I should have sent you to the Convent school. Queen's getting slack.'

I followed her in the kitchen. 'But Nanny, please. I can't be the only one who doesn't buy the tickets.'

'How much for them?'

I went and got the tickets from my backpack. 'A hundred each.'

Nanny fold her arms and set up her face like rain. 'Tina, you must be joking.'

'That's cheap. Most fetes nowadays cost a lot more.'

'Hear you! Since when you know what fete does cost?'

'I know from people in my class.'

'You tell me where I going to find two hundred Trinidad dollars for fete tickets that we not even using?'

I sucked my teeth.

'What you just do?'

'Nothing.'

'I hope that was nothing in truth, because if that was a steups it go be me and you today. You not too big to get a good cut-tail.'

'Is not fair. I want to go.'

'You too young for fete. And Tina, I can't make no donation of two hundred dollars. You know how things tight.'

I sucked my teeth good so she could hear. 'I don't ever get to go anywhere except where you want to go and all you ever want to do is go to church.'

'Go to your room.'

'I don't want to.'

'Go right now before I put two hot lash on you.'

So that is her last word. Carnival is the devil's work. Really? I don't know what planet she living on. She doesn't seem to understand that I am fourteen and a half. I will be fifteen soon and then sixteen next year. I could leave school and get a job when I'm sixteen. I don't care what she says, I am going to be Bumping and Wining in three weeks' time. Endless boys from the college next door will be there. The thing is how I going to find the hundred dollars for the ticket. Aunty Indra no better than Nanny, so no point in asking her. Granny Gwen has money but I can't see her supporting a fete. I've heard enough about Satan in Carnival from Nanny to have to hear it from Granny Gwen too.

It's now two weeks to go before the fete, and the only talk in school is who wearing what. Most girls going in denim shorts, and if you have a shiny top then you're like the coolest thing ever. I tell people that I haven't decided yet if I feel like going. Charmaine said I could go with them. Her parents could pass for me on the way to the fete and drop me back home after. This is the lime of the year. Everybody who is anybody going to be there. It will be like so amazing. I tried Nanny again but she threatened to hit me with the broom if she heard one more word about that so-and-so fete.

One week before the fete and the girls trying out different hairstyles in lunch break. Charmaine is going to have some tiny plaits in her hair with red and silver beads to match her top. Another girl was showing us how to do the latest eye makeup – thick lines of kohl on the eyelids. All I can think about is going to this fete. Even the teachers stop giving us homework because they too busy with the organising to have to mark it. I wish my Dad was around. He would be one of the dads helping in school and he would take me to the fete with him. He would tell Nanny she is over-reacting and that it's normal for girls my age to party. And he would have a hundred dollars for the ticket – no problem – because he would have a big job and a nice ride.

This afternoon when I came home I went straight in front the TV. Nanny wanted to know why I was not doing my homework. She didn't believe me when I told her I didn't have any. She started on about how I'm lying, and to bring my books for her to see. That was it. First I can't go to the fete and now I lying about homework. So I emptied the backpack on the floor right by her foot. I told her she could search the books for homework if she wanted. Then I stamped off to my room and slammed the door as hard as I could and locked it. Nanny started to bang on the door, trying the handle and yelling at me to come out now and clean up the mess and how I am rude and that is no way to treat my books. She could scream for the whole street to hear. I. Don't. Care. This blasted old woman is ruining my life. Thanks, Mummy. Thanks a lot for leaving me alone here with this hateful old witch.

I have to find my Dad. It's the only way out of this hellhole of church and church people. Once she let me go by a friend during the Christmas holidays. Once. And she doesn't think it's right to invite girls to our house. When I ask she says that I see them Monday to Friday and I don't need to see them Saturday and Sunday too. Well, up yours, Nanny. That evening I never came out of my room to bathe or eat or anything. When I was fed up I turned off the light and went to sleep. Next morning I got up early and went to school before Nanny got up. The cleaners were still sweeping the classrooms when I reach.

You know the old woman was waiting for me on the veranda when I came home after school. She said she nearly went to the school but she didn't want to shame me in front of everybody, but if I ever carry on like that again she will come to the school and give me one beating I will never forget for as long as I live. Imagine that. I am taller than her already. If she so much as lay a finger on me she will regret it. But I didn't say anything. I play cool and went and had my shower. When I came out she had left a plate of food covered on the kitchen counter. I ate her tasteless rice and stew lamb, went to my room and took off the light so she would think I was sleeping. I don't have anything to say to her. She didn't have to put up with the teacher making fun of me in front the whole class when I returned the fete tickets today. They could all go fuck themselves. Yes, I know the F word and the C word and plenty more.

While everybody feting down the place on Sunday I will be in church for the nine o'clock service followed by a super interesting day in the company of Miss Celia. Oh, and guess what I find out? Miss Celia only done gone and give away my Boo-Boo. I can't bear to think where my baby dog is now. Every time I think about it my stomach doubles up and I want to cry.

Anyhow, Nanny is going on a Bible retreat after church, so I have to stay with Miss Celia until she pick me up around seven in the evening. Well, praise the Lord. Yeah right. Life is so unfair. I am not asking for anything special. Why must I always be the one who can't have this and can't do that? My Mom would never have treated me like this. Our home was always happy with whatever we had.

Nanny does make me feel like is my fault we never have enough money for anything except school uniforms, school books, and a few dresses for church. People must be fed up seeing me wearing the same old clothes week in, week out. I have exactly two pairs of shoes – one for school and one for church – but I am always being told that I should be grateful for everything I have. Of course I am grateful, my mother dead and nobody has a clue who my father is. If that is what I have to be grateful for in life, then screw life.

Saturday rolled up and I guess everybody in my class was either shopping or by the hairdresser fixing up for tomorrow while I home. Nanny decide is time the windows see a little water and soap. They so dirty that when she looks out she can't see the neighbour big orange house properly. She only want to see people business. By the time I worked my way through the house it was lunchtime. I was so dog-tired I flopped down on my bed to chill out. About an hour later I heard Granny Gwen's voice, and right after Nanny calling for me to come say hello and give the old sweaty lady a kiss. After that they settled down on the veranda.

I swear I didn't plan any of it. It happened so quickly, and I have to admit it was kind of easy-peasy. Even so, my heart started racing and I felt like I was burning up. My hands were trembling. I could hear my breathing loud. Granny Gwen would never miss it. A woman like her have so much. The battered brown leather handbag was flopped on the kitchen table. I unzipped it as carefully as I could. Her black purse almost spilled out. Inside the notes were rolled up tight and shoved in. There were a few hundred bills. I only took a single hundred dollar bill. I'm not greedy. One hundred for the ticket and not a cent more. She had more money in that purse than I have ever seen since I born. Why should she have all that and I can't even go to a stupid little fete? I am not asking for much – just a chance to hang with kids from my class.

I crumpled the note and put it in my pants pocket, zipped the bag and left it exactly as I had found it. The scriptures say thou shalt not steal. Maybe I should put it back before anybody realised what happened. But then, what if I get caught putting the money back? And I will save up and give it back same way I took it. She is always saying I am like another granddaughter, so she would want me to have this small loan. Yes, it's a loan and a little one for a woman with a big hardware store.

I could hardly believe it. I actually have the ticket money. I don't need to buy anything when I'm there. The question now is how to get out of staying by Miss Celia. All afternoon I thought about it while Nanny and Granny Gwen chatting and reading Bible. When Nanny called me it was to say goodbye. Granny Gwen was already holding her handbag when I came out. Her son Mr. Robin was waiting in the car outside. My heart was racing. There was no need for her to check her purse before she left, but I was so afraid today she would have some reason to open it. But she left without anything happening. Even if she missed the money later she would never know it was me. Never in a billion years would she think I had taken money from her purse. I think I'm home and dry. Now all I have to do is ditch Miss Celia.

I started after dinner pretending to have an upset tummy, and I kept making trips to the bathroom every half hour. Nanny gave me some tablets but I flushed them down the toilet. By the next morning I told her I was still not feeling well, and I should stay in bed for the day. I was really sorry to be missing church and seeing Miss Celia but I had to be near a toilet or else there could be an accident. The dumb old lady believed me. She left at eight o'clock in the morning and I didn't expect her to come back before seven in the night. I deserved to go. Still, part of me felt a little queasy about the way she put out biscuits and cheese for me before she left. As soon as I figured she was down the road I called Charmaine and she said get ready because they picking me up about eleven.

I blow-dried my hair nice and straight and put on my

only jeans and my best top that Aunty Indra had given me Christmas gone. Nanny never lets me wear makeup but I borrowed some of her powder and blusher and a little lipstick. Charmaine's mom noticed I locked the front door and wanted to know where my grandmother was, and I told the truth. She was at a church retreat for the day and I was happy to be out with them rather than by myself. When we got to the school I told them I had to buy a ticket. Charmaine's Dad also needed one. He bought both and would not take my money. I never expected to have extra money in my pocket. Or maybe I should keep it to put back in Granny Gwen's bag next Saturday.

The fete was sweet for so. Everybody who was anybody was there liming, and plenty boys from the school opposite came. I dance down the place until my top was soaked right through with sweat. I did worry a little that someone might go back and tell Nanny I was at the fete, but she doesn't know a soul in my school except Priya, and of course Priya not here. To be honest, it was a funny experience because I was having a good time, but in the back of my mind I kept thinking that if Nanny ever found out she would skin me alive. As soon as six o'clock reach I was looking to go home. And that is when the trouble started.

Charmaine's family were having a ball and they didn't want to leave yet. They only saying I should relax because my grandmother know I'm with them so she wouldn't be worried. Well, I know better. I only spent ten dollars on a drink and doubles so I have more than enough to take a fast maxi-taxi rather than the bus to get home. It seemed like no taxi running. Five minutes gone. Six minutes. Seven minutes. Oh Jesus, please let me get home before Nanny. Nine minutes and a taxi finally stop. Thank you Jesus and all the saints. It was a quarter to seven when I unlocked the front door and ran straight in the shower. You wouldn't believe this but as soon as I turn on the tap I heard Nanny's voice calling for me. My dirty top and jeans were on the bed. I had to pray she didn't go in my bedroom before I came out.

'Tina? You feeling better?' asked Nanny from outside the bathroom door.

'Yes, Nanny. I'll be out just now.'

'You eat something?'

'A little.'

'They had food at the retreat and I bring some for you. Is pelau. I not sure you will want that but it was all they had.'

'No, I fine with that. I coming out now.'

I opened the bathroom door slightly, checked that Nanny was in the kitchen, and fled to my bedroom. I stuffed the dirty top under my bed, flung on a nightie and came out. I thought that as soon as she looked at me she would know exactly where I had been, but she didn't. We ate the pelau, she went in her bed early, and that was the end of that. Can you believe how lucky I am?

Well Carnival came and Carnival went. Nanny did not even like me watching it on the TV. 'Look at them girls. They not shame who see them carrying on so? And it look like once they see the camera they behaving more bad.'

'They want to get on YouTube and be famous.'

'What is that tube?'

'Is just a website with videos.'

'I hope you ain't watching that.'

'No, Nanny.'

Does she really think I won't watch YouTube? Clueless.

Granny Gwen has not visited since that time with the purse. I have eighty dollars left. I have to get another twenty before I could put it back. Soon. I know what I did was a sin and I know I have to put the money back. Sometimes I think about it and feel shame. Imagine I took money from an old lady and I lied to my Nanny who took me in when I didn't have a home. I'm glad they never found out. I promised Jesus that if he let me put the money back in Granny Gwen purse without getting caught then I will never do something like that again. I'm not a thief. It was one time and it will never happen again. The fete was fun, but to be honest I was scared even when I was jumping up with Charmaine and the other girls. Saints above, don't let Nanny or Granny Gwen find out anything, I begging you.

Two weekends passed and still no Granny Gwen for a Saturday lime. We saw her in church so I know she still alive. By the third weekend when she didn't visit I asked, as if I couldn't care less, why we were not seeing Granny Gwen. Nanny said that to be honest she was not sure why. All she could think was that for Lent Granny Gwen want to stay home. Maybe the truth is Granny Gwen knew I took that hundred note, and instead of causing a scene she decide to stay clear of us. She might think I will take money again. Maybe is stew she want me to stew. She biding her time till she nice and ready, and then she will bust the mark. But I pray she never did miss that money and we not seeing her for some other reason.

Every time I think of the blasted money it scrapes the inside of my belly raw. I have the whole hundred now. All I need is a chance to put it back. It look like no one Nanny knows has seen me at the fete. Is only this f-ing money business hanging over my head day and night. If my mother was alive, none of this would have happened. Or if I had my father around he would be looking after me. We would go places together. He would know about stuff like YouTube and what young people like. He would have bought the fete tickets and given me more than enough pocket money. I will never stop praying that somehow, somewhere, he knows about me and is looking for me. I know before I die he will find me. He will find me and take me away to live with him. I know he will.

Granny Gwen has blanked us four straight weekends

now. I must get the money back to her somehow. This coming Saturday Nanny having a few church ladies for a special Bible study, and I am hoping Granny Gwen in that. I am counting off the days until Saturday because I can't take this pain much longer. Even if she didn't miss the money, I know what I did was evil and God will punish me. It could be today, tomorrow or next year, but one day I will have to pay for my sins. The Lord sees all and knows all that we do on earth. My punishment is coming and when it come it go be one big-ass trouble.

Saturday morning finally reach. I am helping to tidy up the house but all I can think about is how I will get to put the money back at last. What if she doesn't leave the purse in the kitchen? She might keep it next to her, as is not her and Nanny alone today. My belly hurting, my head hurting, and my skin feeling dry-dry. I have learnt my lesson good and proper. Jesus, please let me give the money back today. I can't manage another second.

'Afternoon. Inside. Good afternoon.'

I have never been happier to hear Granny Gwen's voice calling from the front gate.

I called back. 'Afternoon. Come. We home.'

Granny Gwen does her duck-waddle walk up the three steps to the veranda.

'How you keeping, Tina girl?'

'Fine thanks, Granny Gwen.'

'Where your Nanny?'

'In the kitchen. I think she cutting up a sweetbread she made this morning.'

The ladies chatted while I got the tea and sweetbread ready. Granny Gwen put her bag on the kitchen table. I was hoping as hard as I could that she would leave it there. When I helped them take the trays out, the bag was left behind.

Another church lady arrived and the three of them settled in. I didn't wait another minute. I checked they had everything and went back to the kitchen. I unzipped the handbag quickly and grabbed the purse. It didn't have other hundred dollar notes in it – just a few twenties. There was no choice. Maybe when she looked in her purse later she would think she getting old and forget how much she had on her. I pushed the purse back in and zipped the bag so fast I pulled the skin on my index finger. A little sting and some blood. It didn't matter. Amen. Amen. Amen. I have made amends. Please forgive me, Jesus. I don't ever want to feel like that again. I could have been caught putting the money back and would have had to confess to taking it first. Anyway, it's over. Over. I am going to watch TV and try to forget this whole nasty business. Of course none of this trouble would have happened if Nanny had let me go to the fete in the first place. Stupid old woman.

[1. Trinidadian street food, a doubles is a sandwich made with two bara (a soft, fried bread) filled with curried chickpeas and garnished with tamarind, cucumber, hot sauce and the herb chadon beni.]

CHAPTER NINETEEN

Bea stood outside Michael's apartment taking deep breaths to steady herself. She was wearing new clothes – grey jeans and a silky white top. Dr. Payne was right. She needed to be getting out more, and Michael's invitation to dinner at his place was something she wanted to do and thought she could handle. They were developing an easy understanding founded on their childhood friendship. Michael also had the knack of being present without intruding – something Bea appreciated.

She smoothed the short bangs off her forehead, straightened her top and dared to press the buzzer. When he opened his apartment door his face looked happy and she thought a little nervous. They kissed lightly on the lips rather than on the cheeks as they usually did. She awkwardly handed him a bottle of wine and a single lily she had picked in the park nearby. His hands were trembling as he accepted the gifts. The red wine he had bought was already breathing.

'Your place is lovely,' she said, accepting the glass of wine he offered. 'Cosy.'

'I've been cleaning all day,' he replied.

She smiled. 'What inspired that?'

'Well, I've been here over a year and the place needed a good tidy.'

She ran her hand along the bookshelf. 'For a computer

person you have a lot of books. We have quite a few authors in common.'

'I do so much on my computer I guess I enjoy the feel of real books. One day I'll get around to sorting them,' he said, raising his glass of wine. 'Cheers.'

They drank in silence as Bea thumbed through books. A timer went off and made her jump.

'You want to come in the kitchen while I finish cooking?' he asked.

'Sure. What's for dinner?'

He smiled. 'I've been slaving over a hot stove for days.'

He took her hand and led the way. She sat at the small kitchen table set with a white cloth and proper linen napkins, sipping her wine while he made a green salad.

'We're having lasagne, salad and garlic bread. For dessert we have strawberries and cream.'

'Don't remember the last time I had such a home-made feast.'

'Wait till you taste it. I know Trini people are super-critical if food is not up to their exacting standards.'

'It smells wonderful.'

While he placed dishes on the table he asked her to put on some music. Bea anxiously flicked through his iPod and settled on a Bach compilation.

Dinner was delicious and the conversation uncomplicated. Bea forgot the horrors of the past months and enjoyed the unfolding evening with this man she had been lucky to find again after so long. Later they moved to his compact sofa and he slowly fed her strawberries. She began to feel uneasy.

'Bea, are you crying?'

'I'm sorry,' she said, wiping her face. 'I didn't even realise.'

'It's not the normal reaction I get when feeding a girl strawberries.'

'It's not you. It's the music. "Air on the G string". Bach.'

She pulled away and sat up.

'Did my father ever go into details about what happened when he left?'

Michael popped a strawberry into his mouth. 'Gosh. Well, if he did, I don't know about it. I was just a kid. Why are you asking?'

'I need to know.'

'I'm sorry, but I don't remember anything.'

'Do you think my Dad remembers the music that was playing? I mean, if it happened to you, would you remember?'

'Beezy, this is an odd conversation.'

She chewed the nail of her left index finger.

Michael leaned closer. 'Why are you asking me about stuff that happened decades ago?'

'Our parents were close. You were next door, for goodness sake. You must have heard every blessed detail.'

He got up and refilled his glass.

'A top up?'

'No. Thank you. I'm sorry. I don't mean to be morbid,' said Bea. 'But this music. It was playing. He listened to it the day he left. When it was all over, he sat there listening to it.'

'A favourite?'

'Don't think so. Maybe he wanted to hear some music. Any music. To calm down.'

'Probably.'

They fell back into an awkward silence. Why was this slimy mess seeping out now? Michael squeezed her hand.

'I'm going to change this music,' he said firmly. He bent close to her face and kissed her forehead. She inhaled his warm, comforting smell. 'It's going to be okay, Beezy. Lie down here and relax while I wash up.'

Her mind drifted to the BBC Radio 4 programme, *Desert Island Discs*, where celebrities were interviewed about the music they would select if marooned – the soundtrack of a life. The 'Air' would definitely be high on her list. What if she dared ask her father? If he had blocked out the events, then bringing them up would be an act of insensitivity, even ruthlessness. It was a silly piece of near ubiquitous music. But nothing could erase the image behind her eyes of his sad, slumped form in the old Morris mahogany sofa, the one with chocolate-brown cushions.

'Play some music, Beezy,' her father had said.

She selected a CD and held it up for him to see.

'Yeah, that one,' he had said. 'That's good.'

Christ, that was a day to forget.

But how do you do the actual physical and mental forgetting? Does Amazon stock *Forgetting For Idiots* with a step-by-carefully-planned-step of erasure? The details had invaded the cells of Bea's body, rearranged her DNA. Putting years and thousands of miles between herself and Trinidad had done nothing to block the memory of that airless July day.

She was a little girl playing in Michael's back yard that day, as they did most days that summer. He was the lucky one with a big garden and a hoard of toys. Over the fence they could hear the sound of water spraying from a hose. Her Daddy was washing the car. By the time she came home he was sitting on the front porch steps staring at a gleaming, spotless white Mazda.

'What time you call this?' he snapped as she walked toward him. 'You know how long I here waiting for you?'

'Sorry, Daddy.' She smiled. 'I didn't know you wanted me to come home. I got sweeties.'

'You always in the people house!' he yelled.

Her smile evaporated.

'Day and night you playing there.' He glowered at her. 'What, you living next door now? I have a mind to throw your clothes over the fence.' He pointed to Michael's house.

'If you like it so much then go live by them!'

The ferocity of his words was like a punch in the stomach.

'Sorry, Daddy. I didn't know I should've come home.'

He glared down at her, his eyes wild.

'You didn't know?' He gripped her arm tight and yanked her closer. 'You didn't know?' His other hand rose as if to strike.

She froze while his hand was suspended in mid-air. He had never struck her or held her so roughly.

'Get out of my sight!' he shouted. 'Get out before I put one beating on you right here in front the whole street.' His mouth twisted in revulsion. 'You disgusting like your mother.' He let out a scary, grunting sound and pushed her away.

She wanted to run but her legs would not move. It seemed forever before she could will them to take her away, first walking tentatively, then faster and faster until she was safely in her bedroom. Her throat felt dry and her hands were sweating. The four o'clock sun streamed through her window. Her mother was probably having an afternoon nap in the next room. Disturbing her would guarantee being screamed at. It was impossible to predict what would happen if they were both angry. Her father's anger was not unusual but she had never been subjected to this irrational, volatile temper. It had jolted her, making her little heart race and her knees shake.

She did not understand. Why would he threaten to beat her for playing where she played every day? Why today? She was his special girl. She wore a lemon coloured T-shirt with 'Daddy's Girl' in black felt letters across the front. Not 'Mummy's Girl'. Mummy didn't even want to be a Mummy. She had said so. Bea took too much of her mother's time and energy. It suited everyone that Bea was, and always would be, Daddy's Girl. And Daddy's Girl got special protection.

He provided his little girl with an invisible, magical force field that no bad person could penetrate. With it nothing bad, absolutely nothing, would happen to her.

Soon his heavy footsteps passed her bedroom on the way to his. 'The door locked!' he shouted, jiggling the doorknob. 'Open the blasted door.'

Silence.

'You better open this door or I go break it down right now.'

Bea heard the door as it banged hard against the wall.

'Oh, Jesus Christ, I was taking a rest,' her mother said. 'Why you have to carry on so?'

'Who was on the phone this afternoon?'

'No one.'

'Stop taking me for a fool. Who were you talking to on the phone? You think I don't know you was talking to that red nigger?'

Bea heard furniture being thrown over.

'I wasn't on the phone. Stop talking like that. Bea will hear you.'

'You lying bitch! I had enough of your shit! You think I stupid because I don't have your fancy qualifications? Eh? You take me for a fool? Answer me.'

'No one take you for a fool.'

'Well, you must really think I dumb not to see what going on right under my nose. I know exactly which red nigger you fucking!'

'Stop it!' her mother screamed.

'You think nobody see you, eh? Well, let me tell you something. I see you.'

'What you talking about?'

'I see you with my own eye park up in the car with him!'

'We were only talking.'

'Oh, so that is how you does talk now?'

'Stop it!'

'No, you stop it! Fucking bitch!'

This was not the first time the neighbourhood had heard their voices echo through the street. Michael must have heard every word.

It's just as well Daddy did not to want me to play next door any more. I am so ashamed to face Michael again.

Bea's head hurt. Her parents went on screaming accusations at each other. Then the strangest thing happened. Bea stopped hearing. In a split second, she became deaf. Part of her knew they were still yelling, but their voices were silent. She shut her eyes tight and tried to control the overwhelming urge to vomit.

Bea floated gently towards the ceiling. The house was so quiet from up here. Up and out she glided into her parents' bedroom. Daddy was yanking a frame off the wall. He smashed it, then snatched the photograph and viciously shredded it.

Careful of the glass, Dad.

Mom, watch out.

He must have thrown the frame at the window because that was smashed too. Glass was everywhere. There were perfume bottles and picture frames on the bedroom dressing table that could break. Better to stay in the corner by the bedside table. Safe for now. Suddenly her ears popped and she could once again hear the shouting.

'I never plan to hurt you. I never wanted it to be so,' her mother cried.

'So what exactly you expected to happen?'

'I so sorry. I didn't mean it. I so sorry.'

The words were swallowed by loud sobs.

'Sorry?' He sneered. 'Sorry? You can kiss my ass.'

For the first time he seemed to notice Bea shaking in the corner.

'Bea, pack your clothes. We're leaving this damn house right now.'

So it had finally come to this. The End. Bea did not move.

'You can't take my child!' her mother screamed.

Daddy pushed his face right up to Mummy's.

'A whore like you trying to tell me what I can and can't do?'

'I am the mother!' she shouted between sobs. 'Is my child!'

He turned to find Bea. 'I said get your clothes. I not making joke. Now!'

Bea floated over and hovered between her parents.

Her mother was clutching the other Bea and her snot and tears were dampening the front of the child's dress. Bea had been warned this might happen one day. But Daddy had told her they would be okay. They would always have each other, and Daddy loved Bea more than anything or anyone else in the whole wide world.

'She's not leaving this house,' her mother cried. 'You go have to kill me first before you take Bea!'

They would live at Granny Gwen's house, safe in the warmth of the extended family. There would always be people around to talk to and play with. And on Sundays Granny Gwen would bring rice cakes from the market and make her special lentil soup. And only Daddy loved her and only Daddy would always love her the most.

'Hurry up, Bea!' her Daddy snarled.

Mummy would be fine. She probably wouldn't even notice Bea was gone. To deserve maternal love she had to be prettier, brighter or better mannered. So why then was her mother howling like a wounded dog and gripping Bea's hand?

'I said she not going. You deaf?'

Bea felt her body floating over to inspect the torn edges of the photograph peeking through shards of glass. It must have hurt too much to see them both young and unbearably beautiful on their wedding day. Where was Daddy now? Ah, throwing his clothes out of the cupboard and into an old black suitcase. He was moving quickly in and out of the room.

Bea stood in the corner with her mother curled up next to her holding on tight. Her father threw another suitcase on the bed next to Bea and then went into Bea's room and yanked the clothes out of her closet.

Bea rubbed her eyes, crying.

'It's time to leave, Bea. Help Daddy pack.'

Disentangling from her mother was impossible. The grip around her was too tight.

'No, baby, you have to stay with Mummy,' she pleaded through tears. 'Stay with Mummy, darling.'

'Don't cry,' said Bea. 'I'll come back to see you.'

'If you leave this house I'll kill myself. I swear I will kill myself.'

'Mummy, don't say that! Don't say that!'

'I will! You know I will!'

Bea knew exactly where she hid the stockpile of pills. The open whiskey bottle was in full view.

Her father was almost done packing while her mother hung onto her tightly.

Would her mother survive the simultaneous loss of a husband and a daughter on this July afternoon?

Tick, tock.

Tick, tock.

Tick, tock.

Bea had to make up her mind.

Tick, tock.

Tick, tock.

Save father or kill mother? Betray father or save mother?

Eeny-Meeny-Miney-Mo
Catch a fellow by his toe
If he hollers, let him go

Eeny-Meeny-Miney-Mo.

'I'm staying with Mummy,' said Bea, roughly wiping her tears away.

Mummy stopped crying. Both parents seemed shocked at the little girl's sudden resolve.

'Don't be stupid,' said her Daddy. 'Get your clothes now.'

'I'm not leaving Mummy,' Bea repeated with the same newfound clarity.

Eeny-Meeny.

Betrayed father.

Miney-Mo.

Saved mother.

He sneered. 'Oh, I see. You think your mother have time for you? All right. But Bea, when I gone, I gone for good. You hear me?'

Her father dragged his suitcase down to the car, then returned to the bedroom for a bag left in the corner of the bedroom. He looked at Bea, telling her with his eyes that this was the last chance to change her mind. She knew from his look of anger and determination that if she didn't follow him she'd never again be Daddy's Girl.

Bea followed him out. As they walked through the living room, her father stopped and collapsed onto the old chocolate brown sofa. He closed his eyes and inhaled loud deep breaths. 'I'm going now, baby. Give Daddy a hug.'

'Daddy!'

He began to cry quietly.

'Come sit by Daddy before I go.'

'Don't go!'

He put his warm arm around her.

'Play some music, Beezy,' he whispered.

Bea held onto her Daddy. In between their sobs they inhaled the 'Air on the G string'.

*

A phone was ringing in Michael's apartment. Bea assumed it was Michael's but soon realised the sound was coming from her handbag. Mira was on the line.

Michael eventually called from the kitchen. 'Is everything okay?'

In a daze Bea walked into the kitchen and told him the devastating news.

CHAPTER TWENTY

Two days later, Bea and Michael were on a plane to Trinidad for Alan Clark's funeral. Michael's company had a project on the island and thought he could combine the funeral with work. Bea was thankful for the emotional and practical support. It was Michael who organised the plane tickets and spoke with Mira. She was there to pick them up at Piarco airport.

They drove in near complete silence, afraid of saying the wrong thing, afraid of each other. Although they had come off a six-hour flight, Bea wanted to drop her bags, change and head straight to her father's house where family and friends had been keeping wake for the past two nights. Michael followed her lead. She had not said much during the flight, and every time she had tried to talk she broke down in tears.

They arrived to a wake in full swing. Cars lined the street and Mira was forced to park some way from the house. It was easy to mistake the scene for a party. Well-dressed women arrived with covered pots of cooked provisions to share. The men were bringing bottles of Old Oak rum, often with fresh coconut water to chase it.

Bea followed the trail around to the back yard. The small space was packed. In one glance she was drenched by a wave of faces at once familiar and unfamiliar. She was afraid she would burst into tears at the slightest mention of her dead father. A group of men playing poker at a plastic table paused to take in the newcomers. One of the men with thick grey sideburns, his cheeks red from drink and heat, raised his hands, beckoning to them to come near.

'You is Alan daughter?' he asked. 'I recognise the face.'

'Yes,' replied Bea softly.

'You now reach?'

'Yes.'

'You come from America?'

'Yes,' she said.

He pushed his chair away and stood up shakily to offer his hand. 'Tate Walker. Please accept my condolences on your father passing. Me and the boys here was real tight with Alan. Every Friday we used to lime with your father, playing poker right here under the chenette tree.'

'Thanks,' said Bea softly. 'Do you know where my Granny is?'

'Granny Gwen right over there. She ain't stop crying since the news. You know he was she eyeball. Granny lived she life for Alan.'

Tate Walker peered behind Bea. She smelt the rum on his breath. 'And you is the mother?'

Before Mira could answer, Granny Gwen had spotted them and pushed her way through the clusters of people sitting around on plastic chairs.

'Well, look at my crosses,' Granny Gwen said, holding Bea in a tight hug and bursting into fresh hot tears. 'I nearly didn't make out me own grandchild. Miss Glenda say she see somebody looking just like Bea so I say let me come see for myself. Let me look at you. I been waiting for you to come.'

Bea sobbed aloud. She felt close to collapsing.

Her grandmother wailed. 'You is all I have now of your father.' She held Bea's tear-stained face in her hand and kept repeating, 'Alan's only child. Alan's only child.'

Gradually she and Bea let each other go. Granny Gwen led her to a group of older women. 'All you know me granddaughter, Bea? She is the one teaching university in America.'

'Hello, Granny Gwen,' said Mira.

'Mira girl, he gone,' bawled Granny Gwen. 'He with the Heavenly Father now.'

She pulled Mira close. 'This is me daughter-in-law. Never mind she and Alan wasn't together when he pass. Ain't she still me daughter-in-law? I use to say that Alan would never meet another woman good like you. But people don't listen to an old lady.'

If Mira was surprised by this interpretation of her marriage and subsequent divorce, she was magnanimous enough to keep it to herself. Bea had told Michael that from early courtship and throughout the marriage, Granny Gwen had kept Mira on the periphery of the Clark family, viewing her with the suspicion and jealousy a lover might feel for a rival. In the years following the breakdown of the marriage they had rarely seen each other.

'I don't know if you remember Corrie and Rupert who were Alan's good friends long time now?' asked Mira, pulling away slightly.

'You mean the friends them living England somewhere?' inquired Granny Gwen.

'Yes,' Mira confirmed. 'This is their son, Michael. You remember little Mike? Well, he ain't no little Mike no more. He's a big man now. A handsome man.'

'Well, oh gosh, I would've never know is you!' Granny Gwen looked him up and down. 'Last time I see this child he was little so,' she said with her hand at hip height. 'Come let me take a good look at you.' Granny Gwen gripped his forearm and Michael kissed the old woman's wet, marsh-mallow-soft cheek.

'Hello, Granny Gwen,' he said with a shy smile.

'You well resemble your mother. Yes man, you is Corrie child. You nice and fair just like she. How your parents them? They well?'

Michael nodded. 'They're fine and sorry not to be here. But they send their love to you. I'm really sorry.'

'I so glad you here to see your uncle bury. Never mind you not blood. Your father grow up here like me own son, you hear. So you is one of me own.'

Granny Gwen sighed and rubbed her forehead as if detained from her grief long enough by these conversations. Tears began silently flowing again and she motioned for them to sit. Bea sat down and covered her face with her hands.

'He left that morning to see a friend living Claxton Bay side,' said Granny Gwen to no one in particular. 'They say the other driver was drunk as a sailor. Is a wonder he only kill one person that day. Wasn't nothing Alan could do.'

Bea looked up from behind her hands. 'How did you find out?'

'My heart must be strong as an ox,' said Granny Gwen. 'They call the hardware. He was driving the Toyota and we have the hardware sign painted on the car door them. The police see the number and call we. Your Uncle Robin was the one answer the phone.' She paused, wiped her eyes and put her hand over her heart.

'I hear Robin bawl out so I run come to see what going on,' Granny continued. 'I had a feeling in me waters before he did even say one word. Then he tell me the policeman want him to come quite by San Fernando General Hospital to identify the body.'

The old lady broke down again and Bea gently stroked her back. 'Just so, just so, I find out me son dead,' whispered Granny Gwen. 'One day Alan here good-good, talking and laughing right under this same chenette tree. Next thing you know he gone and dead.'

She wiped her face. 'Is not right. Is not right,' she said from behind her hands. 'A mother never supposed to have to bury one son. Now I burying a second one. I can't believe he not going walk in here any minute now.'

Granny Gwen's tears flowed uncontrollably. Mira was quietly crying too. Occasionally Granny Gwen plunged into her blouse and removed a small, stained handkerchief that she used to blow her nose loudly before secreting it again in the folds of her ample bosom. Bea looked so small and lost. Faced with pure raw grief she did not know how to comfort Granny Gwen, or herself for that matter.

People continued to pour into the yard. Bea felt dehydrated so she and Michael made for the makeshift bar under a tent.

'This is a good wake, yes,' said the bartender who Bea did not know.

'Yes. Good turnout,' said Michael.

The man next to him quipped, 'At least nobody ain't get shot.'

All eyes at the bar looked at him.

'Man, all you didn't see the papers today?' he went on, beaming at his audience. 'A young boy get two bullet in he stomach point blank when he was in a wake. And the wake was for a next young boy who did get murder the week before. It have nowhere safe these days.'

Another man shook his head. 'When you see thing like that going on it must be drugs and gang in that.'

Bea took her fresh lime juice and went to sit down. She propped her head in her hands and sipped the drink. A steady stream of silent tears rolled down her small face. She felt like a scared sad child. Her Uncle Robin, Alan's brother, came and led her through the crowd of family and friends, introducing her to everyone. Wherever Bea went, Michael followed. Death was in the air they breathed.

During the long night, Bea accepted condolences, listened

to stories about her father, and heard updates on lives she seemed to have fallen out of step with. Missing second cousins were found to have moved to Toronto. Wendy who lived two doors from the hardware had finally received her green card and migrated to New York.

'When your father went New York last year for holiday, he went and spend a day by Wendy. I think he carry some of my homemade pepper sauce for she,' said Aunty Doris, Uncle Robin's wife.

Bea was quiet.

'Everybody liked your father, Bea,' said Aunty Doris, absently stroking the gold cross that hung on a chain around her neck. 'He didn't have a single bad bone in he body. Alan always had a joke to tell you. That man was a happy, happy soul.'

Michael put his arms around Bea and she sobbed aloud again, her whole body shaking. He was holding her tight when a man about their age came up and bent down to give her a hug.

Michael let go to make way for him.

'Beezy, I'm so sorry about Uncle Alan. It's such a shock to everybody. I can't believe he's gone.'

'Charles!' she said, looking up. 'Michael, this is my darling cousin Charles, Aunty Doris' son.'

'So my uncle have to dead for me to see you, Beezy? Like you forget you have family in Trinidad?'

'Don't say that, Charlie. You know you're my favourite cousin.'

Charles gave her another tight hug.

'You don't remember Michael, do you?' asked Bea, holding Michael's hand. 'He lived next door to us on Sydenham Avenue in St. Ann's.'

Charles's eyes widened.

'No way,' he said, reaching out to shake Michael's hand. 'You're the little boy from the orange house? I remember your family had one sweet Julie mango tree. How you doing, man?'

Michael smiled and chatted easily with Charles until interrupted by Aunty Doris.

'All you see that red-skin girl over there in the tight-tight black jersey?' asked Aunty Doris. 'That is Kim. I think she and Alan had a little something going on right before he passed.'

Bea glanced at the woman. If it was true, then Alan had been dating a woman roughly the same age as his daughter.

'And look over by the drinks,' said Aunty Doris, pointing with her chin. 'You see that old Indian lady in the blue dress talking to Mira? That is Mrs. Ramlogan, and the little girl is her granddaughter, Tina.'

She paused. 'Town say that Alan once had a thing going with Mrs. Ramlogan daughter. But it's real sad because the daughter died in a car accident. The little girl Tina is the dead woman daughter. If what they say is true, maybe that little girl is your half-sister, eh Bea?'

Michael gave a little laugh. 'It sounds like your Dad had a full life.'

Bea shot him a dirty look. 'I don't know if I can be proud of my father being the village ram goat,' she said, roughly wiping her eyes.

'I didn't mean it like that,' said Michael.

Bea turned to look Aunty Doris in the eye. 'You really think that little girl is related to me?'

'I don't think so. Is probably only old-talk. Your father never did anything that make me think is he child. I only telling you what the parish say.' Aunty Doris turned to Michael. 'You take a plate of food yet? It have plenty dhal-pouri roti and curry goat.'

'Thanks, Aunty,' said Michael. 'But I'm okay for now.'

'Bea, is time you accept your father for what he was,' said Aunty Doris, taking her hand. 'Everybody here loved him and none more so than Granny Gwen. No woman was ever good enough for she son. Alan never say nothing, but I telling you this, Bea. I feel that he would still be married to your mother if it wasn't for her interfering all the time.'

'That's all far in the past,' Bea replied.

As the night progressed more stories about Alan were exchanged. A teacher from the local primary school told how Alan gave freely of his time to coach the cricket and football teams. Someone from St. Theresa's church made a point of finding Bea to tell her that Alan never failed to give generously at Christmas time. Bea wondered if he died knowing he was so well loved. Tears laced with regret trickled down her cheeks.

It was well past midnight when an overwhelming exhaustion suddenly hit Bea. She looked at Michael and could see that he too was drained of all energy. They walked through the thick throng of people in search of Mira. A tall man who had the same straight nose as Alan and was about the same age was hugging and consoling Mira. As they approached, Mira pushed him gently aside. 'You all look like you ready to leave,' she said. 'Say hello to Uncle Kevin.'

'Hello, Bea,' said the man. 'My condolences.'

'Thanks,' said Bea. 'Sorry, but I think we need to go. I'm really tired.'

'Well, I will see you all tomorrow if God spare life,' said Uncle Kevin. 'Nite, Mira.'

He bent down and kissed Mira gently but directly on the lips.

CHAPTER TWENTY-ONE

very freaking day is an argument. Today is about the
cooking. It is Charmaine's sweet sixteen party and
that means I am out the house. Apparently I should
cook beforehand and leave food for Nanny. She going to be
alone but I have to boil rice and fry fish for her. You would
think her hand break. She going on and on about how since
I finish my high school exams that I should be doing the
cooking. But I didn't know that mean if I'm going out I still
have to cook before I can go out. When she out doing her
church meetings and Bible study and is me alone I make
do with biscuit and cheese or open a tin of sardines. This
blasted woman want a full meal left on the stove. I told her if
she wanted cooked food she could make it herself.

'Tina, I could never talk to my grandmother the way you
does talk to me.'

'Whatever.'

'You feel because you nearly sixteen you can behave like
a big woman. I have seventy-two years. You should be trying
to ease me up now and not making more trouble. How hard
is it to make a little bit of food for me, eh? How hard?'

I steups. 'I still have to do my hair and iron my clothes
for tonight.'

'When I was your age I was bringing money in. Every
Friday I used to come and put my whole pay in my mother

hand. When she take what she need for the house is only then I get something for myself. I don't ever tell you to get a job and put one cent towards the house. You have a roof over your head and food in your belly. Since your mother passed, God rest her soul, you never want for nothing.'

'I said I will get a job. I need a little break first.'

I sat down by the kitchen table and started to undo my two plaits.

'You ever hear me say that you have to work?' said Nanny. 'I glad for you to go back to school and get your A levels or whatever them does call it these days.'

I kept undoing the plaits. 'Boring. I have zero interest in doing more school.'

'Your teachers say how you is a bright girl but you don't apply yourself. You forever distracted.'

Nanny on a roll today.

'Please don't go over that again. Results supposed to be out next week.'

'You have a plan? What you going to do if you don't get the marks to do A levels?'

'I'll find a job.'

'And is where you getting a job with no qualifications?'

I took up the comb and started pulling it through my knotty hair.

'Thanks. Thanks a lot. The results ain't even out and you write me off already. Can't you stop bugging me all the time?'

'You going nowhere fast. Your poor mother must be turning in she grave. You uses to be so smart. I remember you reading before you even reach big school. Now is only boyfriend and liming I hearing about.'

That was it. I dropped the comb and went right up in her face.

'Why you always have to bring up my mother? You think I happy? You think I want to live with you and all your fucking Bible shit?'

The swift slap across my face was a shock and before I know what was happening I got another one. By the third slap I felt the sting. I held on to her hand and twisted it away. She start to bawl for me to stop. I was blue vex.

'Who you think you slapping, eh? Bitch. What give you the right to slap me?'

Nanny give me one hard look. 'As the Lord is my witness you are going straight to hell and damnation. Satan have you good.'

I left her right there and slammed the door to my bedroom. Then banging started on the door.

'You are nothing but a little slut. I take you in when nobody wanted you. Nobody. And this is how you treat me, Tina? You curse your grandmother? You hurt my hand? You take the Lord's name in vain? This is how you show gratitude for all that I do for you? All the sacrifice I make for you?'

Now she bawling and crying like somebody from church dead. I wish she would shut the fuck up.

With the sticky afternoon heat and all the craziness I must have dozed off because next thing I wake up and hear one set of pounding on my door.

'Tina, come out here now! You hear me? Open this door right now!'

Oh great. The old bitch only gone and put Aunty Indra in the mix now, so I ain't getting no peace. I opened the door and Aunty Indra was standing outside with hands on her hips like she is some bad woman.

'Tina, get yourself in the living room right now. I have a few words to say to you.'

I hope she not going to be too long. I still have to iron my clothes for the party. She and Nanny sit down on the sofa and I sit down opposite in the armchair.

'I hear something from your Nanny that I can't believe. You hurt your Nanny hand and then you curse her using the

B word and the F word? Tell me that is not true.'

Nanny started to cry again. I don't have nothing to say.

'Answer me, Tina. Did you do what Nanny tell me?'

'Yeah. But she slap me hard first. Three whole times. Across my face. What I suppose to do? Stand there and take the blows?'

'What make you feel you can hit my seventy-two year old mother and curse her? You just a pissing-tail little shit. I feel like knocking you down but your Nanny tell me to spare you.'

I am thinking she should shut up. Stupid.

'We have put up with all kind of bad behaviour from you that this family has never seen before. We had the shame when the principal call us in because you cut school and went liming with a boy. You take money we give you for school books and buy headphones. I didn't even know headphones could cost so much. But you crossed the line today, Tina. You crossed the line. I don't want my mother to have to deal with this kind of abuse in her old age. She should be taking it easy now and instead look how you have her in tears.'

I choked. Whatever happen I am not going to give her the satisfaction of seeing me cry.

'I never wanted to live here in the first place,' I blurted out.

Aunty Indra ain't missing a beat.

'And where you think you was going to live? If Nanny didn't take you in, out of the pure goodness of her heart, you would be in an orphanage. You wouldn't have a decent house and your own room and everything you need. You don't appreciate the sacrifices people make for you.'

I stopped listening. Aunty Indra was going on and on. All she wanted was to see me cry. Fuck them. I have to find my father and move in with him. He will want me no matter what. They must know who he is and out of bad-mind they keeping it from me. They can't stand to see me happy. I will find him. If it's the last thing I do I am going to find him and leave these damn backward people alone.

Before Aunty Indra left she banned me from going to Charmaine's birthday party. She really think she can ban me from my best friend's sweet sixteen? I texted this guy Ken who is so cool and he said he will pick me up around eleven. Best to make real sure Nanny sleeping. Besides, no good party does get going until about eleven thirty.

And man, it was a party and a half. They had it around the swimming pool with a bar on one side and a dance floor on the other. Lanterns were hanging from the trees and flashing disco lights made the dance floor look like they expecting John Travolta to make an appearance. Everything was perfect. And Charmaine looked like a princess in this tight strapless maxi dress. All the cool people were there. Oh, the cake. Wow. It had two layers – like a wedding cake with beautiful pink roses tumbling down one side. If you dreamt about how to do your party you would want it to be like hers. My sweet sixteen is next month and I will be lucky if I get so much as a cake and then it will be the same fruit cake Nanny always bakes at home no matter what the occasion. They don't care that I hate fruit cake.

*

Results coming out today. Aunty Indra pull up nine o'clock on the dot for us to go to the school and hear what I get. I don't care because I am no Priya with her straight A grades. She's already doing her A levels and always making out that she's better than me. And Nanny forever telling people how proud she is of Priya and calling Priya her favourite grand-daughter. You ever hear her say a good word about me? Hell will freeze over first. I am just the orphan they pick up from the garbage.

I passed five subjects. I got a B in English Language and four C grades in English Literature, Maths, History and Geography. I didn't expect to get Geography. The Geography teacher never explained anything in a way that you could picture it in your head. Still, I taking my C and run. Charmaine and her mom were there. She did better than me, as expected, but then again she did go for extra lessons six days a week. She got five B grades and three As and was waiting to see the principal about doing A levels. Aunty Indra was talking to Charmaine's mom, no doubt telling her how useless I am. Then all of a sudden I heard her shouting.

'Tina, come here!'

We were in the courtyard and Aunty Indra's voice was so loud and so sudden it wasn't only me who turned around.

'Yes, Aunty?' I said walking fast so she would stop talking loud.

'Come here,' she said, looking me hard in the eye. 'Charmaine's mom was just telling me about the birthday party and I want to hear it from you.'

Christ. Why today? Why here in front everybody? I looked down.

'Answer me when I speaking to you. Did you go to Charmaine's birthday party last Saturday?'

I didn't say anything.

'Didn't I specifically ban you from going because of how badly you behaved towards your Nanny? These people know how you curse your grandmother using the F word?'

It seemed like the whole courtyard had stopped what they were doing and were checking out the action my family providing.

'I'm asking you again. Did you go to the party when you were told not to?'

'Yeah,' I said softly. I was trying hard to hold back the tears but they had begun plopping directly on the ground in front me.

'How did you get to and from the party?'

I kept my head down. 'Ken drop me.'

'Ken who? And how old is this man you know with car?'

Charmaine's mother stepped closer in and tried to put her arm around Aunty Indra's shoulders.

'Indra, is okay. Ken is a nice boy. I sure nothing happen. And Tina behave herself in the party. I didn't see any kind of foolishness.'

Aunty Indra shook herself free. She squeezed my upper arm real tight and her long nails dug into the soft bit of flesh you have underneath your arm.

'You are a disgrace, you hear me? A damn disgrace. You sneak out the house to go in car with a man none of us know from Adam?'

People were coming up closer, not even bothering to hide their interest in Aunty Indra's performance. I was crying as quietly as I could.

'You are a total disgrace, Tina, and from the looks of these grades you're a dunce too.'

Aunty Indra was breathing hard and started rubbing her temples.

'Well, you could say goodbye to all your friends right now because you not seeing any of them again. Everybody else going on to better themselves. You will have to find a job fast because if you think you getting a single dollar more from me you think wrong. Now come on.'

She pulled me by the arm and marched me out the school gates. Everyone was watching. Even if I had the grades to stay on, I could never come back to this school.

CHAPTER TWENTY-TWO

The very thought of burying her father exhausted Bea. She was drained of emotional energy and unable to sleep in spite of acute tiredness. By five o'clock she was wide awake, dreading another day of constant visitors paying their last respects. The wakefulness was complete: she knew it was pointless trying to sleep, so she sat outside on the balcony. The cool morning breeze whipped through her thin cotton nightshirt, but she didn't mind. Spread out below in twinkling lights was a map of still sleepy Port of Spain.

Mira had bought this house almost two years before Bea left for university, but it had never felt like home. Her bedroom had been hastily converted into an office. For this unexpected homecoming, her mother had done everything possible to make the house on the hill welcoming. But Bea could never trust that the house would always be there for her to return to if she was weary or down on her luck.

She wanted nothing more than to quietly enjoy the breeze, but the congestion of thoughts in her mind got thicker and louder and the tears began to flow. This grief was like nothing she had ever felt. It was pure acid that burned straight through flesh to bone. Yet it seemed unreal, as if it was happening to someone else. Other wretched losses had been mere rehearsals for the heart and mind to survive this loss.

Mira came out, took one look at Bea's tear-stained face and offered to make what she remembered as her daughter's favourite breakfast of fried bakes and saltfish buljol. Bea wondered if this truce would have occurred without her father's death. Soon she was following a comforting aroma into the kitchen – onions, garlic, tomatoes and saltfish, sizzling in hot olive oil.

'You want Lipton tea while you waiting?' asked Mira, looking up from stirring the pot.

Bea nodded. 'Thanks.'

'Ten minutes and I go done frying these bakes,' said Mira. 'You think Michael will eat bake and buljol or I should make eggs and bacon for him?'

'No, I'm sure he'll eat anything.'

'It's real nice to see him after all these years.'

'Yes,' Bea said. 'It must be fate.' She looked around the compact, tidy kitchen. 'Can I help?'

'No, man. You sit down. Is not every day I get to make breakfast for my one child.'

Bea took her mug of tea into the living room and snuggled into an armchair. 'You know what's happening today?' she asked.

'I think they taking clothes to the funeral parlour. They will bury him in a suit and tie. And they have to meet with Father John to finalise the service. Tonight is wake as usual.'

'You don't have to go if you don't want to,' said Bea.

'I don't mind. I had nothing against your father.'

'Funny how Granny Gwen loves you now that you're not related.'

'Maybe that's why,' said Mira. 'And she softening up in she old age.'

They heard the gate click as it was opened, then a dull thud as something crashed on the paved driveway.

'That was the van dropping today's papers,' said Mira.

'I'll get it,' Bea volunteered. 'What do you take?'

'The *Guardian* and, as it's Friday, *Trini Expo* should be there too.'

Bea stepped out in bare feet on the cool paving stones. She found the papers in the middle of the driveway, tied together with string. She untied the bundle. The *Guardian* was headlining a new offshore drilling site to be developed by an American oil company. An opposition senator claimed that the deal was corrupt. If forced, he was prepared to name the government officials involved.

She sat in the armchair, flipping through the rest of the slim paper. Prominently positioned on page three was a photograph of a pretty young woman in gown and mortar. Proud parents announced that Michelle Ali had obtained a Bachelor of Science degree from Florida State University. Bea saved her favourite part of the paper, the classifieds, for last. A Christian lady was looking for work caring for the elderly or operating a bread van. A holy man with psychic powers, direct from Chennai, would be in Trinidad for the next two weeks only and available for personal consultations, including matters of marriage, dealing with enemies and financial security.

'Food ready,' called Mira. 'You eating now or you go wait for Michael to come down?'

'I'm eating while it's hot.'

'Well, come in the kitchen then,' said Mira. 'And bring the papers with you.'

Bea continued reading and could not help laughing out loud at the adverts. 'There's one here for special oils that you can buy to cleanse yourself, including Money Drawing Oil, Man Trap Oil, Boss Fix Oil and wait, the Oil of Oils, Influence and Victory over Evil Oil. All available in small, medium and large.'

They sat at the small square Formica table, scrutinising the papers together and relishing the feast Mira had prepared.

Bea remembered she'd left the other paper in the living room. 'Let me get *Trini Expo*,' she said, getting up from the table. 'I haven't looked at that rag in years.'

'*Trini Expo* does tell you what really going on,' said Mira.

Bea picked it up from the arm of the chair where it had been tossed. Across the front page was splashed a colour photo of two crumpled cars slotted together. In the top right-hand corner was an inset of a dead man's face awkwardly squashed on the smashed windscreen. The words and picture merged together. All Bea saw were white and black dots. Her hands shook and then her world went blank.

Mira heard a thud as something heavy hit the wooden floor.

'Bea!'

Mira bent over her. Bea's eyes opened slowly. She opened her mouth to speak but no sound escaped. Mira saw the paper clutched in her hand and prised it out of her fingers.

'Oh me Lord,' cried Mira. 'Oh Father in heaven. Oh my God, look what they put in the papers! Oh, Jesus! How they get that picture?'

She helped Bea into the armchair.

Michael came rushing down the stairs.

'What's happening?' he asked frantically. 'I heard shouting.'

Mira trembled. 'What kind of people would take out a picture so and put it on the front page? Who would do a thing like that?'

'Mira? Bea, you all right?'

'The papers,' said Mira in a hollow voice. 'Look, Michael.' She pointed to the newspaper. 'Take it away. I can't look at it again.'

Michael picked up the paper.

'This is disgusting,' he said, putting his hand over his

mouth. He looked at Bea slumped in the armchair and reached for her hand. 'It's okay. You don't have to see it ever again.'

Mira steadied herself and sank onto the sofa. They sat silently while *Trini Expo*'s colour photos were created and recreated a million times behind their eyes.

Michael broke the spell with a deep sigh. 'Can they do that?' he asked Mira. 'It can't be legal to publish those horror pictures.'

'Who going to stop them, eh?' asked Mira. 'This is the kind of thing people want to see when they buy the paper. They do this all the time. Once on TV they even show the rape of a disabled child. Trinidadians get accustomed to this violence, day in day out. It don't bother them any more.' She stood up. 'Oh God, I better phone by Granny Gwen. The old lady go drop down dead if she see this first thing in the morning.'

She rushed off to the phone in the kitchen. From her side of the conversation it was clear that Uncle Robin, who was staying with Granny Gwen, answered and had already seen the paper and hidden it from his mother.

'Robin, if I was you I would sue they ass,' Mira said. 'It might be news but that is people family and you can't treat people so. Look, Bea fall down and faint when she see the picture. Is a lucky thing nothing else ain't happen to she. You tell me if these people them have a heart. What, them ain't have a father or a brother too?'

There was a pause.

'Well you never think it going happen to you, eh,' said Mira. 'How you going make sure Granny Gwen don't see it at all, at all?'

Again there was a pause.

'Okay,' said Mira. 'Well, try, boy. Do what you have to do. You want me come and stay with Granny Gwen while you see them? I done bathe and dress.'

Another pause. 'You sure Doris coming now? If you not sure, I go be there in two twos … All right, then. Later.' Mira hung up.

She took her time coming back into the living room. 'Bea, you okay? You want water? You want to lie down? Come lie down. The shock have to work itself out of your system.'

'No,' said Bea. 'What are we going to do about this? They can't get away with it.'

'Your Uncle Robin say he going straight to the head office,' said Mira. 'Let's wait and see what they have to say.'

'Have you ever seen anything like that before?' asked Bea.

Mira sighed. 'I was telling Michael, the truth is they does run picture like this in the papers all the time. Mind you, not bad like this one showing everything. A man get shot in the road and you will see a picture with the man right where he fall down and dead. People think is normal to see that on the TV and in the papers. Is just another shooting or a stabbing. That is why we living with burglar-proofing bars on the windows.'

Mira turned to look out the window. 'I don't like to keep dog, but even I thinking about getting one for protection as is me alone living here.'

Michael sighed. 'It's going to take more than a guard dog to live here with any sense of security.'

CHAPTER TWENTY-THREE

Chenette was in season and Granny Gwen's legendary chenette tree, almost two storeys high, was laden with clumps of small green fruit. Granny Gwen's late husband Ignatius had spent his entire working life at the agriculture ministry and had planted a number of different fruit trees from the seeds of particularly sweet specimens. There was a pomerac tree, Long mango and Julie mango trees, several orange trees, a soursop and a cherry tree. But Ignatius's prize was the chenette, positioned for the right amount of sunlight, fed, manured and watered through the dry season. His dedication had paid off, and decades later his granddaughter Bea sucked on the sweet fleshy fruit while she helped to put out soft drinks, cheese paste sandwiches, mini meat pies, cookies and iced vanilla sponge cake to feed those who would be coming all day to pay their respects to Alan Clark.

Aunty Doris gave directions about where to put the food. Uncle Robin sorted out the bottles to take for recycling, and put soft drinks in coolers full of ice. Michael and Charles cleaned up. Mira and Uncle Kevin arranged chairs. Granny Gwen was in her bedroom getting ready to face the day.

People began trickling in almost as soon as the brunch was laid out. Most had seen or heard about the newspaper article and whispered their outrage. There was no disguising the collective disgust and trauma ordinary people felt when faced with these bloody pictures. It was not the final image of a person anyone should endure.

Bea was surprised that she had stopped crying constantly and took this as a good sign that she was coping better. But she was constantly exhausted and longed desperately to go back to bed. Between her and the world was a solid glass wall, blocking sound and feeling as she was slowly anaesthetised by searing grief. People spoke to her and she was able to carry on conversations, but all feeling, good or bad, had disappeared.

Mira came to check on her. 'You all right?'

'You want anything?' asked Uncle Kevin from behind Mira.

'I'm fine,' said Bea weakly.

'Don't worry, I'll stay close to her,' said Michael.

As they walked off Michael gently nudged Bea in the ribs. 'Remind me, please. How is he your uncle?' he asked.

'Who? You mean Uncle Kevin?'

'Yes,' said Michael. 'I don't remember him.'

'He is some sort of half-brother. He and my dad were roughly the same age. I always assumed Kevin was Grandpa's outside child. I'm really not sure. And there is some connection with my Dad's eldest brother who died young, but no one has ever talked about it.'

Michael held her hand in his. 'Maybe now you're all grown up Granny Gwen might tell you.'

'I doubt it. It's one of those family things. Uncle Kevin's always around. But his surname isn't Clark,' replied Bea. 'He's a Foster. Kevin Foster.'

Well-wishers interrupted their conversation, asking where they might find Granny Gwen. Bea went inside to find her. From the moment she climbed up the stairs into the house she felt soothed. She had always liked this old house. Granny Gwen kept it clean and tidy, ready to receive important visitors. Immediate family members were not allowed into the proper living room where crocheted cream antimacassars lay straight and undisturbed on the backs of the red upholstered chairs. Pink and white silk flowers, dulled by a layer of dust, stood proud in a vase on the sideboard. The dark wood sideboard was full of glassware and china reserved for relatives visiting from abroad or those deemed higher up the social ladder. Bea smiled as she glanced around the room. The house had remained unchanged for as long as she could remember.

'Who out there?' came Granny Gwen's voice from the bedroom. 'Robin, is you?'

'No, it's Bea,' she called back.

'Ah, I thought it was Robin,' said Granny Gwen, walking into the living room. She was trying to zip up her dress.

'Let me help you, Granny Gwen,' said Bea, taking hold of the zipper.

Granny Gwen pulled her dress hem down, then beckoned Bea to sit down on the red upholstered sofa.

'Granny, how come you letting me sit down on the good chairs? I don't think you've ever let me before. But Charlie and I used to sneak in when we were little and sit on them when you weren't looking.'

Granny Gwen laughed. 'Well, you get big now,' she said, snuggling next to Bea. 'I don't think you going to dirty it up.'

'Promise, I won't,' said Bea.

They sat for a moment in silence.

'I so glad you here,' said Granny Gwen patting Bea's hand. 'When you get old like me you doesn't know when next you go see your family that living all over the place.'

'I should come back more often,' said Bea.

'Please, child. For your grandmother sake.'

Bea pushed a stray hair off Granny Gwen's forehead. 'Well, you still have Uncle Robin and them to keep you company.'

'Yes,' sighed the old woman, but the tears had already begun to leak out. 'You know that I did have another son who dead.'

'Yes,' said Bea.

'Matthew was nineteen, nearly twenty, when he dead,' she said, wiping her eyes. 'Then I bury your grandfather Ignatius, God rest his soul. That was another trouble.'

Bea hugged Granny Gwen tight.

'Granny, what about Uncle Kevin? I don't think anybody has ever explained how he's related to us.'

Granny Gwen stiffened and her face hardened. 'Go on, child,' she said. 'You better go tell everybody I coming down just now.'

Bea sensed the sudden chill in Granny Gwen's voice and left quietly. The old woman didn't seem to notice. She was lost in another space. She sighed and sank back into the red sofa, her head resting on the crocheted antimacassars.

Alan, her youngest, was only a newborn baby when she had buried her first-born, Matthew. Less than two years later she had gone back to church for her husband Ignatius's funeral. Ignatius had been chatting to her under the chenette tree when he leaned forward and collapsed in front of her, a lifeless heap. The man had barely reached his half-century. Matthew gone. Ignatius gone. Now the diminished family was preparing to pay its last respects to her sweet baby Alan.

Why hadn't the Lord taken her instead? Why was she made to suffer the anguish of burying a husband and two – yes, two – sons? And there had been other, less visible losses. Between Matthew's birth and Alan's, a span of twenty years, only one baby, little Robin, had made it to full term alive. Six miscarriages. Six babies who never made it into her arms. Still, a brood of three boys was a reasonable show. The Lord was merciful, and just as he took away her Matthew he had given her a consolation prize. She regretted that it had taken

Alan's death for her to accept that gift.

As she moved about the living room, adjusting a chair here and a curtain there, she soothed herself with a lullaby she used to sing to her babies.

Dodo petit popo
Mammy gone to town
To buy a piece of sugar cake
And give baby some.

Some nasty, stinking, drunk man coming back from a fete. Drinking whole night. He should be dead. Is he should be laid out in Chatoo Funeral Parlour. Not Alan. Not her last precious child. But she had Kevin, who was practically his twin in age. Through the window she could see that he was outside today, helping as if he had always been within the fold of the Clark family. Looking at him, she felt a surge of guilt about the Saturday market visit so long ago, and how she had denied him. Her legs weakened and she sat back down again. The memories came flooding back.

★

'Mistress Clark, how you going?' asked Marva, the fish lady. 'You look like you going drop baby any day now.'

'Child, I not due for two more weeks,' replied Gwen. 'At least that is what Dr. Sanatan say.'

'What you think it is? I feel is a girl you making,' said Marva. 'They say when you belly round so is a girl. If it's a boy baby it would have poke out more in the front.'

'Well, a girl child go be nice,' admitted Gwen. 'Two boys is a handful.'

'And I hear Matthew girlfriend Prudence had she baby Wednesday gone,' said Marva.

Gwen's smile collapsed, and she felt the skin on her face tighten and burn. 'Is true that little Jezebel get sheself pregnant, but that is not my Matthew doings,' she declared. 'That little madam barely sixteen and already she's the village mattress. I bet she don't even know who the father is. Trying to put that on my son. Ah, Jesus.'

'So you ain't going to see the baby?' Marva persisted.

Gwen supported her aching lower back with her left arm and shook her head. 'What I going see it for? That child ain't nothing to me.'

But Marva was not giving in. 'And what about Matthew?' she asked. 'He gone and see the baby yet?'

'Why?' snorted Gwen. 'Is not he flesh. I tell him don't go unless you want to end up paying for another man child.'

'How you sure so?'

Gwen was beginning to tire, but she knew that her every word would soon be repeated up and down the market. A firm denial was required before she could go home to rest her aching back. 'I ask Matthew and he tell me is not he child,' she said. 'He say Prudence worthless. Sleeping with every Tom, Dick and Haripersad. Imagine you only have sixteen years and making baby. The harlot. She should hang she head in shame.'

Marva threw a cup of water over the kingfish, red snapper and marlin laid out on the wooden tray in front of her. The fish gleamed in the sunlight.

'Don't get vex with me, I only talking what I hear,' she said. 'Town say that the child is the spitting image of Matthew. The baby have he same straight nose. If I was in your shoes, Mistress Clark, I think I would have to go and see with me own two eye before I say for sure that it not my flesh and blood.'

Marva had gone too far. Gwen felt her body burning with anger. 'I not setting foot in no low-class house,' she declared through gritted teeth. 'If they so sure is Matthew baby then let them bring the baby by we.'

'You know they can't come by you,' said Marva calmly.

'Them is poor poor people. They already shame how Prudence make baby and no father there to see about the child. How they could come by your house?'

Gwen had stopped listening. She picked up her basket and waddled to the taxi stand. This village slut was not about to ruin Matthew's life. He was a handsome young man with a good job at Trinbago Life Assurance Company in Port of Spain. Matthew had prospects. That girl had her own family. And of course it might not be Matthew's child, no matter how straight the baby's nose.

The teenaged Prudence christened her baby boy without a father being named. Water was sprinkled on his tiny forehead and Kevin Foster was welcomed into the fold of the church of God. As fate would have it, on the same day Kevin was christened, Gwen gave birth. Despite Marva's predictions, it was another boy. Ignatius named him Alan, meaning 'precious'. Gwen was exhausted but relieved. Bitter past experience had told her not to hope until she had seen the little one wriggle, breathe and cry, and she had counted ten perfect tiny toes and ten perfect tiny fingers. After all those dreadful losses Alan was indeed a precious baby.

Gwen's labour had been difficult and the doctor insisted she stay in bed for at least a week before facing the world. She had not wanted to jinx the well-being of the baby, so there was little paraphernalia to welcome Alan. With Ignatius at work, and Robin still a young schoolboy, it fell to Matthew to gather basic supplies for his baby brother's arrival at home. He was dispatched to Nadia's Mother and Baby Supplies on Frederick Street with a list.

'Matthew, you going take bus or taxi?' his mother asked.

'As is Saturday, I prefer bus,' he replied. 'Them taxi drivers does drive like they mad. I see one the other day overtake three car and only just miss bouncing a maxi-taxi that was speeding coming up the road.'

'You have the list?'

'Yes, Mama.'

'I forget to put Johnson's Baby Powder. Add that on for me please.'

She adjusted the wriggling baby in her arms. 'You coming back home straight?'

'Yeah, I think so,' said Matthew.

'Well, if you see Ali selling doubles by Independence Square, buy two for me. That man know how to make a doubles. I feeling to eat something so. But hold the pepper. You not supposed to eat pepper when you feeding baby or else the baby stomach go burn him.'

In later years Gwen would often reflect on that list: two dozen cotton nappies, Vaseline, one pack of wash cloths, five baby vests, a bottle of Limacol and one Johnson's Baby Powder.

That shopping list had been Matthew's death warrant.

People were anxious to tell her the details. Marva, who knew everything, gave Gwen an account as she had heard it. At the bus station, Matthew had seen Prudence holding her brand-new baby, and next to her the baby's grandmother. He seemed to panic and tried to hide behind a concrete pillar. But it was too late. They had spotted him. Matthew emerged from behind the pillar, hands in his front pockets, whistling.

'Morning,' he said, looking beyond them. 'All you look like you going in town.'

'We only going up the road,' said Prudence. 'The baby have his one-month checkup today.' She hesitated, then looked up at Matthew. 'You want to see the baby?' she asked softly. 'He's sleeping.'

She pulled the blanket back a little away from Kevin's tiny body and moved her arms so he could be seen more clearly. The infant was fast asleep, his tiny hands clenched in fists. Matthew had looked dizzy.

'You not feeling good, boy?' asked the grandmother. 'Like

you see a ghost? Is just a little baby.'

'I good,' he said. 'Yes, man. I good. You make a nice-looking baby, Prudence. He have a name yet?'

'Kevin,' Prudence said shyly. 'My father chose it.'

Matthew had looked unsteady. The baby's grandmother held his wrist. 'You don't look too good,' she said. 'You want an orange? Let me peel one give you.'

'Thanks,' said Matthew.

The old lady took a good-sized orange with rough green-and-yellow skin from her string bag and peeled it with a penknife. She cut it in quarters and offered the pieces to Matthew. He sucked them quickly.

'This orange sweet for so,' said Matthew. 'You get these in the market?'

'Is from the tree in we yard,' said the grandmother. 'You want a next one?'

'Thanks,' said Matthew. 'I didn't take tea this morning. Me belly hungry for so.'

Matthew had barely finished this second orange when their bus pulled into the station and the women left. The last they would have seen of him was when he looked up briefly from the orange and waved.

By the time Matthew's bus pulled in fifteen minutes later he had collapsed and was dead. The cause of death remained unknown. But village voices suggested that Prudence's mother had worked obeah on that orange to kill the man who had wronged her daughter.

What took place next was even murkier. Some say Prudence came and offered Kevin to a grief-stricken Gwen, who rejected him outright. Others say Gwen went to the girl's house, took a long hard look at the baby, and informed the family that the boy was not her grandson and she wanted to hear nothing more about it.

Whatever the truth, the ban had clearly not been total, and Kevin had slowly leaked into their lives. Today, weighed down by grief for Alan, Gwen knew she must accept that Kevin was Matthew's son and her grandson. Deep down she had known it for decades. It was time to make amends.

CHAPTER TWENTY-FOUR

I don't want to see anyone. Not now. Not after the way Aunty Indra carried on in front the whole school. For the past few weeks I've stayed home. I get up early and cook food that I'm not eating and go back to bed. If I'm hungry I might have a few salt biscuits. Some days I don't even bother to change out of my nightie. I mean, what exactly is the point? I don't have the grades to do A levels and I don't have the first clue how to get a job. If she talks to me at all, Nanny's only interested in when I am going to look for a job and start paying rent. She says that if I want to act like a big woman then I can mind myself.

Aunty Indra doesn't want to have anything to do with me. Imagine she and Uncle Ricky have banned me from seeing my own cousins because they're afraid I would be a bad influence on them. Fine. Since I'm not going to any stupid church services either I'm not likely to see them anyway. The family might as well put me on the street because that is how it feels. Mummy, are you watching down on all this? And Daddy, where the hell are you?

I turned sixteen last week. No cake – not even the fruit cake I don't like. No gifts. In fact Nanny barely said happy birthday. But now I'm sixteen I wonder if I can get any information about my father from the Registry of Births. I must find my only close blood family left. Sometimes I have this nightmare where I look and look for my Dad and when I finally track him down it is to find that he died the day before. I miss my Mom but mostly I feel angry that she didn't tell me who he is. What was so shameful? If he's a married man, so what? That is no big deal these days. Maybe he was mixed up in drugs or something. But my sweet mother would never have had a child with a bad-john. I love my Mom with all my heart. How could she leave me?

This morning when I was cooking corned beef and rice for Her Majesty she came in the kitchen with the newspaper.

'The papers full of jobs,' she said. 'You look at any?'

I didn't answer. She can't even say good morning first.

'I see at least two jobs you could apply for.'

I have nothing to say to that witch.

'Well, I leaving the papers right here and some bus money. I want you out of the house and looking for a job today. Today. Today. Today. You hear me?'

'Yes.'

'Good. And when you come back home I want to know where you went and what they say. This damn nonsense of you lounging around whole day like the Queen of Sheba stopping today self.'

Last time I look we living in an old wood house in St. James, not Buckingham Palace, but it's not worth answering back. She will use it against me and get Aunty Indra on my case again.

The *Guardian* has twenty-seven positions vacant. The first one I had to get a dictionary to understand it. A full time phlebotomist required. That is somebody who opens your veins to let blood. I can barely look when I get a cut so no way I could open up people veins for bloodletting. What kind of people have bloodletting done to them in this day and age? If you ask me that sound like obeah, but I not calling that number so we will never know. A few adverts are for housekeepers with experience and references. There is one needing a live-in carer for an elderly lady in the San Juan area. No mention of experience or references and I get to move out of here. The other two jobs I thought might suit me were for 'multitasking workers in a café' near Woodbrook and the receptionist at a rehab centre in Petit Valley. I would look so cool behind a desk with my nails painted.

I called the live-in carer number first. No answer. Is the middle of the morning so somebody must be home. I tried about five times before a lady answer. Once she hear I'm sixteen she put on one obscene laugh.

'You ever change adult pampers?'

'No.'

The lady start to laugh again in a really annoying high-pitched voice.

'You strong enough to turn a body that have over two hundred and fifty pounds?'

'I don't think so.'

'I eh think so either. This not the job for you, dearie, but I sure you will find something else. Jesus helps those who helps themselves.'

It's a relief that I don't actually have to go for an interview. No way I'm changing dirty diapers from some old fat woman. I feel like vomiting just thinking about it. When I get old I hope I die before I have to get someone to change me when I go to the toilet.

Next call, the receptionist at the rehab centre. A man answered the phone first ring and I asked if he knew about the job.

'Yes, man. We looking for a well-spoken computer-literate young lady for the front office. You ever work as a receptionist?'

'No. I just left school. But I did computer studies.'

'How much years you have?'

'Sixteen.'

'No, that won't work. I need somebody who know what they doing.'

'I learn fast.'

'Darling, don't take this the wrong way, but you will need training up and I too busy for that. I'm sorry. Good luck, you hear? Don't take on all this talk about recession. It have people hiring out there.'

I put down the phone. How am I going to get trained if no one will give me a job?

The advert for 'multitasking workers in a café' was sounding better after the last two calls. A man who answered the phone sounded like he was running a marathon. He explained that he was expanding and wanted two more staff. Since the morning start he already had ten calls inquiring about the jobs, so he plan to see everybody tomorrow and I should come for ten o'clock.

'If you afraid of hard work don't bother coming for no interview.'

'I'm not afraid of hard work.'

'Good, because you can't stand up only looking pretty-pretty. You will have to be taking orders, washing wares, mopping the floor and prepping the meals.'

'I could do all that.'

'You ever work in a café before?'

'This will be my first job.'

'Well, we all have to start somewhere. See you tomorrow.'

The first problem was finding the café. I thought I knew town but I never saw this part before. The café was pushed up behind a construction site and packed with dusty-looking workers in big boots and hard hats eating at small metal tables. The manager, Mr. Morris, was a tall black man with his hair in a white net. He took one look at me and said he didn't think I was right for the job.

'How old you say you is?'

'Sixteen.'

'You think you could manage the men in here? They could get real crude sometimes. A good-looking chick like you with your tight jeans and make-up might can't take the hassle.'

'Please. I need a job. I will manage.'

He sighed. He steups. He looked to the heavens.

'All right. I know I going to regret this, but I'm giving you a chance. You could start now?'

'Right now?'

'Yes. Right now.'

'Thank you sir, Mr. Morris. Thanks a lot.'

'Okay. All you have to do today is take the orders and pass them on to Gerry here.'

'I could do that in my sleep.'

He handed me an orange apron with 'Men At Work Café' printed in green.

My first customer slammed a ten-dollar note on the counter.

'Sweetness, a portion.'

'A portion of what?'

'A portion,' he said with a steups.

Mr. Morris looked at me and sighed. 'The man want a portion of chips.' He turned to the customer. 'That's all you want?'

'Yeah.'

I wrote down the order.

'Man, give me a cold Coke too. Your drinks them cold?'

'Sure,' I said. 'One Coke.'

I wrote it down and passed the note to Gerry who seemed to be already stuffing chips in a bag.

Another customer was raising his voice at me. 'Sister. Look me here. A man hungry.'

'Yes, please?'

'Two egg and bread and a mauby drink.'

The men began piling through the door. It had started off with a queue but that broke down in no time.

'Reds.'

I didn't look up.

'Reds.'

I watch him hard. 'My name is not Reds.'

'So what you name then?'

'What you want?'

'Bread with egg and cheese and an orange Fanta.'

'Okay. Coming now.'

The man turned to my new boss.

'Morris, I glad you finally get a nice red girl for me to look at in here.'

The customer turned to me. 'You is family to Morris?'

'No.'

He turned back to Morris who was busying at the cash register.

'Well Morris, if you don't mind I going to have to carry this lovely lady for an ice cream later.'

'Behave yourself,' said Morris. 'She's only sixteen.'

'Sixteen.' He licked his lips. 'Cool. You can't make a jail for that.'

I gave him a hard stare. 'Look, I don't want to go for no ice cream with you.'

'Well, hear she. Like reds feel she too good for me.'

Morris touched my arm. 'Don't bother with him.'

'All right then, sweet sixteen. I go check you out tomorrow.'

In fairness I have to say that most of the customers didn't trouble me. They were tired hungry men who wanted food and to get on with their day. Once the rush was over I had to help wash up, dry the wares, and wipe down the tables. The afternoon was less busy but still a steady line of people taking a little shelter from the hot sun with a cold drink and maybe a currants roll or a slice of sponge cake. All the staff get to have a cold drink and a sandwich that they take whenever they can. There's no set break times and you don't ever really stop because there is always something that needs doing.

We closed at five sharp but it might as well have been midnight because I was wiped out. Mr. Morris said I did well for a first day. I nearly fall asleep on the bus home. Nanny was sitting on the veranda rocking.

'You gone whole day. I hope that mean you find a work.'

'Yes. I working in a café in town.'

She wanted to know where it was exactly and what it was called and if the owner is a Christian man.

'How much they paying you?'

'Ten dollars an hour.'

'That is cash or you have to pay tax?'

'Cash.'

'All right. When the week done I go work out what you have to give me for rent.'

She looked me up and down. 'They give you a uniform?'

'No. You wear an apron over your clothes.'

All I wanted was to take off my shoes. My feet were killing me. I didn't even want to eat – just a shower and my bed. I had to be back at the café for eight o'clock in the morning. One thing is sure – if I stay in this job I'll save plenty money because I'll be too tired to go spend it in the mall.

Within a few days I understood the rhythm of the café and how to deal with the men that want to get fresh. None of them mean anything – is only talk, and if you don't encourage them they end up treating you like a normal human being. It's a long day on your feet. With traffic I have to leave the house by seven to make sure I'm on time. And when I finish is still rush hour. It takes anywhere from thirty minutes to a whole hour to reach home. I am so exhausted when I reach home that I only want to shower and go in my bed. I don't see much of Nanny thankfully since I don't want to get my head bite off every time I open my mouth.

First Saturday I had the day off Nanny came at me as soon as I woke up.

'Don't think because you giving me a little piece of money that go be enough. I expect you to cook and clean when weekend reach. I getting too old to have to keep house when it have a healthy young person living under my roof.'

I didn't say anything. I just vacuum the house and clean the kitchen and bathroom. I'm not cooking. She could starve for all I care. I tried calling Charmaine to go for a little lime in the mall but she said the work you have to do for A levels is ten times the amount we had before and she don't have time to go out. She sounded different. When I told her about my job all she said was that she's glad I found something. I texted Ken but he hasn't texted back. Maybe he has a new number. Whatever. I don't need them. The girls at work planning a beach lime next weekend and I in that. I think Gerry, who is like the main cook, is the one driving us to the North Coast. It might take most of my money but I going to get a new bikini to wear. I'm looking real thin these days.

I've been thinking it's time I made a serious attempt to find my father. Someone must know something. I am going to swallow my pride and beg Nanny to tell me.

I waited till the afternoon when she was rocking in the veranda and reading the Bible.

'Nanny, I sorry to bother you, but I want to ask you something.'

She didn't look up. 'What you want?'

'I finish school. I'm working for my own money. I giving you rent. You don't think is time you tell me who my father is?'

She laughed one nasty laugh. Actually it was more like a pig snorting, with a laugh at the end.

'You think I would put myself through all this trouble to bring you up if I did know who you father was? Man, I would have sent you to live by he long time now.'

She began rocking harder. 'No, child. Your mother take that name to she grave. But your father couldn't have been a decent body. Why else it so secret that her own mother never find out his name?'

Okay. I don't know why I expected anything different from the old witch. I hope she dead soon. The only other person in the world left who might have that secret locked away is Aunty Indra. I doubt she will want to help me, but is not like I have a choice. When she came to drop a bag of oranges for Nanny I walked her out to the front gate.

'Aunty Indra, I know you still vex with me, but I have to ask you something.'

She let out one steups. 'You right about that. What you want? I hope is not money you want because your Uncle Ricky and me don't have nothing more to give you.'

They certainly not teaching forgiveness at St. Theresa's church.

'No, Aunty.'

Maybe I should leave it alone. I want to but I can't.

'I was wondering, now I'm working and thing, if you could tell me who my father is. It only natural I want to know. And I big enough to take the truth.'

She bit her lip. 'If your mother wanted you to know then she would have told you. But she passed now and that is that. You can't live your life expecting no father to come carry you away. Is you and you alone have to make something of your life. And let this be the last time you bother me with this foolishness. I have enough worries of my own.'

That was so kind and helpful. Thanks for nothing. Bitch.

CHAPTER TWENTY-FIVE

A lthough as a child Bea had frequently sat in these pews, this was the first occasion when she really examined the flooring of St. Theresa's Church. Between rows of shoes, it was clear that the mosaic of large black and white tiles was not in the best condition. Hairline cracks had created a secondary pattern and time had ground the white closer to a dirty grey and left the black lacklustre. It did not help that it had rained earlier and the crowd of perhaps two hundred people packed inside the small church had each brought a little of the damp earth indoors. Father John's words interrupted her thoughts.

Dearly beloved, we are gathered here to commend our brother, Alan Jeremiah Clark, who has been called home to the arms of Jesus Christ our Saviour who is in Heaven.

It needed a proper clean on hands and knees with a solution of one part vinegar to three parts water. After that, if the tiles still looked dull, they should try one of the specialist tile-cleaning liquids sold at the hardware.

Let us stand and join in singing hymn number 714, 'Through all the Changing Scenes of Life'.

At a push they could even try a mild solution of bleach and water, but that risked damaging the tiles further. Bea wondered who was in charge of decisions on tile cleaning. Was it the priest? Perhaps a particularly involved lay member with special knowledge of tiles? Or was there a church committee entrusted with such decisions? Maybe, thought Bea, the issue fell through the cracks. Ha, ha, ha. The congregation was singing.

Oh, magnify the Lord with me,
With me exalt His name;
When in distress to Him I called,
He to my rescue came.

The black and white tiles faded into blocks of colour in her mind. Black and white. All light and no light. Bad and good. Dirty and clean. Base and sophisticated. Hell and Heaven. The pews were flooded with black cloth, draped, stretched and pulled over brown skins.

According to Aunty Doris it was becoming quite acceptable to wear alternative, bright colours. She had even heard of a man whose deathbed wish was honoured when everyone wore yellow to see him off this earthly existence.

'The Lord be with you,' Father John proclaimed.

Her funeral would be an all-white affair.

'And also with you,' responded the congregation.

If white was good enough for the queens of mediaeval times then it would do for her.

'A reading from John 14, verses 1-6,' said Father John.

White was the colour of mourning for millions of Hindus. She made a mental note to wear more white.

In my Father's house there are many dwelling places.
If it were not so, would I have told you that I go to prepare
a place for you?
And if I go and prepare a place for you,
I will come again and will take you to myself,
so that where I am, there you may be also.

Bea wondered if her maternal grandma seated a few rows behind had worn white when her husband died. In spite of all her misgivings about the living Alan, this grandmother did her duty with an appearance. The congregation was asked to stand. It was that wonderful hymn asking to be made a channel of peace, to bring love where there was hatred, and to pardon those who injure us.

Bea's mind drifted to other funerals she had attended. Great-Aunty Sonia had been given quite a send-off. Was it really ten years since her cancer-riddled body had been laid to rest? Back then the family had been unable or unwilling to channel inner or outer peace. From the moment of death to the descent of the coffin into the earth, her husband, children and step-children publicly raged and tore at Great-Aunty Sonia's memory. No one could forget the moment her stepson, emboldened by the weed of wisdom, seized the briefest of pauses between hymn and scripture reading to leap to his feet. Those present in that packed church twittered for months, perhaps years after, as they recalled his incoherent but impassioned speech setting out the reasons why his father should never have married the now deceased blood-sucking bitch in the first place. It had taken three male relatives to forcibly remove him from the church. Bea smiled to herself that this would never happen at a funeral in Boston.

Father John announced that Bea would deliver the eulogy. She felt an imposter taking centre stage. Her wish was not to speak at all, but Granny Gwen had insisted.

'How it go look if you don't say two word in the church?'

'But Granny Gwen, I can't talk in front of all those people. Uncle Robin should be doing it, or one of Dad's good friends. I bet one of them really wants to do it.'

'So what you have all them big degree for?' asked Granny Gwen scornfully. 'Your father work hard-hard to make sure you always had the best of everything. This is how you show your respect?'

The old woman had turned away muttering. 'Young people today too damn ungrateful. Think they get big all by theyself like nobody ain't help them.'

Bea stepped up to the podium. 'I have been asked to speak about my father.'

Someone rushed up to adjust the microphone downwards to her mouth. 'I have been asked to speak about my father,' she repeated in a disconnected, newly amplified voice. 'He was a popular man who was much loved by all who knew him.'

A loud deep cry rose from somewhere on the left side of the congregation.

'Oh God he gone! Oh God Alan gone!'

Everyone turned to try and locate the cries. It soon became apparent that the guttural sounds and loud pleadings to the Almighty were originating from a petite woman, yellow-skinned with jet-black straight hair and oriental features.

Bea's mind raced. There really are more than fifty ways to leave a lover.

Get that stupid song out of your mind, Bea urged herself. Concentrate.

The woman's cries ebbed and flowed. 'Oh God he gone! He gone! Why Jesus had to take away my Alan?'

People stared at each other and whispered about the woman they did not recognise as either a family member or friend. Those sitting closest tried to pacify her, but the wailing continued to cut into the sacred atmosphere.

After about thirty long seconds of this explosive grief, Father John whispered in Bea's ear that they would pause for a hymn to give the lady time to compose herself and then continue with the eulogy.

Bea returned to her seat and Father John directed the organist to move along to the next hymn. But even through a hearty rendition of 'The Old Rugged Cross' the howling and distressed cries could still be heard. As the organ faded Bea was beckoned to the pulpit for a second attempt.

'All you carrying on like I ain't here,' the woman bellowed.

'I ain't see me name with the death notice. You could leave me out but this is a public church and all God's children welcome here. Treating me like the man never love me.'

'We pray that our sister and others in the congregation will now be comforted by the words of Beatrice Clark, Alan's only child,' said Father John.

'Well, we know that not true,' laughed the unknown woman. 'Gwen well know that I did treat the man like a king. Now he gone and dead. Oh, God help me!'

The unknown woman had cornered the market in popular grief, and throughout Bea's brief eulogy there were occasional high-decibel cries bemoaning the loss of Alan Clark. Despite stiff competition, the stranger's grief retained pole position to the end.

Bea cleared her throat. 'I have been asked to speak about my father. He was a popular man who was much loved by all who knew him.'

She paused and took a deep breath. It was now or never.

'Truth is, I don't remember when we last spoke. But we have been actively engaged in a joint project. Over the last two decades we have been building a wall of silence. When he died the wall was near completion.'

Bea shifted her weight from one leg to the next and glanced up at the congregation. Everyone was concentrating on her short form. Even the wailing Chinese woman looked momentarily rapt.

'The building materials we used are testament to our innovation and persistence,' continued Bea. 'We stacked block upon block using whatever we found at hand. Sometimes we worked away using resentment and anger. Those are materials you can count on to withstand hurricane-force winds. At other times pride would be added for fortification.'

Bea felt the burning of two hundred pairs of eyes in this church with standing room only. She had made it this far.

There was no turning back.

'But a huge amount of rejection, dejection, regret, self-preservation and denial were harnessed as well, until the wall of silence was a solid and deafening structure. While we worked there were continual challenges, assaults that the wall of silence barely endured. There were even incursions that threatened to undermine its very foundations. Once or twice I thought the whole barricade would tumble down.'

Her voice broke and she took a deep breath to steady herself. 'Since I have lost my fellow builder I can only give you a partial history of attacks on the integrity of the wall as I witnessed them. One of the hardest to repel was the sight of my father on his side of the wall. Every time I saw him I wanted to smash a brick and reach over.

'Daddy, you have died young and so will forever be preserved in my memory with a lean, muscular body and handsome, rugged face. Pity I did not inherit your good looks and, ahem, height. I can still see your thick head of hair, always well groomed, and your elegant hands. Experience taught me to look quietly so that I could glimpse that beautiful smile lighting up your eyes, or watch you walk away with your deliberate, measured gait.'

Bea dared to look up at the congregation. There was a look of disbelief on some faces, mere surprise on others. No one looked bored.

'The wall of silence managed to withstand the assault of these periodic sightings of my father. But when they were accompanied by touch you could actually see this huge fortification shake as if it were at the epicentre of an earthquake. With the Dutch courage of Johnny Walker, he occasionally reached over the wall to give me one of his warm bear hugs. Lately these have been rare. It is unclear how many embraces our old wall would withstand if we administered this stress test now. It certainly caused cracks and crevices in the early days when, as a child, I seized every opportunity to literally hold on to my Daddy in the time we had together. Such a shame. So simple an act might have blown the whole wall apart.'

Bea's eyes welled up with tears and she could barely read from her script. 'Territory demarcated, divided, enclosed, protected. We were walled in, walled up.'

The tears were now big drops blotting the printed pages, but she had to keep going. It was almost over.

'And like Hans Christian Anderson's story about the little match girl,' she said through tears, 'I wish a little light, as small as that from the box of matches you always carried in your pocket, Dad, the one you used to light your cigarettes. I wish that light would magically transform this wall into one of Granny Gwen's light net curtains and I could see you alive and well once more. And like the little match girl, no price would be too high if we were on the same side of the wall.'

CHAPTER TWENTY-SIX

If people would please stay out of my damn business I can get on with my f-ing life. They wanted me to get a job and I did. Now they don't like the friends I made at the café. They don't like me going to the beach come weekend. The pay not good enough. Nanny wants me to ask Mr. Morris for a raise. How I going to ask for a raise when I lucky to have a job at all? She doesn't realise how hard things are out there. Yes, I know he is paying me a little bit less than the others, but I am younger and I've not been there a year yet.

Aunty Indra thinks he's taking advantage of my age and making me do too much for the pay. She wants to come down to the café and talk to him. How will that look? My Aunty Indra coming in my workplace to talk to my boss? They didn't give a shit about me, now they care so much they want to come and ruin my job. I have begged them to please leave it alone. I will ask for a raise when the time is right. I reminded them I didn't exactly have a choice of jobs. Every day they don't appear at the café is a blessed relief.

And both Nanny and Aunty Indra have this really annoying habit of talking about me in front of me, as if I'm invisible. You should hear them. Once I heard Nanny saying to some stranger that I should learn to do hairdressing. People does always need their hair do, recession or no recession. Aunty Indra wants me to learn to cook properly so I can get a job in a hotel kitchen or a fancy restaurant. She is convinced there are always chef jobs because Trini people like their food. But Nanny doesn't agree. It seems I am so hot up with myself I better off doing beautician work. I could do nails. Not once have those blasted witches taken a second to ask me if I want to do hair or nails or cook. And I don't see why anything has to change. I am doing fine, thank you very much. They should f-off.

Is one thing to talk about me like this in the family, but Nanny's mouth never tired. Granny Gwen came for a Saturday visit. She doesn't make it so often any more but when you think you haven't seen her for a while she pops right back up on the veranda drinking tea and quoting scriptures. The old lady ain't reach too long before I heard Nanny bad-talking me. She's carrying on about how I am happy to settle for a job in a café where I only getting paid ten dollars an hour and the minimum wage is twelve.

I feel like cussing the whole lot of them, but I took a deep breath and went in my bedroom with a magazine. While I living under the bitch roof I have to learn to chill. Instead of being proud that I get a job she can't resist putting me down in front everybody who set foot in this house and probably half the people in church too. Don't think it ain't crossed my mind to put a drop or three of castor oil in she food. That would shut her up for a good while.

I was bored hiding in my room away from the old ladies so I decided to do over my nails. The red colour is chipping off. It's hard to keep them looking good but I like to try. I was lying down on the bed letting them dry properly when someone knocked on the door. Is Granny Gwen calling for me. If my nails get smudged I will be real vex. I managed to open the door carefully.

'Yes, Granny Gwen? You going now?'

'I getting ready to go but I wanted to ask you to come by

me tomorrow.'

'Me and Nanny?'

'No. Just you. I want you to come and spend a little hour with an old lady. You could do that for me?'

'Of course I will, Granny Gwen. What time?'

'Come about four o'clock. You want me to send the car for you?'

'If you don't mind. Bus does run slow on a Sunday.'

'No problem. Good. So it's me and you tomorrow. You will get to taste my home-made coconut ice cream, and the tree have chenette for so.'

'Okay. Thanks, Granny Gwen. Tomorrow then.'

I closed back the bedroom door carefully. No smudge. Now what was that all about? She has never asked me to come visit her alone before. I wonder if she saved up speaking out all this time and she finally ready to confront me about the hundred dollars. If she asks I will have to play dumb. She can't prove a thing after so long. Or Nanny might have put her up to this. She probably beg Granny Gwen to "talk some sense" into her wayward granddaughter. I have no bone with Granny Gwen. I will go tomorrow, eat some ice cream, get a bag of chenette and come back home in time to catch *The Simpsons* on TV.

Of course it was wishful thinking that I would get off easy with only coconut ice cream. Granny Gwen showed me around the house. I had only ever been on the outside patio where they seem to spend most of the time. This time I went inside. She has a nice sitting room that is perfect. I don't think she allows anybody in there, much more let people eat and drink in it. And the bedrooms all have beautiful quilts with matching pillowcases. I can't imagine actually sleeping in such a pretty bed and messing it up.

The dining room is a separate room with a huge mahogany table and eight matching chairs. The table is set with fancy plates, glasses and napkins like she expecting the prime minister or Brian Lara for a visit. We sat down in the kitchen and it was then I realise what was missing.

The house was empty.

Granny Gwen is living in this big house all on her own. I thought her son Mr. Robin who runs the hardware lived here with his family, but she said he has his own place. Mr. Kevin, a half-brother or cousin, I'm not sure how he's related, has always been here the few times I visited, but again this is not his house. Granny Gwen is alone.

'You don't get lonely here, Granny Gwen?'

'You know my big son Alan who died used to live with me. Is he that I miss when I here by myself. The Lord knows why He chose to take him. We don't know His plans.'

'I went to the funeral. I was little but I remember it had a lot of excitement.'

Granny Gwen laughed.

'At the time I was so vex, you hear? But now I look back and laugh. Alan was always in some confusion with the ladies.'

She took the ice cream out of the freezer.

'How much you want? Two scoops or three?'

'Only one. I have to look after my figure.'

'Alan was a kind soul. Everybody liked him. And I have one granddaughter from him. Bea. She ain't come to look for me since the funeral. But young people today busy. I suppose she will make it back one day.'

I tasted the ice cream. It was creamy with real coconut flavour. You can't buy this in Hi-Lo supermarket.

'Granny Gwen, this is real delicious. If it was in our freezer it wouldn't last a day.'

'I glad you like it. When my grandchildren were growing up I used to make all the time. Now is only when I feel like it I do a batch.'

I never knew Granny Gwen had had such an interesting life. She wasn't always this old church lady. She showed me pictures of her when she was young. Gosh, she was pretty in her high heels and makeup and fancy dresses. And she was skinny like a size zero. She told me how every Saturday she and her friends used to go to dances up at a girls' college that close down now. And her husband was one good-looking man too with his black hair all slicked back with a ton of hair cream and his drainpipe pants. And the albums were full of pictures of her children. I didn't know she had lost a son before Mr. Alan. This poor lady has really seen some trouble.

Then she said she had a special picture to show me. It was of a little girl standing behind her birthday cake with candles glowing.

'Who this remind you of?'

'That is super weird.'

'I don't know how long I been meaning to bring the picture to show you.'

'Who is it?'

'That is my granddaughter Bea when she was about ten or eleven. But it could have been you. I can see your face in it. I tell myself I must show Tina how she resemble my granddaughter for so. You could pass for Bea's sister easy-easy.'

I took the picture and looked at it again. 'But Granny Gwen, I don't look like her now. At the funeral I remember she was so short. I'm five-eight.'

'Yes. Poor child. That is from her mother side of the family. Her mother Mira must be five foot at most. That family is a set of short people.'

'But I must say we did look alike at that age.'

'You see, for me there is still a resemblance. I think that is why I take a liking to you from the start. I saw little Beezy in you.'

I concentrated on scraping up the last of my ice cream because for some reason my eyes had welled up with tears.

'You want more ice cream, Tina?'

'No thanks,' I said, wiping my eyes quickly. 'Like you want to make me fat?'

'You have a long way to go before anybody could call you fat.'

'I wish you were my granny.'

'Never mind, child. You should think of me like a next granny.'

The place was cooling down so we went outside and sat on the chairs under the chenette tree. It had bunches and bunches of the little green balls of fruit. I love when you crack the shell and suck the pink flesh. When I was small I used to be afraid of swallowing the seed inside, though now I don't know why because it ain't a tiny seed.

'When the driver come back I will ask him to pick some for you. The tree only ever have sweet chenette. My late husband, God rest his soul, planted all the fruit trees, but this one is my favourite.'

It was turning into such a nice visit. No one barking at me. No one telling me off because my skirt too short or my nails too long or they don't like how my hair do. I wish she was my grandmother instead of the witch rocking in the veranda back home.

It is so easy talking to Granny Gwen. I told her about the café and how the men like to call me 'Reds' but I could give as good as I get. And I told her how the staff does treat me like the baby. Gerry gives me a drop home any time he can and the girls and I meet up to lime in the mall sometimes. Granny Gwen asked if Gerry is my boyfriend. I had to laugh. She has clearly never seen how ugly Gerry is. I'm sorry. He has a good heart but that cannot make up for his four gold teeth.

And while we laughing I couldn't help but think of the wrong I done this old lady taking her money. Yes, it did get put back, but that is not the point. I took from this sweet person who has only ever shown me kindness. It's at the tip of my tongue to tell her, but what will happen then? You can imagine the trouble that would cause once Nanny hear? And Granny Gwen would never invite me again to come over for ice cream and to sit so peacefully under her chenette tree. I wish I could tell her, though. Maybe there will come a time when telling her won't be so bad and she would forgive me and there would be no bad blood between us. But that day is not today.

'Tina, you look like you loss away.'

'Sorry. It so quiet and calm here.'

'How much years you have? Is seventeen?'

'Almost eighteen. Why?'

'Your Nanny been talking to me.'

So all the ice cream and sweet talk was to soften me up for the kill.

'Tina, she worried about you.'

I got up and shook a branch of the chenette tree.

'She don't have to worry about nothing. I have a job. I paying rent. What more she want?'

Granny Gwen let out a deep sigh. 'She find the place you working a little too rough for a girl like you from a good Christian home.'

'I never complain.'

'Well, I have a better idea.'

'What?'

I am so glad now I didn't confess about the money.

'Why you don't come and work in the hardware back office? The girl we have could teach you how to do secretarial work.'

My head was spinning. Granny Gwen kept talking, which was great because I did not know what to say.

'Nanny say how you not even getting the minimum pay he suppose to give you. I could pay you well and you will be working in a nice little office where nobody will trouble you.

This hard work on your feet whole day can't be easy.'

I finally looked her in the eye.

'Nanny put you up to this? You all had a good gossip about me and decide everything before I even reach here today? I wouldn't be surprised if she hand in my notice for me already.'

'No. That is not what happened. Yes, your Nanny give me the story about your working, but it was my idea to offer you a job here.'

I looked away.

'I swear on my late husband's grave that I ain't say a word to a living soul. To be honest I ain't even check with me son Robin. But he will do what I tell him. Is you I asking. And if you don't want it that is not a problem. I will never say a word to your Nanny.'

I can't understand why she would be so nice to me. I am nothing to her and if she really knew about me she would not be making this offer.

'I don't know what to say, Granny Gwen.'

'Look, think about it for the week, and when I come by you next Saturday you can tell me if you want the work or not.'

I don't know what to do. I like that I have a job that I found all by myself and don't owe nobody nothing. This new offer is somebody going out of their way to help me. I don't think I felt wrapped up in so much kindness since the time when I was little and Miss Celia used to give me bottles and bottles of sorrel at Christmas.

CHAPTER TWENTY-SEVEN

It was dusk by the time the casket had been properly covered with earth and flowers placed on the fresh mound. It had drizzled, that annoying constant drizzle, too slight to justify an umbrella, but eventually it made everything and everyone damp, humid and sticky. The unknown wailing woman had asserted herself further by staying at the graveside and joining in the singing of 'Amazing Grace' and 'Kum Ba Yah' as they lowered the casket into the waiting hole.

Bea nudged Aunty Doris and asked if she knew who the woman was.

'Truthfully, I have never seen that woman before today.'

'And what about the little girl and her grandma that were at the wake? They're here today. You think she is my half-sister? Should I go talk to them?'

'I told you before, I don't feel that is true. Don't go creating any kind of confusion.'

'But what if it is true?'

'If they have something to say they would have said it by now. That child must be at least ten years old.'

Aunty Doris sighed.

'Bea, your father was the life and soul of every fete from Port of Spain to Point Fortin, but he was also the village ram goat.' She put a finger on each side of her head to form little horns. 'I surprise is only one woman behave bad in the church. After family the first two pews was full of woman who he love up on. God rest he soul, but Alan Clark couldn't keep he thing in he pants.'

Bea had heard enough. Let that be Aunty Doris's mean memory if she wanted. Her father was not that man.

A posse of men who had not quite made it all the way inside the church had set themselves up near the graveside under a sprawling flamboyant tree with flasks of Vat 19 rum. They had joined in at the graveside only long enough to throw packets of cards and sprinkles of rum on the coffin before the fresh earth was shovelled back into the hole. Wherever he was, they wished Alan Clark could make a game of five-card stud and take a drink of rum like he used to do with them every Friday.

Bea kept her eyes firmly cast down. Behind her she could hear Mira and Michael talking in hushed voices.

'It would've been a shorter service, but that crazy woman didn't know when to shut up,' said Mira. 'And nobody even know who she is. That is Alan all over for you.'

'But it was a good service,' said Michael.

'When the fat fellow got up and sang 'You Lift Me Up', that was nice.'

'Yeah, he had an amazing voice.'

'I think he is one of Alan friend from school days. His face familiar,' said Mira. 'I must ask Granny Gwen about him.'

'And Bea's holding up well. She looks good in the circumstances,' said Michael.

Mira twisted her face. 'Yes, but the sleeves on that blouse too long and the skirt don't have no shape. You would think she could dress better.'

Back at Granny Gwen's place the mourners gathered one last time to collectively grieve the loss of the man they had known. Bea was fenced in by well-wishers, many of whom were puzzled that she did not recall them by name from childhood. They certainly remembered her. A few minutes alone to compose herself would have eased the strain, but there was no escaping the throng encircling her. In the distance she could make out Michael and Mira standing together, their arms around each other for comfort. Uncle Kevin was talking to them. She caught his eye and he waved to her. So many people wanted to relay their condolences and hear about her absent years. The news would be passed on to the less fortunate who had not secured an audience with Alan's daughter who had made her home abroad and was now fatherless.

When Bea eventually managed to push her way through to Michael he was with a group of her relatives. Mira was begging him to have more tuna sandwiches or a slice of cake – he looked in need of someone to fatten him up a bit.

'Mira, leave him alone,' said Uncle Kevin. 'He's a big man. If he want food he go eat.'

'I only looking after him little bit,' she replied, and squeezed Michael's hand. 'I'm so happy you come. You grow up real handsome. I hope Bea treating you good. She don't know how lucky she is to get a man like you.'

Bea attempted a weak smile to hide her embarrassment as Michael playfully reached forward to put his arm around her shoulders.

Again they were interrupted. People needed to share their shock and grief with Bea before she vanished to a place they needed a visa to visit. Bea rubbed her face dry, tried to smile, and continued to field the good wishes and enquiries with whatever grace she could muster. Gradually she managed to reduce the volume of voices swirling around her. In her mind there was no annoying drizzle that would not let up, no groups huddled under the chenette tree, no coffin in a fresh grave. There was no Mira, no Michael, and no Granny Gwen. There was no unknown Chinese woman who had cried loud and long. There was no little girl who might be her blood relation. There were no neighbours. There were no strangers. Nothing could reach her.

The lack of serenity continued into the next morning. Granny Gwen wanted to discuss Alan's will. Bea went alone, leaving Michael to work and then go sightseeing with Mira. She had tried to avoid the meeting altogether by making it clear she neither expected nor wanted anything. But Granny Gwen had insisted she and Uncle Robin come alone to the house. Alan, it was soon revealed, had left all his worldly goods to his surviving brother Robin.

'I feel bad he only mention me,' said Uncle Robin. 'You is his only child. He should've left it all to you.'

Bea smiled and sipped the weak milky tea Granny Gwen had offered. 'I'm okay. He knew you are the backbone of the business.'

Robin wrung his hands. 'Take anything you want,' he said. 'Anything at all.'

Bea reached over and gently touched his hand. 'It's okay,' she said. 'Really, I don't want anything.'

Robin paced around the room. 'And it seems he had a piece of land in Toco of all places,' he said. 'I have no idea why he gone and buy land so far behind God back. Man, years ago I went up there to see them massive leatherback turtles lay eggs. But that is the only good reason I know to go Toco.'

Bea continued to politely sip the lukewarm tea she hated, hoping that nothing in her body language betrayed the gnawing well of hurt that was filling her belly. It was not the money. Alan had not been a rich man. But not to have been mentioned at all was unexpected. Was she dead to him before he was to her?

When they had talked enough, and Bea had reassured them several more times that she did not want an inheritance, she was released to return to Mira's house. She tore off the jeans and T-shirt she had been wearing and curled up in a ball in bed wishing she never had to get up again. In spite of every story she told herself about being loved, about not being rejected, there was no denying her father's ultimate act. Bea knew this familiar pain of rejection for which there was no consolation. She sobbed hard into the pillow until her head throbbed and her stomach knotted. She tossed around in bed. Slowly the day passed through noon, slipped into afternoon, slid into evening; and still the pain refused to yield.

When Mira and Michael returned, the house was in darkness. Bea heard them open the front door, telling each other that she must not be home. She did not answer their calls, and hoped that when they did discover her they would think she was asleep and go away. Which was indeed what happened.

'You remember all the places we went today?' Mira asked Michael.

'Some,' said Michael. 'I don't recall Trinidad having fancy restaurants like the sushi place we had lunch at the other day. We could've been in Boston.'

'One thing we should have done today was buy some doubles to bring home,' said Mira.

'My favourite,' Michael laughed.

'I buy mine from a man named George in Woodbrook,' said Mira. 'Man, that doubles is the bomb. But you know what is the best part? Right next to George have a lady selling doubles too. Is only George ex-wife! And look, nah. She have a big sign saying buy your doubles from George's X. Only in Trinidad, yes.'

'And thanks for the shark and bake sandwich,' said Michael. 'I love Maracas beach for that, plus the views out to the sea as we were coming through the Northern Range mountains were spectacular. It was like a postcard.'

After that Bea could not make out what they were saying.

They seemed to have moved from the kitchen to some other part of the house. They were probably in the living room or outside on the porch, enjoying the night breeze. Pretending to be asleep until the next morning was impossible. With a huge effort she pulled on her jeans and ventured out of the bedroom. The house was quiet and dimly lit. They were not inside or on the porch. The hallway clock chimed eight.

She thought she heard faint laughter coming from outside. She walked out onto the porch and into the garden. The only illumination came from the twinkling city lights below. Following the sound of low voices, she walked around to the back of the house and there on the little bench were Michael and Mira laughing and talking. Mira's hand appeared to be touching Michael's. Bea felt her blood turn to ice.

'Is now you wake up?' asked Mira, straightening up and putting her hands in her lap. 'We didn't want to bother you.'

'How was today?' asked Michael.

'All right,' said Bea, folding her arms.

Michael rose. 'Have my seat.'

'Yes, sit down,' said Mira. 'Plenty stars out tonight. The sky clear-clear.'

'No. I need to go back to bed,' said Bea, rubbing her temples. 'I have a massive headache.'

With that she turned and fled back into the house, locking the bedroom door behind her. She took deep long breaths. Maybe their hands had touched accidentally for a brief moment and she happened to arrive at that precise instant. But why sit in the dark out back? Why not sit on the comfortable porch chairs with the ceiling fan and light fixtures?

There was a knock on the bedroom door.

'Bea, it's me,' said Michael.

She sat still, holding her breath, but he would know she was awake. 'One second.' Bea closed her eyes for a moment and, with a long, noisy exhalation, she rose and opened the door.

'You okay?' asked Michael. 'You didn't seem so well.'

'Yes. Fine,' she replied, coldly.

He raked his fingers through his hair and asked her again: 'How did it go this morning?'

'He forgot to mention he had a daughter.'

'Oh, Bea,' he whispered, pulling her close for a hug.

Bea allowed herself to be held but did not reciprocate.

'Oh dear,' he said. 'That is mean. Gosh. I don't know what to say.'

Bea tried for a little longer to make conversation, but the effort was too much and she pleaded to be left alone to rest. He tried to kiss her on the lips, but she moved her face so the kiss barely brushed her cheek instead. Later she crawled into bed without taking off her clothes, pulled the blankets around her foetal figure and rocked and cried and rocked and cried through the endless night.

Everything's all right, she told herself. In two days she would leave Trinidad and she need never come back.

CHAPTER TWENTY-EIGHT

Bea woke early and was surprised to find Michael already sipping tea on the front porch. He offered to share the pot he had boiled a few minutes before, but she declined. It was enough to sit and watch Port of Spain coming alive. She was anxious to ask Michael about what she had seen the night before, or what she thought she had seen. But in this new day it all seemed absurd. She was tired of imagining things. What if he didn't care for her the way she cared for him? What if he was attracted to the older woman fussing over him?

'Why are you up so early?' she asked.

'Had an important email to deal with,' he replied.

'And?'

'You know my firm is bidding on a project in Trinidad. They have more meetings here next week and want me to stay on for them.'

'So you're not going back with me tomorrow?' she asked, looking out at the tankers waiting in the bay beyond the city.

'No,' he said slowly. 'But I'll be back soon. The meetings are scheduled for three days at the end of next week.'

'I see.'

'I spoke to Mira about it last night and she insisted I stay here.'

'Well, it's her house.'

'Only if it's okay with you,' he said. 'Otherwise I could stay in a hotel. The firm will pay.'

'No need,' said Bea. 'If she invited you then knock yourself out.'

They sat silently concentrating on the sky as it changed from purples to light blues. Bea announced she would have a shower and head out to say a last goodbye to Granny Gwen and to her father's grave. He declined to join her, claiming work had caught up with him. Mira was due back in the office that morning and would take Michael downtown, while Uncle Kevin would be Bea's chauffeur. An hour later his car horn sounded and Mira rushed to greet him. They disappeared into the kitchen while Bea went to get her shoes and bag.

When she walked back to the kitchen to let them know she was ready, there by the kitchen sink was Uncle Kevin bending over Mira, his hand up the back of her blouse. There was no mistaking the intimacy of the scene. Bea immediately walked backwards, trying to be soundless, but they had heard something. Mira's hushed voice asked if they had been seen. Uncle Kevin reassured her that it was probably a stray cat.

Bea went back to her room and sat on the edge of the bed, her heart racing. Colliding thoughts bombarded her mind. Even though she had suspected they were lovers, she could not process what she had seen. When had Mira taken such a keen interest in Uncle Kevin? He had always been around, a shadow at Clark family events, but he had never emerged as a whole person. He was either Alan's half-brother or a distant relation adopted into the fold. His exact affiliation had never been clear. Still, he was related to Mira's ex-husband. Bea knew she was unfairly judging them, but her instinct saw it as incestuous.

How long had they been together? What would Uncle

Robin or Granny Gwen think if they found out? Maybe they already knew, though she doubted it. Of all the men Mira could have had, she had latched onto one from a family she had never liked. Now Bea would have to gather herself to be with Uncle Kevin. She would be saying her last goodbyes to her father with this trespasser hovering around. A knock at the door brought her out of herself.

'Bea, you know Kevin waiting on you,' said Mira. 'Hurry up.'

She couldn't hide in the room forever, though right now it seemed the safest place to be. Everyone was in the kitchen talking about the rise of casinos in Trinidad, and Uncle Kevin was explaining to Michael a hugely popular national gambling game called Play Whe.

'You ready?' he asked.

Bea forced a smile. 'Ready.'

'Okay. See you tonight,' said Michael and kissed her on the cheek.

'I'll see all you after work, then,' said Mira.

Bea felt lightheaded with all the unanswered questions, hemmed in from all sides. It was not her business who Mira slept with, but while they were at the graveside thoughts of Mira and Uncle Kevin intruded on her silent conversation with Alan. The flowers on the grave were fresh enough to stay there a while longer. A headstone would be coming within the next week or two to mark Alan's place next to his father Ignatius and brother Matthew. Granny Gwen was always boasting that she had been the first to buy a huge family plot when this cemetery opened. There was enough room for her and all her boys. Back then it had cost a whole fifty dollars.

'I sure he at peace,' said Uncle Kevin, fixing a bunch of flowers that dangled precariously on the grave. 'He was at peace in life so he must be at peace in heaven.'

Bea felt the tears welling up. 'Doesn't feel real.'

'You don't come home enough,' said Uncle Kevin. 'Maybe now you will come to see his grave and pay your respects.'

'I will,' said Bea. 'And Michael might have to be in Trinidad for some time if his firm wins the contract they are bidding on, so I have another excuse.'

'Really?' asked Uncle Kevin.

'Yes, he's not going back with me tomorrow.'

'So where's he staying?' asked Uncle Kevin.

'With Mira.'

Uncle Kevin twisted his face and rubbed his chin. 'Well, if I were you I would keep an eye on that situation.'

Bea was taken aback. 'What do you mean?'

'Nothing,' he said, and turned to walk back to the parked car. 'Just watch out for yourself. Young boys these days.'

'Michael isn't like that,' she retorted.

He didn't reply.

Bea climbed into the passenger seat desperate to press him further. Did he mean that all men were untrustworthy, or Michael in particular? Anyone who had met Michael would know what a decent person he was. She wanted to leave the island having made amends with Mira and Granny Gwen, but the morning's events were pushing her to an edge where she could no longer trust herself.

The mood did not lighten when they called at Granny Gwen's to say goodbye. The old woman was sitting alone on a chair under the chenette tree staring into the middle distance, occasionally rubbing her eyes.

'Kevin, boy,' she said. 'I glad you come and bring Bea.'

Granny Gwen pulled Bea down to her for a sweaty hug. 'So you going back America tomorrow, darling?'

'Yes, Granny Gwen. Back to Boston.'

Granny Gwen beamed at Kevin. 'Well, look at that. I have a granddaughter working quite in Boston. You know how proud Alan was of she? He was always telling people about Bea.'

They sat and chatted while Granny Gwen reminisced about the son she had just buried. Alan the devoted son. Alan the sharp business man. Alan the heart of every social function. Alan perfected in death. Kevin joined in, reminding them of the many good times he had shared with Alan, including a party on the lush muddy banks of Matelot River where they barbecued meat, drank rum and talked nonsense until sunrise. It was overwhelming to Bea, these shared memories. She closed her eyes and let the tears escape. Granny Gwen leaned over and held her hand.

'Bea, I sorry you didn't get nothing from the will,' she said. 'But I hope you will keep the little thing I sent for you.'

'What thing?' asked Bea.

'Mira didn't give you what I sent?'

'No. What was it?'

'Is nothing expensive, but it was your father special gold cufflinks. Those cufflinks used to come out the box once a year for the Christmas morning service. After that it would get put straight back in the box till Christmas reach again.'

'I remember them. Thanks. I promise to treasure them.'

'And don't go giving no man that, you hear?' said Granny Gwen, playfully nudging her in the ribs.

'Of course.'

'If you have a son and you want to give him, that is a different matter.'

'I understand.'

Granny Gwen held Bea's hand and they both cried as they said their goodbyes. Bea promised to make the gap between visits shorter and to phone once in a while to check on the old lady. But there was more to come. Before they could leave Granny Gwen turned to Uncle Kevin.

'My boy, is you and Robin left,' she said. 'You must come see me. I not going to live for ever.'

'Yes, Granny Gwen. I will pass and check you out.' He put an arm around the old woman.

'Come and eat lunch Sunday,' she commanded. 'I cooking macaroni pie, stew chicken and red beans. And I'm making my coconut ice cream. You know my ice cream better than any of that Håagen-Dazs they does sell in town.'

'Thanks, Granny Gwen,' he said. 'I'll see.'

'Man, you could do better than that,' she said. 'Robin and Doris coming and you should come. I want the whole family here Sunday if God spare life.'

He smiled and gave the old lady a squeeze. 'Okay.'

Granny Gwen opened her mouth to say something then closed it again. She paused and looked ready to spring fresh tears. With a deep sigh she slowly got up and held onto Uncle Kevin's forearm.

'Bea, I want you to hear this too,' she said. 'As Jesus Christ is me witness, I want to say something. Kevin, I know I didn't treat you good when you was growing up. And I know things was hard for you. I was grieving for Matthew for so long, and Alan was only a baby, born weeks after you. But I not making no excuse. I already bury two sons and I want to make sure I don't dead without saying how sorry I am.'

Her words gave way to noisy sobbing and she held on to Kevin for support. He was rigid, staring at the ground.

'Kevin,' she said, struggling to control her quivering voice. 'You is Matthew son. If I show you a picture of Matthew you will see how much you resemble your father. You have his same nose and his build. This is your rightful family, boy. You belong with we.'

There was silence. Granny Gwen let go of his forearm and sank back into her chair. Kevin was roughly wiping his cheeks with the backs of his hands. Bea sat trying not to move a muscle. This was the first time Uncle Kevin's relationship to the Clark family had been acknowledged. Alan, almost his exact age, had been his uncle, not his half-brother. Grandpa Ignatius had not strayed as Bea had imagined. Uncle Kevin was not an uncle – he was her cousin. Her mother was sleeping with her daughter's cousin. Bea wasn't sure if this made things better or worse.

Kevin's creaky voice cut through the silence. 'I don't know what to say.' He took a deep breath. 'Is all right, Granny Gwen. We good,' he said. 'Is all right.'

Before she could answer he had bolted and sped off, leaving Bea and Granny Gwen to sit under the chenette tree each lost in their uneasy thoughts.

CHAPTER TWENTY-NINE

Bea was left stranded at Granny Gwen's, so she called Mira. There was no need to explain what had transpired, only that she had stayed at her grandmother's and would be grateful for a ride home. From the way Uncle Kevin's hand had been thrust up her blouse, Mira would know the details of Granny Gwen's confession soon enough.

'And can I bother you for one more thing?' asked Bea.

'Yes?'

'Granny Gwen said you have some cufflinks for me?'

'I'm busy now, but remind me later,' said Mira.

Bea ripped herself away from a tearful Granny Gwen. The old woman repeatedly reminded her that she was all that remained of Alan, and with this came a duty to spend time together. The last thing she told Bea was that Alan's old home also belonged to her and as a granddaughter she was always welcome, at any time and for as long as she wanted. The house with the living room sealed off for special occasions, the chenette tree that never seemed to stop bearing fruit – these would be waiting for her.

There was only one more goodbye to say. When they got home Mira did not even change out of her work clothes but went straight to the kitchen to cook Bea's favourite foods for their last supper. Bea interrupted the preparations to ask for the cufflinks again. They were her bond to Alan and she wanted them now.

'Oh, Jesus, you bothering me about the cufflinks when I cooking?' asked Mira. 'You can't see my hands in flour? Let me finish making the roti.'

Bea tried to control her anxiety. 'If you tell me where they are I can get them myself.'

'They're somewhere in my bedroom. Probably in the safe,' said Mira. 'I'm not sure. You go have to wait till I done in here.'

'I could open the safe,' said Bea. 'Could you give me the combination?'

Mira continued kneading the dough with her fists.

'That safe have all kind of things in there,' she replied, wiping the sweat off her brow with her forearm. 'Let me open it when I done.'

As Bea turned to go Mira added, 'I don't know why you so hurry. Is not like you could wear them.'

Dinner was a feast. Michael, Bea and Mira ate the softest dhalpouri roti. It melted with the curried channa and pumpkin, and with the tender curried goat seasoned with herbs like the pungent chadon beni, a spicier version of coriander, fresh from the garden. Bea tried to show her gratitude by being cheerful even though the day's events had left her depleted, longing to retreat to some small space where she would be safe. But where was that safe place that would ease the anxiety rising in her belly?

Michael, who might have comforted her, seemed to have shifted his focus entirely to work and was preoccupied, talking excitedly about being part of the team bidding for the Trinidad project. He found it thrilling to know the country again as an adult. Bea's isolation seemed to be in direct proportion to his exuberance. Nothing could be more terrifying than sinking further into Trinidad. To be caught in the incestuous world of Mira and Uncle Kevin, Granny Gwen and the endlessly circling caravan of relatives, would unmask her. On a small island, where everyone lived in each other's pockets, it would be impossible to hide the times when she fell into the deep dark pit and feared the world. The cycle of falling into that pit and trying to crawl back up would be exposed. Soon, everyone would know she was an imposter, fresh from a psychiatric facility.

Michael insisted on washing up the dishes after dinner. Bea made her excuses and went to finish packing. While she was filling her hand luggage with her favourite Indian sweet – the fingers of fried dough rolled in sugar called kurma – she heard the doorbell and, soon after, Uncle Kevin's voice. He was talking to Mira and Michael. Bea could hear him settling down to a plate of warmed-up leftovers.

Bea brooded over the cufflinks. If she didn't get them she would have nothing of her father. It might be a trivial piece of jewellery to Mira, but it was everything to her. She found Michael and Mira laughing in the kitchen as they fought over the washing and drying of dishes. Uncle Kevin was mopping up goat curry with a piece of roti.

'Bea,' said Uncle Kevin. 'Sorry if I left you stranded today.'

'Not at all,' she replied.

Turning to Mira she asked about the safe.

Mira sighed. 'I will deal with that later. You can't see we have guests?'

When Michael and Mira were briefly in the living room Uncle Kevin turned to Bea. 'So you eh get your cufflinks yet?'

'No,' said Bea.

'Well, make sure Mira give you them.'

'She'll give me once she has a minute.'

'I know she has them.'

'I'll get them later tonight.'

Mira and Michael came back into the kitchen, and Bea excused herself to finish packing. She didn't leave her bedroom until she heard Uncle Kevin leave and his car horn toot-toot as he drove off. She listened to the night sounds of the house being locked up and curtains drawn tight. She waited until Mira was in her bedroom before she went in. Mira was sitting at her dressing table combing her hair.

'You know I was looking in the safe and the cufflinks not there,' Mira said.

She grabbed her handbag off the floor and began digging around in it. 'I wonder if I leave them in the office?' she mumbled to herself, pulling papers and cosmetics out of the bag. 'When Granny Gwen gave them to me I was on my way to work. I thought I brought them home but they must still be in my desk drawer.'

Bea bit her already short nails. 'Can we go get them?'

'You mad or what?' Mira laughed. 'The office lock up long time and the guard don't come till around seven in the morning. By that time your plane should be taking off.'

Bea sighed. 'I really need to have them.'

'Sorry, but I don't think they here.'

'I guess Michael could bring them for me.' Tears welled up in Bea's eyes.

'No problem,' said Mira.

Leaving without this gold remnant of Alan was agonising. She was Alan's only child and had not made a fuss that he left her out of his will. But it was her right to at least have this token. It was a talisman, infused with Alan's DNA. Surely Mira understood this. She should have handed them over when Bea first prodded her. Now Bea would be leaving Trinidad without even this shard of her father. Until she had those cufflinks, he was utterly lost to her, buried in a grave with his first family, who now claimed him for eternity.

Bea went to her room and sat with her arms folded tightly around her stomach. She had to get to bed. To catch the early flight meant leaving the house before dawn. Her jumbled thoughts were interrupted by a knock on the door.

She jumped up, expecting Mira had found the cufflinks after all. But it was Michael.

'You okay to travel back on your own?'

She didn't reply.

'Here, let me help you lift the suitcase out of the way.'

'Why wouldn't I be okay?' she snapped. 'I've always looked after myself.'

'Of course you can take care of yourself,' he said. 'I'm only sorry not to be going back with you.'

'Well, I'll be fine,' she huffed, hugging herself.

'I'll see you off in the morning,' he said.

'No need. It'll be too early.'

He sat on the bed. 'Come here,' he said, his arms wide open.

She hesitated, then allowed herself to be hugged. He kissed her closed lips.

'Wake me before you leave.' He got up and closed the door softly behind him.

It rained heavily during the night. As the water drummed on the roof, Bea tossed, sobbed and rocked.

A statue with no head.

Alan crying to the music of Bach.

Strapped down in an ambulance on a dreadful winter day.

Long shiny hair tumbling down to her waist.

Dumped at Pizza Hut.

He said he came for the waters. But it's the desert, came the reply. I was misinformed, he said.

A continuous horror film played behind her eyes. Only sleep might have released her from the madness. The cufflinks. She had to have the cufflinks. Daddy's precious cufflinks, or else he was lost yet again.

When the alarm sounded she got up exhausted from the losing battle with sleep. The bedroom window framed a still night sky. Raindrops spattered on the glass. She showered and changed quickly, stuffing the last dirty clothes into the suitcase, then gazed around the room in case she had forgotten anything. She did not want to leave a single item behind, however insignificant.

Mira brought her a cup of tea, but she had only taken a few sips when they heard the taxi beeping its horn outside. Bea got up quickly and went to Michael's room while Mira hurried outside to stop the taxi driver from waking the neighbours. Michael was in a deep sleep when she bent over and softly kissed him. He didn't stir. She looked at his calm face and thought she saw the happiness he seemed to have found on this trip, reconnecting with everything he had missed about the island. Bea couldn't wait to flee.

As she turned to leave, the light from the corridor fell on two small, shiny objects on Michael's bedside table. She stopped, picked up two gleaming squares and rolled them around in her palm. Her heart pounded. Cold sweat coated her skin. Each with a tiny diamond in one corner, they were undeniably hers, her sole inheritance. Christmas morning mass with the Clark family, and Alan would hold her hand tight to keep her from getting lost among the packed congregation. She could still see his hand in hers, the gold cufflinks with the little diamond pulled through the double cuffs of his best white shirt.

She clutched the cufflinks in her hand. This did not make sense. Why would they be in Michael's room? She hesitated, then pushed them deep into the front pocket of her jeans.

'Come on,' Mira called. 'Is nearly quarter past and the taxi waiting.'

Bea opened her mouth, inhaled deeply, then bit down on her lips.

'You have everything?' asked Mira. 'You have your passport? And what about your purse? I pay for the taxi already so don't give him nothing.'

Bea continued to bite her lips, unable to look at Mira.

'Thanks,' she said, looking at the rain, pelting down on the roof of the taxi.

Mira gave her a hug. 'The suitcase in the car trunk already. Safe flight.'

Bea walked out from under the covered porch and opened the back door of the taxi. She paused, then turned around, opened her mouth and closed it again.

'You forget something?' asked Mira.

Bea sighed. 'No,' she said. 'Nothing. Thanks again for everything.'

'Call when you reach to let me know everything all right,' said Mira.

Bea stood next to the open car door.

'Go in the car. You getting wet,' urged Mira.

When she didn't move, Mira asked again if she had forgotten something. Bea was afraid to answer. The pain welling up inside her chest might overflow, and she had no idea if it would escape as a cry or a scream.

'Look, if you forget anything I will send it with Michael,' said Mira. 'The rain coming down hard. Get in the car.'

Bea took a deep breath. 'The cufflinks,' she said softly.

'What?' shouted Mira. 'I can't hear you.'

'The cufflinks,' she repeated in a hoarse voice. 'Where are they?'

'What you worrying about that stupidness for?' asked Mira. 'Get out the rain. Your top already soaking wet.'

Bea did not know how to say that they were safe inside her pocket. Angry and confused, she got into the car and they drove slowly down the steep, slippery drive. Before they reached the end of the road she burst into tears. In spite of all her promises to Granny Gwen and to Mira, there was something final about this journey. She touched her front pocket to feel for the cufflinks. In a few hours Michael would wake and find them missing. It didn't matter. Alan was snug next to her skin, and this time he would not be leaving. Pity she had been forced to steal him away like this. Can you steal what is rightfully yours?

CHAPTER THIRTY

Bea's inbox was full of text messages and emails from Michael, all unanswered. In the days since returning to Boston, she had managed to return to work, but little else. It was still a shock that her father was gone for good. He had been so absent, and now death had severed any hope of making amends. There would never be another conversation, another Sunday lunch together, another beach outing. Sometimes she thought she had imagined the whole funeral, the haunting picture in the newspaper. It was incredible. Alan was dead, gone before his time.

The issue of the cufflinks, on top of these feelings, made her extremely fragile. Her thoughts swung between fear of what Michael might say when confronted, and anger that the situation had arisen at all. The cufflinks, always with her, were a constant reminder that one day – today, tomorrow, a year from now – she would know the truth of how they ended up on her boyfriend's bedside table. Part of her wished she could slink away without ever speaking to him or Mira again.

But the cufflinks were unrelenting, burning her temples so that when she was having a cup of coffee, or reading an article, their image was always a headache superimposed on her mind. Sleep brought no peace. The cufflinks were a scorching reminder that she must confront what she already knew.

One evening after work, when she had been back in Boston about a week, she realised time had run out. She had to deal with this now or risk another major relapse into depression. She tried further delaying tactics. She took a long soak in the bath, sipping a neat double Scotch that she didn't like. Although she hated smoking, she inhaled two cigarettes, one after the other. But absolutely nothing stopped the rising sense of heartbreak. Something warned this would be pain she would carry forever.

Bea got into bed with the duvet up to her chest, lit a third cigarette and dialled. Neither Michael nor Mira answered their mobile phones. She kept trying every few minutes until finally Mira picked up on the house phone. She sounded happy to hear from Bea and anxious to know how she had settled back into Boston. Bea had no space for such pleasantries and interrupted her mid-sentence.

'I know what you did with my father's cufflinks,' she said flatly.

'What are you talking about?' asked Mira excitedly.

'The cufflinks,' said Bea deliberately. 'What did you do with the cufflinks?'

'I didn't do nothing with them.'

Bea dragged on her cigarette. 'Liar,' she said, exhaling a puff of smoke.

'What did you just call me?'

There was no going back. 'You lied to me,' said Bea. 'You're lying to me now.'

'I never thought I would see the day when my own child would disrespect me so.'

'You should have thought of that when you were giving away my father's cufflinks.'

'I don't know what make you feel you could talk to me like this.'

'Uncle Kevin not enough for you?'

'Bea, shut your dirty mouth. I can't believe what I hearing.'

'You took my father's cufflinks and you gave them to Michael. You gave them to my boyfriend – at least I thought he was my boyfriend.'

Bea heard Mira sucking spit through her teeth. 'Michael was only keeping them safe for you.'

'Every word you say is a lie.'

'Stop saying I lie to you. I don't know what happen to you. You gone mad or something?'

'I found the cufflinks in Michael's room before I left. You pretended to look for them when all along you knew you had given them away.'

'I didn't know you would carry on so for a stupid little thing like that.'

'Why did you lie to me?'

'He's a man. He could use them. What you want with cufflinks?'

'They belonged to my father.'

'Oh, yes. Your loving father who always had more time for he woman them than you. And if Granny Gwen didn't take pity on you, you wouldn't even get that from him.'

'Don't talk about my father like that.'

'Yes, well, you didn't have to put up with the horrors I went through.'

'Can't you stop now? He's dead, okay?'

'Thank God.'

'I never want to see you again,' said Bea flatly.

'Well, Bea, I do everything for you and I fed up. I put up with enough shit from you all these years. Fuck you.'

Bea slammed the phone down, stunned. She had told her mother that she did not want to see her again. And what was worse, Mira had not resisted.

Fuck you.

The last bridge had been burnt.

When her phone rang later she saw it was Michael's number. Things couldn't get worse. She might as well get it all over and done with in one night. She gulped down the last dregs of her refilled whiskey glass and answered the phone. Michael wanted to know what had happened. Mira was hysterical. What had Bea done to hurt her mother? She explained that Mira had given him the cufflinks that were rightfully hers.

'Mira said you wanted me to have them.'

'That's not true.'

'So you're upset that I have them?'

'It's not that.'

There was a pause. Bea pulled a blanket around her shoulders.

'Mira said you were really nasty to her.'

'She cursed me.'

'Bea, grow up.'

'So you're taking her side?'

'You should see how upset Mira is.'

Bea took a deep breath and closed her eyes.

'Well, I'm upset too.'

'You can't speak to your mother like that.'

'Some mother.'

'She's a wonderful person, Bea. She's kind and bright and generous.'

'Hold on a minute,' said Bea.

She poured herself another whiskey and took a gulp.

'Bea?'

'I'm here.'

'Well?'

'Fine. She's wonderful and I'm the bitch for wanting my father's cufflinks.'

'I haven't even seen the cufflinks for a while.'

'That's because I took them before I left.'

'So you have them anyway,' he said. 'What's your problem?'

'Stop taking her side.'

'I think you should apologise to your mother.'

'I think you should go fuck yourself.'

Bea could hear him sigh. 'I'll speak to you again when you've calmed down,' he said. 'Goodbye, Bea.'

She did calm down, but they never spoke again. It seemed fitting that in a world where the real and virtual were constantly merging, a relationship with a computer engineer should end when later that night she deleted him from her list of phone contacts. A petty, cowardly act, it smothered the last breath of hope.

CHAPTER THIRTY-ONE

Out of nowhere Charmaine called me last night. The A level exams just finished and now she's hanging around waiting for results. In two weeks she's having a birthday party and wants me to come. I have not heard a squeak from that girl for nearly a year and she still pretends to be my best friend. I suppose it's nice of her. Of course there will be a bunch of people from my old school at the party. Do I really want to tell them about working in Clark's Hardware back office? They're all gearing up for university to become something big working in a nice office and making real money. Priya started at the University of the West Indies last September. She wants to be a lawyer. Aunty Indra keeps going on about how she will have to send her away to do her Masters because the girl is super-duper bright. We all know it's because she doesn't think any Trini man is good enough for her precious Priya. Marriage to a foreign would be the jackpot for this family.

At least no one expects me to become anything much. I think once my Mom died that was it. If I had a father things would have been different. He would care about me meeting someone nice and having a pretty home. Nanny only praying that Lord Jesus please I don't get pregnant any time soon because she's too old to mind the child while I go knocking about town. If I had a baby she would be the last person I would want looking after it. Her spitefulness alone would sour the baby's formula.

The real joke of course is that they carry on like I busy screwing any and every man I meet in the hardware when I have never done anything more than kiss a boy and that was a while back. If you like to look good, and you have a figure, Nanny and Aunty Indra have it on church authority that you must be a whore. I don't like to bad-talk anybody but Priya could do with losing a little of that baby fat she has round her middle, and the double chin doesn't exactly make her a supermodel. I know, I know. I will be hit by lightning or something so for even thinking such evil thoughts about my cousin. I wonder if she's still a virgin. I heard talk about a boyfriend but I haven't actually seen the body yet.

The person who is expecting a baby is Margaret in the office. She is twenty-five and happily married to a decent if boring-looking man who picks her up every day after work. Before I was hired she alone ran the office with Mr. Robin. When I came along she wasn't resentful or suspicious like I was there to take her job. Margaret should have been a teacher because she is so patient. Every day she has taught me a little bit more about stock-checking, dealing with orders and answering the phone properly. It's only been six months and I cool about everything I have to do. Margaret never makes you feel stupid. And another thing I am grateful for is that if I make a mistake she always corrects me when the boss man not in the office. She is a real sweetheart.

Her due date come and gone. You never see a belly so humungous and her feet swell up like two tree trunks. The only thing still fitting them hooves is cheap rubber slippers. But the girl have hard ears and she not going to stop work till the very end. If she doesn't watch out the baby will be born right here in Clark's Hardware. I'm worried about her not taking it easy and she's worried about me managing on my own. I'm going to be cool. I might not be able to do everything as fast as she does, but I will get it done, and I promised her that I will check and double-check everything. It's not that Mr. Robin is a horrible boss, but he doesn't have a lot of time for liming and chitchat. He wants his work done and he wants it done now without any big set of drama. I respect that about him and the fact that he always treats me like a grown-up.

And another nice thing about working here is that Granny Gwen always spoiling me and Margaret. Only yesterday she made cupcakes for her church group meeting and dropped by with some for us. It's the little things like that I appreciate. I don't miss the café. That was hard work and it's true Mr. Morris was taking me for granted. When I said I was quitting he didn't pretend to want me to stay. He said my job would be filled by the next day, so that was that. I saw the girls for a while and then – you know how things go. You don't see each other and eventually you stop calling. Whatever. That is what life seems to be like, for me at least.

I keep thinking about Margaret and her husband having a new baby any day now and I know it shouldn't but it gives me a pain inside. That baby will grow up knowing exactly who its parents are. Why I had to be different? Margaret has heard all about my invisible father and doesn't have any time for my talk. According to her I had best forget about finding him because he could be living in Timbuktu for all we know. If no one will talk, and there is a blank on my birth certificate next to 'father's name', there isn't much that I can do. So why can't I give up hoping? I know there is someone who does not know he has a daughter, and when we finally find each other both our lives will be complete. Until then we are coasting along, though of course he don't actually know that he missing a daughter.

This morning when I came to work Mr. Robin announced that Margaret went into labour and they are in the hospital. I wanted to go straight away but of course I have to stay and keep the office going. And even though I see her every day I must remember that she has her own sisters who are probably with her. Besides, I can't let Margaret down on the first day she isn't in the office.

Whole day half of me excited to know when the baby coming, and the other bigger half worried that I'm not going to manage the office by myself. I don't know how I end up running the people office and I'm not even nineteen properly. How they expect me to do this? But I hardly finish thinking like that when the phone start ringing and it never stop for most of the day. And touch wood – everything get done properly. Mr. Robin checked my work and he said he was impressed. I don't touch the biggest clients but if an ordinary body can't find what they need I can check stock and place orders up to a certain amount without Mr. Robin's approval.

Around lunchtime Granny Gwen reach by the office with a big plate of food for me. I told her thanks and that she mustn't do this too often. You could smell the yummy food before she even open the office door. Is one set of macaroni pie and baked chicken with her juicy gravy that going to stay on my hips and behind. I can't afford to lose my figure or I will end up a spinster living with Nanny till one of us drop down and dead.

By the time we ready to close there was still no word about the baby so Mr. Robin phoned Margaret's husband. Seems they did go to the hospital but then they were sent back home and now she is ready to go in again. I thought when you get labour pains that was it. You push and push and you get your baby. Yikes. Poor Margaret's been in pain since about four o'clock this morning. When I am having my baby I going to do like them celebrities and get cut. And I hear that if you and the doctor agree he could take out a little of the extra fat while you already cut open. If you want to keep your man you better be able to make baby and look hot before the baby is three months, six tops. Come to think of it maybe I won't have kids. I don't want to end up with a hanging belly like Aunty Indra.

Well. Margaret's baby is a real Trini because it wasn't going to let nobody hurry it up to be born. It was around nine o'clock in the night that I got a text to say Margaret and the baby fine. They've called him Karim and visiting is tomorrow after four. It was such good news I even forget me and Nanny are not talking and I went to tell her.

'I glad for she, but don't let this give you any ideas. Margaret is a grown woman with a proper husband. She waited till she had everything line up before she make a child.'

Nanny can bitch as much as she likes because nothing is going to stop me from smiling. If you check I might even be smiling in my sleep tonight.

This morning Mr. Robin tell me we could go see the baby as soon as the hardware closed. Granny Gwen said she leg paining so it end up being only the two of us representing the hardware. Margaret is not a big lady normally but she make one hefty little pumpkin – a whole nine pounds. He's not wrinkle-up like how some babies come out, but you can't pretend that this baby is anything but ugly. Karim has one big head and it covered in fine-fine black hair. Of course you can't tell the mother her baby's not going to win any of those cute baby contests that they carry in the papers. And Karim did have that pure new-baby smell and soft-soft skin. I'm sure as he grows he will get better-looking. Well, I hope so for the child's sake.

But the biggest surprise was Mr. Robin. You would never tell from his businesslike face in the office that he would be such a softie when it comes to babies. Once he had the baby in his arms nobody else get a hug-up. Only when the child started to bawl for his Mummy that Mr. Robin finally let go of Karim.

On the way back to the car park I had to say something.

'Mr. Robin, I never put you down for liking babies so much.'

'I can't help it. Something about a new baby always makes my eyes water.'

'How many children you have?'

'One son. We lucky to have him. My wife could get pregnant but she couldn't keep the baby so easily.'

'Still you got one.'

'I'm not complaining. My mother had the same problem. Apparently I would have had a lot more brothers and sisters if she didn't miscarry.'

'What's your son's name?'

'Charles. He's my eyeball. But I always wanted another child or even two more.'

I had to laugh. I have never heard a man talk like this before.

'You laughing at me, Miss Ramlogan?' he asked and put his arm around me tight. He didn't let go. We were almost by the car and he was still holding me and walking. I could barely breathe but when I did inhale my nostrils were full of his aftershave. My brain went dizzy.

He opened the passenger door and let me go as he walked around to his side. Thankfully he put on the radio because I didn't know what to say or where to look.

'I sure you hungry,' he said after a few minutes. 'Let me buy KFC before I drop you home.'

'You don't have to do that, Mr. Robin,' I said. 'It will have food home.'

'No, man. It late. You must be hungry and you can't say no to a box of chicken and chips.'

And that is the truth. I could eat KFC every day. You see how I going to end up fat if I don't check myself.

Nothing else happen. Well, not much. We got the KFC. I ate it in the car. He saved his for later. When he dropped me out he leant over and gave my hand a little squeeze and I could feel his pants brush up against my leg. I'm going straight to hell because my heart started beating hard-hard in my chest and all I wanted was for him to kiss me. Don't ask me to explain because I don't understand it either. How you can see somebody day in, day out and never feel anything for them and in one evening all of that could change?

As soon as I reach inside the house I went straight in the bathroom. My panty was soaking. I put my hand down there. Oh God, I have never wanted a man this much. I have to have him. I bite down on the hand towel in case Nanny hear anything or get suspicious. Then I flush to make sure she don't come by the bathroom door. When I got into my bed a little later I was shattered. I wanted to dream about him but I never remember my dreams in the morning.

To be honest, I was a little frightened about going into work this morning. I mean he only gave me a hug-up and bought me a box of chicken and chips. The whole thing is in my mind alone. He's my boss. And Granny Gwen's son. And he has a ring on his finger. And he has a son. He not young. Lord Jesus, you and I both know he's not interested in a silly young girl that his mother took pity on and forced him to hire. Is a good thing I figured all that out in my head before I reached the office because when I got there he was normal Mr. Robin, busy-busy and hardly noticing me. I felt shame about the way I got so hot last night in the bathroom. Lucky thing he's not a mind reader or I would have to take my handbag and head out to look for a new job pronto.

Everything was normal that day and the next day and the next, but I felt more and more shame that I ever had those feelings even for one evening. Somebody up there saved me from making a complete jackass of myself. I don't know how old Mr. Robin is but he old. Look how I throwing myself at a man old enough to be my father. In fact he might even be older than I think because someone pointed out his son the other day and is a boy bigger than me. I've seen the wife a few times, but now whenever I see her I look at the woman differently. I imagine them doing it and what that must be like. She's not good-looking but she not ugly either. You would pass she straight. But you can't know what does go on when the lights go off. She could be one porn star in the bedroom, pole dancing on top Mr. Robin. I better start going back to church yes – if only to stop thinking about this man and he wife doing the dog.

One way I am hoping to get my mind off lusting after Mr. Robin is by meeting someone else tonight at Charmaine's birthday party. If the sweet sixteen was the warm-up then this is going to be a fantastic fete. I bought a gorgeous silky halter top, white jeans and red heels that I not even sure I can walk in much more dance down the place in. But they looking super cool and that's why I buy the last size eight in the shop. Nanny took one look and pronounced them ungodly shoes that only ladies of the night wear. She need to get out more and see that anybody with good legs sporting six-inch heels these days.

And the party was worth all the dressing up and the hairdo and the makeup. The music was rocking, the food was good, and they had magical white lights in all the trees and in the ceiling of the dance section. And I swear that more than one man had his beady eye on my skinny white jeans. I even catch Charmaine's old half-dead uncle checking me out. But these young boys here are just that – boys. I plan to only give the goods to a real man and nobody who rubbing up on me tonight qualify.

So having failed to get a man I best be concentrating on doing a good job so I don't give Mr. Robin a reason not to like me. After work I try to spend time with Margaret to help out with the baby. Most days she is knackered, and because she's breastfeeding there isn't much I can do with Karim. What she really appreciates is if I do a little cooking or wash some of the baby clothes as they don't go in the washing machine. She's so grateful for the little help and company that I try to go at least twice a week. I take pictures of the baby on my phone to show the rest of the staff. Nobody else mention Karim's big head, so is best if I keep my mouth shut. How a nice-looking girl like Margaret and a reasonable-looking father make one ugly baby so?

One evening I was getting ready to dash out to Margaret's after work when Mr. Robin stop me. 'If you rushing to go by Margaret, let me give you a lift. I going that way myself.'

'I not going to turn down a ride in a car with AC to hustle up in a maxi-taxi,' I said. 'You sure is not out of your way, Mr. Robin?'

'No, man. Give me five minutes and then come outside. I will pull up in front,' he said with a big smile.

'I could come with you now.'

'No. Give me five minutes and I'll meet you in front.'

Whatever. I used the time to run in the bathroom, wash my face and fix my lipstick.

He was waiting outside. I got in the front seat of my fancy ride. I wonder if people thought that I was stepping out with my boyfriend or if they thought he must be my father? It wasn't a long trip but we had a good talk. When he dropped me off he said he would be finished what he had to do in about two hours, and if I want he will come back for me. Well, I wasn't going to refuse. He is not going to blow the horn or anything. I must come outside around seven-thirty and he will be park up on the street. And he said not to mention to Margaret he dropped me. He doesn't want her to feel that since I started working she is any less important or that he likes her less. I understand that and I am the last person who would want Margaret to feel bad. She is like my sister.

That was Tuesday. Now every Tuesday I get a lift to Margaret's house and then a ride home later. First week he asked if I wanted to stop by the Savannah for coconut water. We park up right there and had a nut each. I like the jelly inside as well and he made the man chop it open for me. He's a perfect gentleman. He ain't try nothing on me. And he asked a lot of questions about what I like to do and my friends and stuff like that. One time he asked if I liked Chinese food. I love sweet-and-sour shrimp and fried rice so he buy some. Another time he asked me if my boyfriend would get vex with me for getting a ride home with him and I told him straight – I don't have anyone. Mr. Robin say he doesn't want any man coming to beat him up when all he doing is buying a little Chinese food for their woman. I kept telling him – I don't have a man.

Each Tuesday we have done something different. We might stop for a roti or just go for a drive. And we never actually said anything but he always stops at the end of my street and I walk the last piece to my house. I don't need Nanny putting her mouth in things and then get Granny Gwen vex. Me and Mr. Robin never so much as hold hands, but people like to talk your business even if nothing going on. He's such a sweet man. Sometimes he has a big Cadbury's chocolate or a piece of cake waiting for me in the car. But Margaret's maternity leave is ending, so today is my last Tuesday ride in Mr. Robin's car. I have been living from Tuesday to Tuesday and now it's almost over. I wanted to say something but I didn't know how or what exactly. When he picked me up after seeing Margaret and the baby he asked what I wanted to do.

'Let's go for a drive.'

He moved his hand from the gear stick and took my hand in his so both our hands were together on the gear and that is how we drove. My heart was beating so loud I felt I couldn't hear anything else. Then he moved his hand and put it on my thigh and started to rub it. Every time he rubbed he pushed my skirt up a tiny bit more. I was afraid to move a muscle in case he stopped. I didn't want him to stop. Ever.

CHAPTER THIRTY-TWO

It was an unusually warm October day and there didn't seem to be a free table outside, but Bea insisted. She had been clear when booking that she wanted to make the most of the exceptional weather during this birthday lunch for Nick Payne. A group of them would be meeting for drinks later, but she wanted to do something special for his sixtieth. Rialto Bridge near Harvard Square was his favourite Italian restaurant.

Her determination paid off, and five minutes later they were sipping prosecco in unexpected sunshine. She asked what he was doing to mark this watershed.

He hesitated, slowly sipping his wine. 'Well, I'm making some overdue changes. Straightening things.'

'Doesn't sound like a lot of fun.'

'It's kind of now or forever hold your peace.'

Bea leaned towards him smiling.

'Tell Aunty Bea what you're doing.'

He laughed.

'I'm serious,' she said. 'Tell me.'

'We're having a good time. I don't want to spoil it.'

Bea sat back and drained her flute.

'I think I need another drink,' she said. 'You ready for a refill? It's your birthday, it's Friday, and neither of us has to go back to work.'

A waitress took their food order and promised to be back with more prosecco.

'On the house,' said the server. 'Somebody has a big birthday today.'

They thanked her and clinked glasses.

Nick sighed deeply. 'You're going to find out soon anyway.' He paused. 'I've resigned and I'm moving to LA. It's past time I settled down. You know my partner lives there and he can't move, so I'm taking a leap of faith.'

Bea stared at him. 'Wow.'

'Yup. We're buying a place together.'

'Well, this is a lot of straightening out for someone who's avoided commitment this long.'

He laughed.

'I think we have to toast to this,' said Bea raising her glass. 'Congratulations, Nick!'

They clinked again and then sat back enjoying the midday sun.

'This is a shocker,' said Bea. 'I thought you were comfortable with the way things were. You have a great job. You guys see each other often for people on opposite sides of the country.'

'Sometimes you have to stop running away,' he said with a smile. 'I'm getting old. It's time.'

As lunch progressed they tried to keep the conversation light-hearted, but Bea could not banish a gnawing sadness that her mentor and sometime doctor would be gone. It was incomprehensible that in three more months there would be no more Nick. He had helped her and shown faith in her. Who else had ever believed in her like this? She ordered another drink.

Bea never made it to his birthday party that evening because she was passed out on her sofa with the television blaring. Too many glasses of wine at lunch, then back home she had mixed a couple of the vodka-and-soda-with-lemon combination she called a 'skinny bitch'. At least she thought it was only a couple. The way her head hurt it might have been three. Could it have been four?

She pulled the window blind slightly open and sunshine whacked her eyes. Outside, Saturday morning was in full swing, pavements bustling with people and children in prams and dogs being walked. She jerked the blind closed. Coffee. She needed coffee. And a glass of water. And where were the painkillers? Her head was pounding. She nestled back down on the sofa, a blanket around her shoulders, and realised she was still in yesterday's clothes. The odd thing was that, terrible as her dry mouth and throbbing head felt, she was perfectly clear about what had to be done.

It had been so long she wasn't sure she still had a valid number. They might have changed it years ago. On the third ring it picked up. A mellow rasping voice said good morning. She recognised it instantly.

'Granny Gwen? It's Bea.'

'Bea? Oh Jesus Christ! Child, is you?'

'Hi, Granny Gwen.'

'Darling, how you going? You don't call me or write me. If you know how I does think about you and I always praying for you.'

'You doing okay, Granny Gwen? You been keeping well?'

'You know I always had a little trouble with my pressure, but the doctor have me on tablet. Otherwise I going strong. If God willing just now I go see ninety years. Imagine that.'

'That's why I'm calling. I want to come to your birthday party if that's okay.'

'How you mean if is okay? Bea, you is my granddaughter. You is the first person who should be there.'

'Thanks. I'll book my flight today.'

'And I hope you staying by me. I have a set of empty rooms here.'

'I don't want to put you out, Granny Gwen. Let me stay in a hotel and come see you.'

'Bea, I don't ask for much. Come stay by your grand-mother. I have a girl does come in every day to help clean and cook a little food. I won't get in your business and anywhere you want to go the driver will carry you. It don't have no fancy hotel go treat you good so.'

'Okay, Granny Gwen. If you're sure.'

'When was the last time you get hot sada roti and tomatoes choka for breakfast?'

'You've convinced me. I'm holding you to that roti.'

'Child, you don't know how glad you make me heart to know you coming. You tell your mother?'

'No.'

She could hear the old lady exhale.

'Wait a minute, Bea. I want to get a chair to sit down.'

Bea could hear furniture being dragged across the wooden floor.

'Bea, you still there?'

'Yes, Granny Gwen.'

'Bea, is time you forget all them problem that you had with your mother years back.'

'Granny Gwen –'

She cut Bea off sharply. 'Don't feel because I'm an old lady I don't know what happening. I know all about the confusion with your father cufflinks and that stupid little boy. Mira had him in she house and parade up and down the town with him as if she was a young thing. I don't know what she was thinking but I know she paid a price. The boy stay must be six months and then he gone he way and is she left looking like an ass. Is Kevin who tell me everything.'

'Well, Mira never tried to contact me once in all this time.'

'Is shame she shame. Everybody does make mistake, child. Everybody. She is your mother.'

272

Bea rubbed her temples.

'I guess I'll see her.'

'For your grandmother's sake, darling. Don't hold on to a grudge so long. Things like that does eat up your inside and you go end up getting heart attack.'

Granny Gwen was almost right. It wasn't her heart she was protecting but her sanity. The conversation wasn't supposed to be like this. Bea rubbed her temples with her free hand.

'I'll call again and let you know my flight.'

'I love you, Bea. God bless you.'

'Love you too. Bye, Granny Gwen.'

*

Two weeks later she was in the gold-and-black dining room of the Royal Savannah Hotel with over a hundred people honouring Granny Gwen in speeches and prayers. It was the first time she was seeing Mira again. They were seated next to each other at dinner and managed a stilted conversation about family and what had been happening in the country in the intervening decade. Bea was grateful for the lively chatter of other guests at their table. There was an old friend of Granny Gwen's, Mrs. Ramlogan, with her daughter Indra, son-in-law Ricky and granddaughter Tina, a beautiful slim mixed-race girl with long slightly wild hair.

'Bea, you know we met a long time ago at your father's funeral,' said Tina.

'I'm sorry. I met so many people that day,' Bea apologised.

'It's okay. I was little. I was there with my Nanny and Aunty Indra. My mom died when I was ten.'

'I'm sorry to hear that.'

'It's okay. I'm just saying because you lost your dad. At

least you still have Miss Mira.'

Bea forced a small, awkward smile.

'And what about your dad?' asked Bea.

The look on Tina's face made her regret asking.

'I don't know who he is. My mom never said before she passed away and it seems no one else knows.'

'That must be difficult for you,' said Bea in her professional voice.

Tina shrugged. 'I haven't given up hope.'

They were interrupted by a call for Granny Gwen to cut her birthday cake, and she in turn wanted Uncle Kevin, Uncle Robin, Bea and her cousin Charles to come up and assist. The DJ played the Stevie Wonder hits 'Happy Birthday' and 'Isn't She Lovely' while Granny Gwen beamed with the joy and lightness of a girl of nineteen rather than ninety. Bea wondered how she could even have thought of missing this moment. How many other wonderful family events had she deprived herself of with her self-imposed exile?

After the cake-cutting Bea avoided returning to the table where Mira sat. She went over to Aunty Doris, Uncle Robin's wife, who seemed less buoyant than she remembered, and was immediately treated to a litany of complaints. Charles was busy with his career and Uncle Robin was working harder than ever to keep the hardware going, which left her alone most evenings.

'Bea, if I didn't know better I would say your Uncle Robin have a deputy,' moaned Aunty Doris. 'That man don't stay home like long time.'

'I think Uncle Robin's past that kind of nonsense.'

Aunty Doris laughed. 'Is true. Who go want a balding old man like he?'

Bea took her hand. 'Aunty Doris, you need to have something that is your own.'

'We have a little group of ladies that does meet up once a week. Sometimes we go cinema or we might go for dinner.

We even went to a casino one time. Otherwise I don't really get out.'

Aunty Doris patted Bea's hand. 'But what about you, child? I know you not married, but you have somebody up there?'

'No. Nobody I see a future with.'

'Well, you can't be looking hard enough. If you come back and live here we would be having big wedding in no time.'

'And how come you haven't married off Charles, then?'

'He have a mind of he own. We introduce him to some nice girls from good families but he always finding fault with them. One too skinny, another one too quiet, a next one he don't like how she laugh. That boy so fussy I don't think he will find anybody that good enough.'

'Charlie will be fine,' said Bea smiling. 'I wouldn't worry about him.'

A waiter stopped and offered them drinks from a tray. They both took glasses of white wine.

'I see you staying by Granny Gwen,' said Aunty Doris. 'What your mother have to say about that?'

Bea sighed. 'Tonight was the first time I saw her. I don't think we have too much to say to each other.'

'How you would feel if Mira drop down and dead tomorrow and you didn't fix things between all you? You have to think about that, Bea. I know she want to make up with you bad.'

'How you know that?' asked Bea, surprised.

'I see she now and then. She didn't have things easy. I know is your father, God rest his soul, but Alan didn't treat her good. She sacrificed plenty for you.'

'I know,' said Bea quietly.

'Then you will make time and go talk properly?'

Bea's eyes filled with tears. She took a sip of her wine and looked away.

'I can't,' she said, wiping her eyes discreetly. 'I thought I could but I can't.'

Aunty Doris held Bea's hand tight.

'Say your prayers and God will give you strength.'

'Aunty Doris, I don't pray.'

Aunty Doris smiled. 'Don't worry. I will pray enough for both of us.'

Bea kissed her cheek, then went outside, past the dance floor where sweaty bodies were getting down to popular soca music she did not know. Beneath the night sky she found a spot – a small bench hidden between palm trees – where her black maxi dress helped her melt into the darkness. She sat down with her head in her hands and cried tears that gushed from deep inside. She had come here to straighten out her life; to do the right thing. Instead she would be leaving more alone than ever, and this time there was no one to share the blame.

As she sat crying and wiping her face on her dress, she gradually became aware of the lyrics of the chutney soca tune blasting out. It was something about a girl named Radica who had left her man, and he keep asking, pleading, why she "leave and go, oh, oh, oh". The tears turned into a broad smile as she got sucked into the easy melody. *Why yuh leave and go? Oh, oh, oh, Radica why yuh leave and go?*

Even the music would not dignify her lack of courage. She got up. A short walk to clear her head and she could go back to the celebrations. It was almost eleven, and surely Granny Gwen would not last much longer. As she neared the swimming pool she bumped into Indra, whom she had sat with at dinner. They were ready to leave and couldn't find Tina.

'I haven't seen her out here,' said Bea. 'But I was going to walk a little before going back inside. I'll keep an eye out for her.'

'Let me walk with you,' said Indra.

They sauntered slowly around the grounds, saw no one,

and were heading back to the dining room when Bea thought she saw Tina in the shadows of a bougainvillea bush.

'Isn't Tina wearing a gold top?' Bea asked, nodding at a gold shimmer in the dark.

'Yes,' said Indra. 'That's her over there?'

They both recognised her at the same time. She was not alone.

CHAPTER THIRTY-THREE

When Mummy died I felt my life ended too. No joke – it was the absolute worst moment of my life. And I never thought anything else could top that. It's like I had two lives – the one before with Mummy and the hell it's been since then. Robin was the first piece of happiness I had in years. Now I wish I never met him.

In fact I wish he was dead. I wish I was dead. When Aunty Indra told me who he was, I literally vomited right there by the pool where we were sitting. She had to hold on to me because I was sure I was going to collapse. Oh God, I want to die. Nothing, nothing, nothing will make this right. Even thinking about it now, days later, makes me want to throw up. The day after I was so sick I must have vomited at least five times.

I took to my bed for three days straight. Aunty Indra told Nanny that I eat something bad at Granny Gwen party and to leave me in peace to get better. Aunty Indra must have sounded concerned because Nanny didn't bother me except to ask if I wanted anything. I wanted to die. I can't scrub myself clean enough. I showered three times today and my skin's still dirty. Soiled and stained. How do you get pure again? To think I loved that man all this time and wanted him to leave his wife. I want to kill myself every time I think of us. It's the most sickening, disgusting thing ever. I never want to have sex with anybody again.

Aunty Indra panicking and want us to keep it from Nanny, but I have no idea how we going to manage that. Of course Bea knows because she was there when Aunty Indra told me. If a brown person could look white she looked white when she heard that news. One good thing is his wife Doris seems clueless. She might have had suspicions but she don't have no proof. We used to be careful like that. Now he better go home with he tail between he leg and make up with his wife or she go leave his flat hairy ass and take half of everything he worked for.

Bea called a meeting in Granny Gwen good sitting room that nobody does ever go in. Madam Bea announced that before she leave we going to have a "come to Jesus" talk. Maybe she's planning to pray on us. All I know for sure is me, Bea, Aunty Indra and Granny Gwen going be there. Bea wanted to have Mr. Robin too but I put my foot down. I don't want to see that man as long as I live. I don't care what we have to say to Granny Gwen, but I am not going back to work there. Margaret can manage easy, and in five minutes they will get a girl to replace me. Lord have mercy, what will Margaret think of me? That's another friend I going to lose.

When Granny Gwen first heard she take a minute then she look at me straight.

'I don't know what it is, but something tell me you had a special place in my family. And now I know.'

She gave me a hug and I started to cry. Poor old lady – she don't know why I really crying. But things was only beginning to hot up. Granny Gwen turn on Aunty Indra wanting to know why is only now she see fit to open she big mouth. Alan had a right to know and once Nalini had passed she should have told him. It was his child too.

'I mean I don't know what it would have been like for poor Tina to know him then lose him the same way her mother dead. Everything in this situation is wrong to me.

All the time I seeing Tina my heart take to the girl. It never once cross my mind that is my own flesh and blood.'

Bea told Granny Gwen not to come down too hard on Aunty Indra because it was a solemn promise she made. But Granny Gwen was not about to let Aunty Indra go just so.

'So Indra, what make you change you mind now, eh? Tell me that? Why you want to go and confuse people brain now when the child done gone and loss she mother and she father?'

Everybody stayed quiet. Something in the way Granny Gwen was talking you know that she mad vex.

'The thing is Tina don't want to work here again,' said Indra.

Now Granny Gwen get even more vex. She stopped hugging me.

'But why, Tina? Young lady, is partly your hardware too now.'

Aunty Indra tried again.

'Granny Gwen, she want to move on and better herself. She might do a course.'

'Well, if she want to do a course, then fine. But she have to know more about the business so she should work here Saturdays at least.'

'No. She don't want to work here again. Leave it. Is her choice.'

'But that don't make no sense, especially now she is family. Of course she should be working in the business. She could go and do whatever course she want but eventually she go have to run the place. I don't know how much more years the Heavenly Father will grant me on this earth. And Robin will want to retire one day. Charles and Bea have they own thing doing. So Tina, is you will have the store to run.'

I couldn't look at her.

'I'm not coming back to work in the hardware ever, so please stop saying that,' I said as firmly as I could.

Granny Gwen rock back in she chair. She face look hard like rock cake. Then she decide to take a turn in my tail.

'Tina, you think I born yesterday? Tell me the truth. What going here? Somebody better start talking real fast.'

Well, I started to bawl. That look she gave me is like she know everything already.

Aunty Indra still trying to keep the peace.

'Look Granny Gwen, nothing happen. But you see Tina and Robin was getting a little too friendly. Is best if things cool off after all this news that he is her uncle.'

Granny Gwen eye open big, big.

'What?' she bellowed.

She took out the handkerchief that was tucked in her bra and mopped her face. 'Let me hear that again? Tina was carrying on with my son Robin? Right here under my nose?'

I don't know why Aunty Indra suddenly being my defender, but she tell Granny Gwen not to let her pressure go up because nothing actually happened. We only making sure nothing ever could happen.

'You damn right about that,' said Granny Gwen.

That is the first time I ever hear a curse word pass Granny Gwen's lips. Imagine if she knew what was actually going on.

'By the grace of God I live to see ninety years and I never imagine I would hear a shameful thing like this happen in my family. Uncle and niece together. Heavenly father. It have no forgiveness for a grave sin like that.'

I didn't plan to speak. It just come out and I said that I didn't know he was my uncle. Granny Gwen gave me a nasty look.

'Lord, the man even older than your father.'

By now the neighbours must be hearing Granny Gwen but she going strong.

'He is a married man. That alone should've been enough

tell you to conduct yourself like a decent Christian, not some she-dog in heat.' She looked out towards the window.

Well, is then I started screaming down the place.

'So what about Robin? Like he ain't have no part in this thing? He pushed himself on me. He wanted me first.'

'You must have pushed youself up on him. Always wearing them tight-tight pants and top that showing your bra clear as day.'

'Well, he is the one make the first move.'

'Never. You little whore. My Robin wouldn't do nothing so.'

'Your Robin is no saint, okay? He is the one who feel me up and tell me all kind of lie how he wife don't want him no more and how he feel like a man again with me.'

Granny Gwen put she hands over she ears and started to bawl.

'Stop your damn lying! You're a nasty liar.'

'I am not lying. Bring him here. Yes, why we don't call him up and bring him here right now and ask him. I bet you won't do that because you know I talking the truth.'

Granny Gwen wiped the sweat and tears from her face.

'Listen, madam. You can talk to your Nanny anyhow you like but don't try that on me. To think of all the things I do for you.'

Suddenly, you know what? I gave up. I had enough. I'm not going to fight with anybody. If they want to call me a whore let them. I deserve it. But leave me alone. The only thing I not compromising on is that I never want to see that f-ing Robin, Uncle Robin, as long as I live. The rest of the Clark family – I couldn't care less about none of them.

All this time Bea was in the corner staying quiet, but then she get up. She said I am her sister and there is no way she going to hide that. Who want to talk could talk and eventually they will get fed up and move on to talking somebody else business.

'Tina is my responsibility now.'

She looked at me and smiled the way Mummy used to smile at me.

Granny Gwen's face fix up like thunder and lightening.

'While you busy talking big, why you don't take she with you? I don't want no little madam who was sweet on she own uncle hanging around here. Lord help us if Doris ever find out.'

'Fine. She can come with me.'

Just like that. I looked at her because I can't imagine that she really mean it. Granny Gwen get in there first.

'How you going to manage the dirty wretch? You don't know the girl from Eve.'

Bea look like she serious.

'She's my sister. That's good enough for me. If she wants to come I am happy to have her.'

Now she asking me point blank if I want to go Boston with her. How I going to answer that when I not even sure where Boston is? I know it have to be near New York because one time Charmaine and her family went on holiday to New York and they drive to Boston to see Charmaine's cousins. It can't be that far if you could drive there.

I burst into tears again. Seems like you only have to say boo to me and I will cry.

'I don't have a US visa so I can't go nowhere.'

'We can organise that.'

Bea came and started smoothing down my hair.

'I used to have hair like yours when I was younger.'

I can't stop crying.

'Tina, if our father were alive he would expect me to take care of my little sister, and frankly you look like you could do with a little break from this place.'

'What if I go up there in Boston and I don't like it?'

'You'll have a return ticket. You can come back any time you like.'

'What if I go and you don't like me?'

She burst out laughing right in my face.

'You and I have been only children up to now. To get a sister is a gift. Any way you look at it, this is a gift from the gods. At least come spend a couple months and let us get to know each other.'

Granny Gwen watching all this. She let out a big, fat steups.

'Take she and the mess she make here. Go along. America is the best place for she.'

Bea walked over to Granny Gwen and put her arms around her. She stiffen up.

'Granny Gwen, you now have another granddaughter and from what people say about my father I'm surprised you only have one grandchild we didn't know about. Don't make the same mistake you made with Uncle Kevin. Seems you liked Tina before today. Don't start hating her now when she is your blood.'

Aunty Indra wanted to know if Bea mean what she say, so she say it again. Then I start to think. I wonder if it making cold? I don't have a single sweater and of course I don't have coat and boots and all them things. You must need stuff like that because people say it does be cold in July much more coming up to Christmas.

'I'll take you to Filene's Basement and we'll get you some clothes. You'll love that store.'

Granny Gwen face still twist up. She mad as hell. But then she get up and stuff her dirty handkerchief back down she front. She look at all of us sitting on her good red chairs with the cream antimacassars and ask if anybody want some fresh grapefruit juice the helper squeezed this morning.

CHAPTER THIRTY-FOUR

Bea opened her powder compact and used the mirror to apply lipstick for the second time. Tina's flight was almost two hours late into Logan Airport. Soon her newly-acquired sister should be bursting through the dark glass threshold that separated the baggage hall from the public waiting area. She stole a glance at her reflection in the partition and smoothed her spiky hair into place. Her jeans and sweater looked old and worn. A dress and heels would have been smarter, but it was too late now for regrets.

Unusually for her, Bea had acted on impulse, though she preferred to think of it as instinct, when she invited the girl to Boston. The subsequent two weeks had been steeped in anxiety. They were sister-strangers. At nearly twenty-one, Tina had never left Trinidadian soil, and this gave Bea the extra responsibility of teaching her to navigate a big city. She would have to learn to use the T, Boston's subway system, and occupy herself while Bea was working. But aside from these practical matters, Bea's worry was this: would they like each other? She did not want to break the heart of a girl who never had the love of a longed-for father and who grieved for the lost love of her dead mother.

Bea was curious too about what they might have in common. She wanted to know everything. Were they both wired with a propensity to slide into black holes? Did they both enjoy hiking? Was Tina a film buff too? The big and little details of each other's lives had to be assimilated with care and tact.

Each time the baggage hall door flew open and Bea caught sight of a young woman she held her breath. How different their lives would have been if all those years ago Nalini Ramlogan had been open about her baby daughter's father. Had Alan really never known Tina was his, or was it an inconvenience he had swept aside? Bea had accepted his playboy lifestyle, but surely even he was not capable of such profound disregard?

And while she breathed in the indignation she felt on Tina's behalf towards Alan, she was pricked by the extent to which Mira had been purged from her own life. They had barely managed an evening of small talk, and neither had reached out to the other after Granny Gwen's birthday party. All that resolve about going back, straightening out her life, and she had returned to Boston as lost as ever. Mira had not been given an olive twig, much less a branch. Alan was not the only Clark to have mastered the art of cowardly denial.

The baggage hall door was opening and shutting more frequently, but no Tina pushed through with a trolley of suitcases. From the mixed ethnicity and dress of the passengers Bea knew it was the flight from Trinidad that was clearing. Tina would be out any minute. Bea pulled her sweater straight. She shoved her hands into the front pockets of her jeans and waited.

An older couple came noisily through the partition. They each pushed a trolley with precariously stacked suitcases of varying sizes. One looked in danger of falling off at the slightest bump. As they pushed past her a large green suitcase came crashing down almost on Bea's feet. The procession halted. And that was when Bea looked up from the suitcases and met her eyes.

It must have been twenty years since Bea had last seen

her, but they recognised each other instantly.

'Eh, but hello! Is Bea?' asked the older woman with beautifully coiffed hair. 'You remember who I is?'

'I know you,' replied Bea. 'You were our hairdresser when I was growing up.'

The woman pulled her trolley aside to let others pass by. Her husband was trying to haul the green suitcase back onto the trolley.

'You don't remember my name?' she asked loudly.

'I'm sorry, but I know we used to go to your salon all the time.'

'Is Judy. How you could forget?'

'Of course. Judy's Hair and Beauty Salon.'

'I recognised your face straightaway. You ain't change one bit. Mira's daughter, right?'

'Yes. Bea.'

'But oh my, you gone and cut off all your hair. You uses to have long long hair and dead straight.'

'It's easier to manage short,' said Bea running her fingers through the spiky cut.

'You used to come to the salon with your mammy. You was a pretty little girl. But now you gone and cut your hair you don't look so good.'

Bea fixed a polite smile on her face, unsure of the best response. The husband took a large suitcase off Judy's trolley and replaced it with a smaller one.

'So you still have the salon?' asked Bea.

'It there, but I don't really do much nowadays,' she replied, adjusting the case so it was better balanced. 'I do two days every week but my son Ranjit is the one running the business now.'

'I'm glad it's still doing well.'

'Yes, man. But we not in the small place you would remember. We move years now and take over a house in St. Clair. And don't think you can come by we just so, just so. You have to make appointment at least a week before you want a cut or colour. We busy for so. Next time you in Trinidad you must come see us.'

'I'll do that.'

Judy leaned forward and propped her elbows on the trolley handle.

'So, you living up here now?'

Bea glanced at the baggage hall door.

'Yeah.'

'And how often you does go back home?'

'Not often.'

The husband came and stood between them.

'This is my husband, Tony,' said Judy. 'This is Bea. You know Mira Clark? Well this is she daughter.'

Bea shook his hand.

'I know your mammy,' he said, smiling. 'But she wasn't on this flight.'

Their trolleys were obstructing other passengers leaving the baggage hall. Tony herded them to one side while Bea kept an eye on the door that was swinging open and shut. Tina must not panic that Bea was late or had forgotten.

'So, is not your mother you waiting on?' he repeated.

'No,' said Bea. 'My sister's arriving.'

Judy straightened up, frowning, her mouth half open.

'We up here to see my son,' said Tony. 'He married a girl from up here. We taking a little holiday to see them before it get too cold.'

Bea smiled. 'You must be a proud papa.'

Judy nudged her trolley gently so the edge of a protruding suitcase bumped Bea's arm.

'You meeting your sister?' asked Judy. 'What sister is this? I never know Mira to have other children.'

Bea took a deep breath.

'It's my half-sister. She's my father's daughter.'

Judy's eyes opened wide.

'Well, look at that. I had to come quite Boston to find out Alan, God rest he soul, had an outside child. All you keep that real quiet because I never hear that talk before. And trust me, I does hear everything in my salon.'

Bea looked away, concentrating on the baggage hall door and hoping Judy would move on.

'So who is the girl's mother?' Judy persisted.

'I doubt you would know her.'

'Try me. Like I say, I know everybody business.'

'It's a woman called Nalini Ramlogan. She died a while back. She died before my father.'

'Wait a minute. I know that family. It have two daughters – the Nalini who passed and another one named Indra.'

'That's right.'

Judy pulled her scarf closer and held onto the trolley handle firmly.

'Well, it's nice to catch up after all these years, even if is in the airport.'

'Nice to see you too,' said Bea.

But Judy wasn't looking at her. She was staring into the middle distance.

'Life strange, yes.'

She looked down at Bea.

'I remember the confusion when that Nalini died and nobody could say who the child father was. And imagine it was Alan Clark child all this time.'

She made to push the trolley but stopped.

'Mind you, Bea, if anybody did ask me about that Ramlogan girl with a Clark boy, I would've bet my bottom dollar on the next brother. What he name now?'

'Robin,' said Bea, her eyes wide open.

'Well, like I said, if she was sweet on any Clark boy, it was Robin, the quiet one. Not Alan. I never liked that Robin. And he was married. Your father Alan was a nice man. He was always laughing and talking with everybody. Robin? He was a tricky one.'

Bea shot her a hard look. 'Why would you say a thing like that?'

Judy sighed.

'Look, don't take me on. Is just I sure when she was alive I did see she a few times with Robin Clark. But that was donkey years now. I could be wrong. Anyhow the Ramlogan lady done pass and you mustn't speak ill of the dead.'

Bea was silent and suddenly cold.

'Anyhow, if they say she had child with Alan, I glad for you to have a sister.'

Bea said nothing. Judy began moving away.

'Well, it was good seeing you. Tell Mira I say hello. God bless.'

Bea managed a half smile, then turned around in time to see Tina coming through the baggage hall door, her eyes frantically darting around. Tina was her sister and nothing would change that. There had been enough mistakes. Together, strangers or sisters, they were going home.

ACKNOWLEDGEMENTS

My parents, Lucy and John Steward, without your unconditional love and support it would have been impossible to complete this book.

Our sons, Anish and Ishan, your encouragement and enthusiasm for this project were invaluable. Home is wherever you are.

Jeremy Taylor, thank you for being so generous with your time and expertise.

Claire Capstick and Trisha Barnes – I am forever in your debt.

Ingrid Persaud was born in Trinidad and calls both Barbados and London home. She came to writing fiction after careers as a legal academic and fine artist. She lives with her husband, twin boys, Rosie the rescue dog, and Jack, the unbiddable Jack Russell. This is her first novel.

Author Photo: Electric Villages
Cover Design: Jane Dixon-Smith

Made in the USA
Middletown, DE
17 August 2017